The Virgin Homicides
A Mahu Investigation

Neil S. Plakcy

This book is a work of fiction. Names, characters, places, and incidents either are products of the author's imagination or are used fictitiously. Any resemblance to actual events or locales or persons, living or dead, is entirely coincidental.

Copyright 2023 by Neil S. Plakcy All rights reserved, including the right of reproduction in whole or in part in any form.

Cover by Kelly Nichols, Editing by Randall Klein

Establishing the chronology of the novels is tricky because *Mahu Men: Mysterious and Erotic Stories*, and *Accidental Contact: Mahu Investigations,* fill in the gaps between novels. Here's the way I organize the whole series:

Mahu
Mahu Surfer
A finalist for the 2007 *Lambda Literary Award for Best Gay Mystery*
Mahu Fire
A finalist for the 2008 *Lambda Literary Award for Best Gay Mystery*
Winner of the 2008 *Left Coast Crime award for Best Police Procedural*
Mahu Vice
Mahu Men: Mysterious and Erotic Stories
Mahu Blood
Zero Break
Natural Predators
Accidental Contact and Other Mahu Investigations
Children of Noah
Ghost Ship
Deadly Labors
Soldier Down
Unruly Son
The Virgin Homicides

This book is licensed to the original purchaser only. Duplication or distribution via any means is illegal and a violation of International Copyright Law, subject to criminal prosecution and upon conviction, fines and/or imprisonment. This eBook cannot be legally loaned or given to others. No part of this eBook can be shared or reproduced without the express permission of the publisher.

Chapter 1
Influencer

My partner Mike and I drove up Aiea Heights Drive past brown-roofed suburban houses with sentinel palm trees and red and purple hibiscus hedges. We pulled into the driveway of the sprawling house owned by the lesbian couple we shared our ten-year-old keikis with. As soon as we got out of the SUV we were besieged by Owen and Addie, who at ten years old were still young enough to love the embrace of their daddies. We took advantage of what we could.

Owen was a miniature Mike, from his unruly black hair to the cleft in his chin. He had a narrow face, like a budding K-Pop star, and a sturdy build. Addie's hair was the same color, but controlled into a sleek ponytail, and her face was rounder, more Hawaiian. She was the better surfer, slimmer, with better balance.

The two of them had an inscrutable twin thing going on, a magnetism that tied them together, and when one got in trouble the other was his or her advocate. I loved them more ferociously than I had thought possible, and just being near them filled me with joy. We hugged both of them in turn, kissing the tops of their heads.

Owen noticed a gold-colored sword abandoned after a recent

costume party, and ran over to grab it. He charged at his sister, holding the sword straight ahead of him.

"Yo, Owen!" I yelled in the voice I usually used only at work, when addressing criminals. "Put that down right now!"

He stopped in his tracks and dropped the sword on the ground. His eyes opened wide and it looked like he might burst into tears. But instead, he turned and rushed toward the luau. After staring at me for a minute, Addie turned and followed him.

"He was only playing," Mike said. He was the good dad, who tossed balls with them and stood up for them. I knew the danger that the world held for them, and I was the one who yelled at them for running in the street or swinging from tree branches. I wanted them to enjoy their childhood but learn how to be safe.

"I used the cop voice, didn't I?"

"You did. Since we don't live with them, and raise our voices over eating cereal and getting ready for school, it matters more to them when we yell at them."

We followed the kids along the side of the house to the back patio where the luau was taking place. I saw Owen and Addie with their heads together, and both of them looked up as I approached.

"I'm sorry, buddy," I said. "I over-reacted. I know you were just playing. But even a piece of plastic like that can be dangerous. You wouldn't want to hurt your sister, would you?"

He shook his head.

"Come here."

He hesitated, and I cocked my head at him and opened my arms.

He rushed over, and I picked him up, holding him under his skinny butt. "Wow, you're getting big," I said, as he wrapped his arms around my neck. "Soon I won't be able to do this anymore."

I leaned in and sucked my lips around a piece of his neck, and made a funny noise as I let go. Owen giggled and I let him down, and they rushed over to the pool, where a couple of their neighborhood friends were already splashing. Mike headed for the food and I walked over to Cathy Selkirk, one of the two moms. The other,

Sandra Guarino, was our state representative in Washington and was away frequently.

We kissed hello, and then she had to run to the kitchen for some emergency, so I shifted to Lui, my eldest brother. Hapa, my favorite Hawaiian band, provided a soundtrack for the party going on around us.

Lui took a sip of his Manhattan, a grown-up drink if there ever was one. He was ten years older than I was, already on that long slide through middle age. He and our brother Haoa, who was two years younger than he was, had been locked in mortal combat forever, each struggling to be better than the other. For a while, Lui was on top, with his career at KVOL, our scrappy independent TV news station, where he had risen to managing director.

Haoa's landscaping business boomed as he got large contracts from elegant hotels and grade A office buildings, and there was a seesaw effect.

There was a sudden eruption of fire across from us, where Lui's oldest, Jeffrey, was trying to grill burgers with his girlfriend Chesa. Both of them jumped back from the grill as Mike rushed in. He was still a firefighter at heart though he now manned a desk, and he expertly doused the flames. He took the spatula from Jeffrey and showed him how to flip the burgers without spilling grease onto the fire below.

"There are a lot of people who shouldn't be parents," Lui said. "But you and Mike were designed to be great dads. I'll bet he wanted to be a fireman when he was a boy so he could rescue people."

I shook my head. "Neither of us knew when we were kids what we'd end up being. He was supposed to be a doctor like his father."

"And you were going to be a surfer like Dad," Lui said.

"Yeah, well, we saw how well that worked out."

He and Haoa had transferred their ambitions to their kids. Each boy and girl went to Punahou, the impressive private school we had all attended, and their fathers scrutinized grades and sent them to expensive extra-curriculars. Fortunately the kids were all working to create their own futures independent of their fathers' desires. Haoa's oldest daughter was a rising star on the surf circuit, while Jeffrey had a great job at the Bank of Hawaii, known locally as Bankoh.

Lui walked away to get a burger, and my son Dakota came around the corner from the driveway, his eyes so intent on his phone that he stumbled over the plastic sword Owen had left on the sidewalk.

He recovered easily enough, with the grace of a twenty-six-year-old who exercised regularly. "What is so engrossing on your phone that you can't watch where you're going?" I asked, as he got close to me.

"Apikela's newest video," he said. Api was the youngest of all my nieces and nephews, a nineteen-year-old student at Honolulu Arts College, where she seemed to be majoring in hair and makeup.

"Api makes videos?" I asked. "About what?"

"Let me show you," he said. I moved in close to look at the display on his phone.

Api's face filled the screen. She was a true island beauty, with the best features of our complex gene pool. Her face was heart-shaped, and you could see our Japanese ancestry by the slight epicanthic fold beneath her perfectly-plucked eyebrows. She had her mother's coquettish eyes and her father's smile. Her skin tone was a mix of our native Hawaiian ancestors and her haole, or white, great-grandmother. It was complemented by an expert application of moisturizer and blush, and her smile was bright, her teeth perfect.

I had to admit that the pudgy little girl I had taught to surf years before had grown into a stunning young woman.

On the screen, Apikela tied a scarf around her head, pulling in waves of black hair. I recognized the pattern as the ulu, a dark green cross with balls at each end, and giant green leaves spinning off on the diagonals.

"This pattern is common in Hawaiian quilts," she said in the video. "Ulu is the Hawaiian name for the breadfruit, a protein-rich superfruit found all over the islands. As legend has it, the god Ku transformed himself into an ulu tree to feed his human family and spread the fruit trees throughout the Hawaiian Islands."

"Looks like someone paid attention in Hawaiian school," I said. All the keikis had gone to after-school enrichment programs in Hawaiian culture when they were small. Those who didn't speak the Hawaiian language at home were introduced to it, and they studied native plants, birds, and fish. I learned how to lash together an outrigger canoe, how to mash poi, and how to dance a very basic hula.

"That's not fair," Dakota said as he paused the video. "By the time I came to live with you and Mike I was way too old for Hawaiian school."

That was true; I had met Dakota when he was a teenager. His mother was in prison and he was homeless. Mike and I had taken him in, mentored and loved him, and helped him unleash his potential. "Well, I'm glad you're watching videos about Hawaiian culture."

"There's way more than that," he said. "Keep watching." He started the video again.

"Breadfruit replenishes the skin's natural lipid barrier, resulting in a glowing complexion," Apikela said. "In the show notes you can find a link to the company that makes the body butter I use. Remember to use the code 'iloveapi' for ten percent off your first purchase."

She smiled at the camera and I thought if I was a girl I'd want that skin. Even as a forty-something gay man I wished I had skin as clear as hers.

She held up the scarf again. "I turned up the edges of the scarf before I wrapped it around my hair, to show off the pattern," she said as she undid it. "Let me show you that again."

"Why are you watching that?" I asked Dakota.

"Kimo. She's my cousin. I have to support her." He looked up at me. "Plus it's cool the way she combines Hawaiian culture with her fashion and makeup tips. And she has good product recommendations. I've started using that breadfruit face wash she mentioned."

Dakota was a handsome young man, and he took better care of

himself than either Mike or I did. He had a row of face washes and skin creams in the bathroom of the apartment he shared with his boyfriend, and both of them collected cleansers and conditioners like they were stocking up for a global shortage.

"She ought to be studying," I said, recognizing I sounded like an old fogy.

"Are you kidding?" Dakota asked. "Do you know how many followers she has?"

I shrugged. "Family and friends?"

He clicked a button. "She has over five hundred thousand followers," he said. "And see the ads at the bottom of the screen? Sephora and Glossier and Clinique. They pay for those, and they also give her free products and pay her to endorse them."

"Really?"

He nodded. "She told me she's going to gross almost a hundred grand this year from ads and endorsements."

"No way."

"Yes way," Dakota said. "I tell you, being an influencer is the path to riches these days."

He spotted Jeffrey and Chesa at the grill handing out burgers and left me in his dust. I smelled the amazing dishes coming out of the kitchen, provided by various members of the family, and after I loaded up a dish I found myself back with my oldest brother.

"Did you know that Apikela is making money from her videos?" I asked Lui, as we stood on one side of the wide backyard. His ancient cocker spaniel, Lilo, nosed around our feet for spilled food.

"I've seen the numbers but I still can't believe it," Lui said. "Jeffrey is handling her investments and he showed me her portfolio. She's nineteen years old and she's studying at that silly arts college, and she already has endorsement deals worth six figures."

"That's what Dakota told me. He's a fan. I'll have to keep an eye out when I'm scrolling YouTube and TikTok."

He raised an eyebrow. "Aren't you too old for a teen obsession like that?" In his mid-fifties, Lui looked like a Japanese statesman on vacation—even in a Hawaiian shirt and neatly pressed khakis, he was so serious that he might have stepped out of a high-level meeting in Tokyo. My aloha shirts were often wrinkled and I usually wore baggy board shorts when I wasn't on duty as a homicide detective.

"Never too old to watch a cute shirtless guy dancing," I said. He frowned but I elbowed him. "Tell me you don't look at half-naked women."

"I manage a television station, Kimo," he said. "That's all I see at work, between surf videos, ads and the Waikiki go-cam we have up at Kuhio Park."

Our conversation was interrupted by the arrival of our middle brother, Haoa, and his wife Tatiana. Haoa had always been the beefiest of us, the one who looked most Hawaiian, but a heart attack the year before had caused Tatiana to put him on a strict diet. He had lost so much weight that he was almost unrecognizable.

That was the peril of getting older. My best friend Harry had survived prostate cancer the year before, and Lui was on a diet of pills for high cholesterol, high blood pressure and who knows what else.

I was lucky to be so much younger than my brothers were, so I saw what was coming and did my best to avoid it. My job was still physical, and Mike had increased his exercise when he transitioned to a desk job, so we were both in decent shape. But we had regular physicals, EKGs and PSA tests and everything else that went with getting older.

Tatiana had lost weight, too, but she'd done it in a way that accentuated her curves, and she had admitted that she had some tucks to remove excess skin. Her hair was still effusive, though, dark blonde curls cascading over her shoulders.

I eventually got tired of balancing my plate and drink, and I sat down at a table in the corner of the yard. I kept an eye on the weather—on our island of micro-climates, a clear blue sky could be swept away by puffy gray rain clouds in minutes. I didn't want the party to be a washout, or drive us all inside. My family is big and boisterous, and we needed that outdoor space to keep us under control.

My family was rooted in our islands, connected to the land and the ocean. Someone always had fingers in the dirt or feet on a surfboard. I had spent a year on the surf circuit when I was younger, and every few months my feet itched to be on a board again. I felt that desire rising inside me and knew I'd have to handle it soon.

When I finished eating, I looked for Mike. I found him on the stone patio playing with Lilo, and my heart cracked. Nearly twelve years ago, when Mike was a fire investigator, a golden retriever had smelled smoke in his house, and woken his family, allowing them to escape. Sadly, their new apartment didn't allow dogs, so Mike had decided to adopt Roby, who was little more than a puppy then.

Roby had begun to limp soon after his twelfth birthday, and we discovered that he had a cancer that affected the lining of the blood vessels. There was nothing we could do for him other than give him as much love as possible for the time he had left, and when it was evident he was suffering, give him a release from that pain.

Mike had been the most affected. I loved Roby, and he was a sweetheart and a sponge for affection, but my partner had mourned him the most. Seeing him play with Lilo reminded me of how much he missed Roby.

That was when the influencer herself made a guest appearance at the luau, though I don't believe anyone paid her to be there. Except for her prodigious income, Apikela might have seemed like a slacker compared to her high-achieving siblings and cousins. Most of my nieces and nephews were adults by then, and a couple of them had chosen to make their careers on the mainland, at least in the short term. The others were with us that afternoon.

After she grabbed a bottle of smart water, she joined a group conversation among Dakota, Jeffrey, and Chesa.

I was standing nearby with a bottle of Big Wave Pale Ale so I easily overheard what they were saying. "You would not believe the loser guys who come after girls at my school," Apikela said. "They think because we're artsy and like makeup that they can talk down to us, and treat us differently from girls at UH."

"Try dating surfer boys." Chesa was a Nisei surfer girl with tattoos and piercings, a real contrast to Jeffrey, who at twenty-eight was almost a carbon copy of his father, though he had a better tan, because he still surfed on the weekend.

"They would rather spend time on their boards than with us," Chesa continued. "I got the best of both worlds with Jeff. He takes me out to nice restaurants during the week, and on the weekends we book up to the North Shore and surf until we drop."

"You are very lucky to have found a career you love that pays so well," Jeffrey said to Api. "Christ, if I was your age and doing as well as you I'd never have finished Harvard."

Chesa elbowed him. "I wish you were the next Internet mogul." She had a degree in marketing from UH and handled social media for a clothing designer who shared her surf-girl sensibilities. "But I'll settle for a surfing banker."

Dakota said, "Did you say surfing wanker?"

"No, that would be you," Jeffrey said, and they all laughed.

I was happy to see that Dakota had bonded so closely with my nieces and nephews.

"Let me ask you a question," Api said, turning to Dakota. "Have you ever heard the phrase 'the male gaze'?"

"You mean the way men look at women as sexual objects?" Dakota asked. "Sure, I took sociology in college."

"Do you ever get that, as a gay guy? That other gay guys look at you like they're imagining how you'd be in bed?"

"That's the way most of us look at each other," Dakota said. "And I can't complain about it because I do the same thing."

"I know what you mean," Chesa said to Api. "It's more than sex. It's the way that men look at us that empowers them while sexualizing and diminishing us."

I thought about what the girls were talking about. Back in the day, when I was coming out, I was afraid to stare at other guys too closely.

I couldn't tell who was gay and who was straight, and I didn't know all the terms like twinks and bears that classified the men I saw at gay bars and indicated whether they might or might not be interested in me.

"It's funny that you use the term gaze," Dakota said. "And yes, I mean g-a-z-e and not g-a-y-s. Because for gay men, it's all in the eye contact. You can see a real Adonis in the gym or a label queen at a bar, but if he doesn't look back at you he's not interested."

"I had a talk with an advertiser last week," Api said, "and she encouraged me to broaden my tutorials to reach out to husbands and boyfriends and convince them to buy products for the women in their lives, but I pushed back. My whole deal is to empower women to look and feel their best, and they don't need men to tell them how to do that."

I didn't end up speaking to Apikela directly at the party, though her comments to her cousins came back to me as I began to investigate my next case.

Chapter 2
The Girl in the Pig Book

Monday morning at work at Honolulu's main police station, I told my detective partner, Ray Donne, what he'd missed at the party. "Apikela hooked her phone up to a TV set in the living room and showed a couple of her videos," I said. "She's a sweetheart and I love her, but I don't need to know what kind of lipstick she prefers and how to keep your mascara from running when you cry."

Ray said, "Sounds better than my weekend. We went to Sea Life Park for the tenth time this year."

Ray and his wife Julie had bought a house down the hill from us in Aiea, only a block from the H1 freeway. It wasn't the best neighborhood in the area, but it was what they could afford, and they were close to us, and to the baby mamas and the twins.

Their son Vinnie had become obsessed with tropical fish, and every weekend when Ray didn't have to work he and Julie took the boy somewhere on the island to swim or gaze through aquarium walls. "Did you ever learn the mnemonic Kings Play Chess On Fat Girls' Stomachs?" Ray asked.

"Apikela is far from fat."

"I wasn't talking about her. It stands for Kingdom, Phylum, Class,

Order, Family, Genus, and Species," Ray said. "Vinnie kept asking us to point out a fish and challenge him to name the whole long list."

"Sounds like fun."

"It makes listening to Doc Takayama talk about fatal wounds a pleasure."

And then, as if calling out the Medical Examiner for the City and County of Honolulu had created a homicide case for us, our boss, Lieutenant Sampson, appeared next to our desks.

"You're up for the next case," he said. "Young woman found early this morning on a cliffside below the Honolulu Arts College."

"That's where Apikela goes," I said, and my heart rate jumped. "Any description of the victim?"

"Caucasian female, blonde, approximately eighteen years of age. That match your niece?"

I shook my head. "Wrong ethnicity, wrong hair color." I felt better, even though I knew somewhere a family was going to get bad news. At least it wouldn't be mine.

Ray and I drove out of downtown and into the mountainside suburb of Manoa, which looks down on our capital city like a rich older sister. The hills were a verdant green, thanks to the frequent rainfall. The first western style coffee and sugarcane plantations were located there, and taro is still grown on irrigated terraces.

We climbed along residential streets lined with palms and colored with the bright red blossoms of the ohia lehua trees. Many of the homes were in a traditional New England style, a tribute to the missionaries who brought their culture with them when they arrived in the 18th century. Manoa is also a college town of coffee shops, boutiques, and yoga studios, studded with Japanese shrines and bamboo forests.

We zigzagged a mile uphill from the University of Hawai'i campus to the Honolulu Arts College, situated on a plateau with views in all directions. It was a cluster of four buildings that radiated like a star from a central stone plaza.

The SUV driven by the Crime Scene Unit had just arrived, and we waved at the techs who were assembling the gear they'd need as we passed.

The patrol officer who'd responded to the initial call, Jimmy Chang, had already used yellow hazard tape to section off an area of stone pavement that had a dark red tinge to it. He finished speaking to a campus security officer and walked over to us. "Hey, Kimo, howzit?" he said to me. He turned to Ray. "Morning, detective."

We all shook hands. I'd known Jimmy for years, since he was a raw recruit on the downtown beat. A few years before he'd graduated to driving a patrol car through Manoa, and it suited him. He was already developing into the kind of heavyset cop whose belly strained against the buttons of his uniform shirt.

"What have we got?" Ray asked.

"The guy over there in the t-shirt and orange shorts is Simon Aquino. He was out for an early morning run when he paused to catch his breath while looking down the mountainside. He spotted the body of a young woman on the ground. He scrambled down to her, checked for a pulse, then called 911."

"This was?" I asked.

Jimmy checked his notes. "Six-fifteen. He says he tries to get out at sunrise, which ties in."

It was a few minutes past eight, and a group of early-rising students were clustered around one side of the perimeter Jimmy had established with yellow police tape. "When I arrived, I spotted that reddish area and it looked like dried blood, so I set up a perimeter tape around it."

"Good job," I said. "Have we gotten an ID yet?"

Jimmy shook his head. "Simon thinks her name is Elizabeth, but doesn't really know her. She's face down and I didn't want to disturb the body, or try and get anyone over to the cliff edge to ID her from her general appearance. All I can say right now is that the pretty dress and sparkly high-heel sandals she's wearing make it look like she went out last night rather than early this morning." He nodded to the group of students already gathering around us. "The ones who are out this morning are wearing t-shirts and rubber slippers."

I'd seen Apikela and her female cousins in the morning, and they often looked like they'd just fallen out of bed. At other times, though, they were dressed to impress even at eight AM.

Ray and I walked over to the cliff's edge, taking care to avoid the area Jimmy had taped off. It looked like dried blood to me, a lot of it. "Head wound?" I asked Ray.

"Probably." He looked at me. "Though if she hit her head when she fell, there wouldn't be so much blood up here."

"You're right. Which makes this look more like a homicide than an accident."

The early sun was blisteringly bright, but fortunately for us it was on the other side of the high-rise, and we saw that the young woman's body was in the shade. The hot sun can do a number on a dead body, making it difficult to establish time of death.

The head tech, Ryan Kainoa, was watching as one of his assistants bent over to take the imprint of a shoe. There was a disturbed path down the hill, dirt kicked up and a branch broken, that seemed to indicate how Simon had gone down to the body to check for a pulse.

"Look over to the left," Ray said, and I followed where he was pointing. "That broken branch is too tall for Simon to have reached. You think she hit that on her way down?"

I looked at the trajectory. I had barely squeaked through geometry at Punahou, so I wasn't comfortable speculating. "Could be. Ryan, can one of your techs calculate that?"

"Larry's good at blood spatter, so he can probably work that out, too," Ryan said. "You need anything before I go down to help them?"

"From the head wound, we're speculating that someone hit her up here and then she either fell or was pushed down the cliffside. So check for splatter up here as well as on the rocks."

"Will do," he said.

"We're going to walk around and see if we can get an ID before the ME's techs winch the body up. How long before that?"

"At least an hour," Ryan said. "Lots of irregular surfaces. And once the ME goes down there with a stretcher and a winch, the scene will get torn up."

One of the coroner's vehicles appeared around the curving drive as we walked over to Simon Aquino, who was sitting on a concrete bench. He stood up as we approached. "I'm Detective Kanapa'aka, and this is Detective Donne," I said. "You discovered the body?"

He nodded. "I like to get out for a run before the sun get too hot." He had the slim build characteristic of Filipinos, and spoke with a slight accent. "My brother is EMT so I knew right away there was something wrong, so much blood around her head. I scrambled down and checked for a pulse, like my brother teach me."

Simon stopped, his eyes wide in remembered horror.

"I know it's tough," I said. "Take a couple of deep breaths."

He followed my advice. "When I couldn't get no pulse, I called 911 from my watch."

He held up his wrist, where I recognized the distinctive square face of an Apple watch. "Then I stay there. So sad for her to be alone."

"Did you know her?" Ray asked.

"I think I see her picture in the pig book," he said.

Ray must have thought that was a slur, because there was a harshness in his tone when he said, "Excuse me?"

"It's a book that colleges put out in the fall," I said. "Pictures of all the freshmen with their hometown and high school, right?"

Simon nodded.

I smiled to put him at ease. "Yeah, we had one of those at UC Santa Cruz when I was a freshman."

"My roommate and I, we went through all of them, looking for pretty girls. She was one of the prettiest. I remember her name Elizabeth, because I knew a pretty girl with that name in high school. And like the girl in photo, she have highlights, on one side, shade of pink."

We collected his contact information and gave him both our cards, in case he remembered anything further. Then we turned him over to Ryan, who took his fingerprints. "We're going to find your prints on anything you touched as you went down the hill," Ryan said. "This way we can eliminate you. I'm also going to need your sneakers."

"How do I get back to dorm?"

"I can give you a pair of rubber slippers," Ryan said, using our colloquial term for what mainlanders and others called flip-flops or zoris. "And you can get your shoes back once we've examined them."

"I didn't kill her," Simon said. "I don't even know her."

"We understand," Ray said. "Like Larry said, it's all about eliminating you and the marks you made."

Simon bent over and began unlacing his sneakers. "I should have kept on going."

"You did the right thing," I said.

Simon frowned, but he handed Ryan his sneakers, took off his socks, and slid his feet into the rubber slippers Ryan offered. He walked away, his soles flapping against the pavement.

Chapter 3
Beautiful Roommate

Ray looked around. "You said Apikela goes to school here. You know anything about the campus?"

"I was up here a couple of years ago for another homicide but I can't say I remember much. Suppose we start with the security guard over there."

We walked over to where a campus guard in a blue uniform stood beside a Cushman three-wheeled security car, a newer model that ran on electricity. The name on his shirt was Zhao, but he looked about as Chinese as I did—the only distinguishing feature was that we both had a similar epicanthic fold over our eyes.

We showed him our badges. "How did you hear about this?" I asked.

"We monitor the police radio in our office in case there's any activity reported up here. As soon as I heard the call I came around to look. That's when I saw Mr. Aquino and he told me what he'd seen."

"Did you go over there?" Ray asked.

"Just to the edge of the cliff, to confirm what he told me. I called the head of security at home, and I waited with Mr. Aquino for the police to arrive."

"Simon told us the girl's name was Elizabeth," I said. "Can you verify that?"

Zhao reached over to the cart and brought out an iPad, and opened an online version of what Simon had called the pig book. He paged through several young women named Elizabeth, finally landing on one who had blonde hair of a similar length. He marked that, and looked through the rest. Elizabeth Lawrence was the only young woman with that first name whose hair color and style matched that of the victim.

"You have her dorm address?" I asked Zhao.

"Mizushima Hall, room 310," he said, and he pointed to the five-story building behind us. It was one of the four buildings that stood at right angles to the central green, where a massive stand of bamboo offered shade and shelter to students who wanted a bit of the outdoors.

The dorm's position gave each of the rooms a majestic view. One side looked up to the Ko'olau Mountains, while the other had panoramic views of downtown and the Pacific. It wasn't possible without going inside to tell which way Betsy's room had faced.

"You want her family's contact information?" Zhao asked.

"Let's hold off until we get confirmation that we have the right victim," I said. "You'll be here for a while, won't you?"

"My shift ends at two, but I'll stay here as long as the boss tells me to."

As we walked over to Mizushima Hall, I said, "Fun fact. In Japanese *mizu* means water, and *shima* means island."

"Doesn't island normally mean a piece of land surrounded by water?" Ray asked. "Sounds counterintuitive to me."

"I'll let you take that up with the Japanese grammar police," I said.

The first level of the building was a wall of glass, and the door was locked, with a swipe bar beside it. Inside I spotted a young woman behind a curved desk, and I rapped on the glass and held up my badge. The door beeped and I opened it.

The round-faced young woman behind the desk wore a name tag that read Su-Kim. We showed her our badges. "What time did you come on this morning?" Ray asked.

"Six o'clock. I'm actually the dorm manager, but the student who was supposed to be here is sick this morning. This desk is staffed from six AM to midnight. In the off hours you need to swipe your badge to get in."

"Were you here before or after sunrise?"

"A few minutes before. I live upstairs, though, so I didn't go outside."

"Simon Aquino says he lives here. Did you see him go out running?"

She nodded. "We rode down in the elevator together."

"Do you know Elizabeth Lawrence?"

"Betsy? Yes, I host a party on each floor at the start of the semester. I can't say I know her well – she's a freshman and school just started a couple of weeks ago."

"Does she have a roommate?" Ray asked.

"They all do. Betsy's is Kimora Tam." She made a face.

"Something wrong with Kimora?" I asked.

"Just that she's beautiful, and knows it," she said. "You know anything about South Korea, detectives?"

I shrugged. "A fair amount."

Ray said, "Less than he does."

"Our culture is all about beauty. Koreans think that a girl with a small face, big eyes, a high nose bridge and a round forehead is pretty." She held her palm out below her chin. "So you can see I don't meet that standard. Kimora does. And she and Betsy only hung around with other beautiful girls."

"You know a girl named Apikela Kanapa'aka?" I asked.

"Api? She's one of the nice pretty girls. She has a YouTube channel where she shows girls how to apply makeup." She held up a tube of pink lipstick. "She gave me this, because she said it was the right color for my skin tone."

I nodded. "She's my niece."

"Oh, you are so lucky! I wish she was in my family."

"Yeah, well, I don't usually ask her for makeup tips."

Ray elbowed me. "Maybe you should."

I curled my upper lip at him, then looked back at Su-Kim. "Thanks. We're going up to room 310."

"Did Betsy do something?"

"Right now, we're just looking into her movements last night or early this morning."

Su-Kim's mouth opened in horror. "Oh, my God! Is that why the police are here?"

I nodded. "Thanks, Su-Kim."

We rode the elevator up to the third floor. The rooms all appeared to be apartment style, no common bath or shower rooms.

I knocked on the door to room 310 and waited for an answer. I knocked again and called, "Kimora? Honolulu Police Department. We need to speak to you."

Another minute passed until I heard a voice from the other side of the door. "I need a few minutes."

Ray looked at me. "Beauty products," he said.

I sighed. "I hope every girl we talk to isn't obsessed with beauty."

"If they're all teenagers? They probably are. This girl I dated in college? She wouldn't let me sleep over because she didn't want me to see her without makeup."

I thought back to the days when I was in the closet, and dating women. I had taken some of them to bed, certainly, but never wanted to stay over because I didn't want to give them the impression that there was a future between us.

We cooled our heels outside Kimora's door for ten minutes by my watch. I was ready to knock again when she opened the door.

She was stunningly beautiful, as Su-Kim had said. She looked like she'd just stepped out of a K-pop magazine, with a long slim face and dewy skin.

We both held up our badges. "Is your roommate here?" I asked.

"Betsy? I don't know. Her door is closed."

She led us into the spartan living room, with an Ikea-style modular sofa and coffee table. There was a galley kitchen off to one side. She crossed the room to a closed door and knocked. "Betsy? The police are here."

When she got no answer, she opened the door. We saw beyond her that the bed looked like it hadn't been slept in.

Kimora looked back at us in confusion. "You'd better sit down," I said, motioning her to the round breakfast table. "I'm afraid it looks like Betsy died last night, from a fall down the hill."

Her expression didn't change. It was as if she was afraid of frown lines appearing. "That can't be right. I saw her at ten o'clock. Right before I closed my door to do some studying before bed."

"Did she say anything about going out?"

Kimora shook her head. "She was texting on her phone, though. Maybe with a guy, but she didn't say and I didn't ask."

She looked at us. "Are you sure it's Betsy?"

"Right now we're basing our identification on two things," I said. "The boy who found the body said he recognized a girl named Elizabeth from the pig book because of the pink streaks in her hair. Any other girl here at HAC who had similar hair?"

"No. Most of the girls here have brown or black hair—lots of Asians, like me. Only a few blondes, and I'm sure Betsy was the only one with strawberry highlights. She was proud of that."

I tried to give Kimora my most compassionate look. "We're pretty sure it's Betsy." "Did she have a boyfriend?"

Kimora shook her head. "The boys here are either geeks or goths. Nobody either of us wants to date. We got an invitation to a party down at UH Manoa this weekend, but we haven't met anyone from there yet."

"Anyone else? You said she was texting before you went into your room. Do you know who it was?"

"I don't. I assumed it was someone from home."

"We're going to need to search Betsy's room," I said. "You're sure no one else came up here after you closed your door?"

"I'd have heard. These walls aren't exactly soundproof."

"Did Betsy often go out late?"

Kimora shook her head.

"If she was meeting a boy, you don't have to cover for her," Ray said.

"I'm not. Like I said, we've only been here a month and we agreed that the boys here aren't worth bothering with."

Ray and I put on blue rubber gloves, and just to be safe, blue rubber booties as well. Kimora watched us, her mouth and eyes wide open. "Why are you doing this if she fell?"

"Because we won't know until after the autopsy if she fell or was pushed," I said.

Chapter 4
Bruise

"Did Betsy ever talk about suicide?" Ray asked.

"No. She was excited to be here in Hawai'i. She loved all her classes. We were getting to be good friends."

Kimora went back into her room, and I heard her fingers frantically tapping on a keyboard, probably her phone.

Ray and I each took one side of Betsy's room, looking for any evidence that might help us make a judgement. Did she have leave any journal entries that indicated suicide was a possibility? Notes about a boy she was seeing, or any reason why she went out after her roommate had already gone to bed?

Ray began with the closet, and I started on the bookshelf over Betsy's desk. The only books there were textbooks, though she had brought with her a well-read copy of *Goodnight Moon*, probably a childhood favorite. She had a spiral-ring notebook for each of her four classes, though very little had been written in any of them. She had done some rough sketches in the notebook for her introduction to animation class, but they were mostly the same head in different poses. In another notebook she had been scrawling geometry problems, lots of question marks and numbers crossed out.

I moved on to Betsy's dresser. The entire right side was filled with tubes and squeeze bottles of various kinds of makeup: pore cleanser, concealer, lip gloss, lip oil, lip balm, eyeshadow, mascara, and a dozen other items whose purpose I could only guess at. She had six different kinds of makeup brushes, a pumice stone, tweezers and various other instruments of female torture.

It always felt like a violation to search through someone's private belongings, but if someone had pushed Betsy down that hill it was going to be a murder investigation, and searching was a requirement.

Propped up beside the portable vanity mirror on the bureau was a half-empty package of birth control pills, and I held it up for Ray to see. "Kimora says Betsy wasn't dating anyone, but she was taking these."

"Those pills are only effective if you take them regularly," Ray said. "Even if she wasn't sexually active with anyone now she'd have to keep taking them. Especially if she and Kimora were planning to go to a party at UH soon."

Ray had found and bagged all her electronics, including a brand-new Surface laptop, a well-used iPad and a Kindle. "Everything's password protected except the Kindle," he said, and he handed it to me.

Betsy's taste in books ran to teen romances and books about vampires, though she also read some science fiction, including Mary Robinette Kowal's books about a female astronaut in the 1950s.

"You find anything else?" I asked.

"Nothing in her closet or her clothes. You want to help me pick up the mattress?"

We removed the stuffed animals from the bed, including a monkey that looked like Curious George. I may not know much about teenagers, but I did know what little kids liked. It was interesting that Betsy was eighteen and sexually active, yet holding onto some childhood toys. She was at that delicate stage between girl and woman, and yet, at her own hand or someone else's, she would never complete that navigation.

We didn't find anything under the mattress, or under the bed. While we did learn a bit more about Betsy from our search, there was nothing that pointed to why she'd left her room the night before or who, if anyone, she was going to meet. Her phone was missing, and if I knew anything about teenagers it was that they hardly ever let go of that appendage. I hoped the crime scene techs would find it on the hillside.

I called Ryan Kainoa's cell and asked him to send someone upstairs with three large evidence bags, for Betsy's laptop, her iPad and her Kindle.

"You don't know her passwords, do you?" Ray asked Kimora as we prepared to leave.

She shook her head. "She never said anything about them."

"We haven't found her cell phone yet. What kind did she have?"

"A gold iPhone 14. Her mother bought it for her as a going-away present."

We waited there until one of Ryan's assistants came up with the bags, and we signed off on all three devices. We thanked Kimora and left her with our business cards, then went back downstairs. The ME's techs were waiting patiently for the crime scene techs to finish, so Ray and I took a slow walk around the campus.

The four-story building ninety degrees from the dorm housed a gallery on the ground floor and administrative and faculty offices above that. Windows there might give a view to where the body had been found, but it was unlikely anyone had been there at night. And even so, interior lights would have prevented anyone from seeing what was going on.

The next building was Manoa Hall, the student life center, including a cafeteria, meeting rooms, and facilities for student services, financial aid, and so on. The fourth building housed the digital arts labs. HAC was a pioneer in such studies, with courses in computer animation, motion capture, and social media.

That reminded me that Apikela was a student there. If she was anything like Dakota or her many cousins, she was probably still asleep, but I sent her a text asking her to call me when she could.

Ray and I walked back to where the medical examiner's team was waiting. Ryan and his crew were finishing up. "Did you find her phone anywhere?" I asked.

He shook his head. "Though if she had it in her hand when she fell, it might have gone farther than we looked. After they take the body away we can do another quick sweep."

I thanked him. "Any ideas based on the position of the body?" I asked. "Can you speculate about a fall versus a push?"

"There's a nasty bruise on the back of her head, and that's probably the source of the all the blood on paving stones. But the ME will have to tell you for certain."

I looked at Ray and we both frowned. I had a sinking feeling what the ME would tell us.

We watched the ME's techs strap Betsy's body to a board, and carefully winch it up. Betsy's blonde hair had flipped over, covering her face, revealing rust-colored dried blood that had caked on her neck.

I looked at the crowd and noticed Kimora standing there with her phone, filming us. As I walked over to her, she hastily put the phone away.

"Do you think you can do something for us?" I asked.

She looked suspicious. "What?"

"Before we call Betsy's family, can you confirm it's her?"

She shook her head violently. "A dead body? No way." She backed away.

A young person in a baggy t-shirt featuring a violent video game stepped up. "I recognize the hair," the person said, in a mid-range voice that, in addition to the clothing, made it hard for me to assign a particular gender. "That's Betsy Lawrence. She's in my English class." The person sneered. "The professor tried to put me in her group for a project and she said no lesbians were allowed."

"Your name is?" I asked.

"Lee Graham. And you can put in your report that my pronouns are they and them."

"Good to know," I said. "But we need someone to look her in the face, just to be certain. Can you do that?"

Lee shook their head. "I didn't hate her that much."

Before I let them go, I got their cell phone number for further questions.

"Anyone else?" I asked.

There was a general mumbling in the crowd that made it clear Betsy was not well-liked, but that she didn't deserve to be killed.

Finally a haole boy standing next to Lee said, "I knew Betsy. I can identify her for you."

I turned to him. He had a mop of black hair on top of his head, and the back and sides had been shaved. "You are?"

"Kyle Goodman. I live down the hall from Betsy and Kimora."

"Good enough. Come with me."

As we led him over to the hearse, he said, "I'm studying animation for video games. It'll be useful to see what a real dead person looks like."

I didn't say anything. By the time we got to where the body rested on the stretcher, someone had pulled a cloth up over Betsy's face. I asked one of the techs to pull it down. Kyle's face went pale, and he looked like he might throw up.

"That's her," he managed to say in a strangled voice. "Betsy. Betsy Lawrence."

He turned away, ran a few steps, and threw up on the pavement. None of the other students who'd been watching moved to comfort him, not even Kimora or Lee, for whom he'd made his gallant gesture.

Ray called the student affairs office at HAC to identify students who lived near Betsy or shared a class with her, and I turned to the crowd. "I'd appreciate the opportunity to speak with any of you who knew Betsy. Help us get a better picture of who she was and how this happened to her."

Ray joined me. "I have to head over to the office to get a printout of students," he said.

"Call me when you're done." I turned back to the crowd. "I know you all have classes to get to or work to do. If you can give me your name and phone number we'll make a time to meet with you that's convenient."

No one stepped forward and I began to get exasperated. "Come on. One of your fellow students has possibly been brutally murdered on the very campus where you're supposed to be safe. Don't any of you care?"

Chapter 5
Trigonometry

A portly middle-aged haole in a neatly pressed aloha shirt stepped forward. "That is the hardly the way to talk to our students, who are certainly traumatized," he said. "I'm Milton Medeiros, Dean of Students here. You are?"

I reached out to shake his hand. "Detective Kimo Kanapa'aka, HPD. Perhaps you can help convince anyone who knew Miss Lawrence to speak with me."

He turned to the crowd. "A terrible thing has happened here, and I want to assure you that the administration will do everything we can to ensure your continued safety. I will be meeting with the director of campus security later today to put together a plan to evaluate any weaknesses in our current system and rectify them. Assistant Dean Laurie Chang is a certified College & University Suicide Prevention Specialist and she is qualified to offer grief counseling to anyone who has been traumatized."

He turned to me. "This is hardly the right place to conduct interviews. I can offer you the Dean's Conference Room adjacent to my office to conduct any interviews you deem important."

"Thank you, sir." The last thing I wanted was a college administrator hijacking my investigation, but I dealt with bureaucracy at HPD so I'd work around him if I had to.

I turned back to the crowd. "We will be getting a list of students who shared classes with Miss Lawrence, as well as those who lived near her, so it would be a lot easier if you stepped forward now rather than us having to track you down."

In deference to the dean, who wasn't leaving my side, I said, "We'll be arranging interviews in the dean's office, or a neutral location if you prefer."

Finally one young woman stepped up and gave me her name and number, and a few more followed. Behind us, the ME's van departed, and with nothing left to see the crowd began to disperse.

Dean Medeiros finally went back to his office as Ray approached with a couple of sheets of paper. "I have the names and class schedules of each of the students on the same floor as Betsy in the dorm, as well as the rosters of students in each of her four classes," Ray said. "Betsy was scheduled for two classes today. The woman who gave me the printout suggested we wait around the classrooms at the end of each session to buttonhole students who might have known her."

He looked around to be sure that Dean Medeiros was gone. "And she told me to watch out for that guy you were talking to, the Dean of Students. He's going to want to keep everything very quiet and not spook the students."

"Yeah, I got that vibe from him. Can't blame him, though. I wouldn't want the parents of a couple of hundred kids calling to worry about safety."

I looked at my iPad. "I have the names of six students who don't have a class until noon," I said. "I'd rather not set up at the Dean's office unless we're forced to. Why don't we go over to the café in the student union building and start calling these students in to talk?"

"Sounds like a plan. And I could use some caffeine, too."

I began calling the students and setting up appointments with them at ten-minute intervals. We took two adjacent tables at the back of the café and began asking questions. I took the first student to arrive, and Ray the second, and we traded off like that for an hour or more.

The first few interviews yielded little we didn't already know. Betsy was pretty, she had some talent at drawing figures, and she was mean to anyone who didn't pass her looks test. As word spread about who we were, additional students showed up.

"She asked me if I knew where to get drugs," one thickset boy said. His name was Carl Sachiko and he had intricate Japanese tattoos on his muscular upper arms. He shook his head. "I didn't know this girl from anyone, and she walks up to me and says, 'You look like you use steroids. You know where I can get some pot?'"

"Not a great way to start a conversation," I said.

"In addition to which I don't use anything. Really pissed me off."

Another young woman, Hailey Meafua, told me about a similar encounter. "When Betsy found out I grew up here, she wanted to know what bars I hung out in that didn't ask for ID. I told her that I was a Christian and signed a pledge not to drink until I'm twenty-one, and she looked at me like I was from Mars."

A handsome blond guy in a T & C Surf Shop t-shirt thought Betsy was beautiful and very friendly. "But I'm like one of the only good-looking guys on this campus, so it wasn't surprising she was all over me."

I nodded. "Did you guys date?"

He shook his head. "I'm here for like two reasons. To surf and to get a marketing degree. Chicks can wait."

I couldn't resist telling him that I had spent a year on the surf circuit after college, and I told him a couple of my favorite breaks on the north shore. By the time he left, we were best buds, and I felt stupid. Just like Betsy Lawrence, I'd been lured in by a handsome face.

And a killer body, if I have to admit. But he was twenty years younger than I was so all I was interested in was looking.

Even if Ray and I were speaking casually with witnesses, it was important for us to record what we heard. We used the voice recorder on our cell phones, and we were careful to first ensure we had the individual's permission to record the conversation.

Once we had that, we stated the name of the person with whom we were speaking, and the date, time and location of the conversation. After the conversation was over, we used my iPad or Ray's to add any notes such as the person's demeanor, or anything else that might have influenced the course of the interview.

The morning went on like that. After the flow of students petered out, Ray and I compared notes. No one had ever seen Betsy drunk or high, though we kept the possibility open that she'd gone out at ten o'clock to meet someone who could get her alcohol or drugs.

"Anything else?" I asked.

"There's no security at the entrance to the campus, so anyone could have driven up here," he said. "Including anyone she might have been chatting with online. Or she could have been meeting a classmate, or another student at HAC."

"Agreed. But we can't ignore what Su-Kim told us, and what other students have confirmed. Betsy was a mean girl, and she could have made enemies at school quickly. It's possible that a girl she treated badly catfished her, convincing her to come out and meet some great guy. And used that as the opportunity to get revenge on Betsy for something she said or did."

That afternoon we haunted the hallways outside rooms where Betsy had classes. We tried to move to a quiet, secluded place where the interviewee would feel free to speak, and we could record the conversation clearly. But sometimes that wasn't possible, and we would note that we spoke to the person in a busy hallway or while he or she was en route to a class.

We caught up with Kyle Goodman, the young man who had identified Betsy's body, outside the animation studio that afternoon. "I figured she was going to get in trouble later in the term," he said, as we walked down the hall together, students ebbing and flowing around us.

"She could draw, for sure, but animation is a lot more than that.

To be a good animator, you need knowledge of trigonometry, algebra, and integral calculus. She didn't know much math and I was sure she'd be coming to me for help."

Kyle looked like he wouldn't mind that at all. He dressed like a classic nerd, in sneakers, black draw-string nylon shorts, and a t-shirt that read "There is a fine line between a numerator and a denominator. Only a fraction will understand."

"Really?" I asked. "You use a lot of math in animation?"

He nodded. "You need to understand trigonometry to know how to rotate and move characters. You need integral calculus to simulate how light bounces around in an environment. Remember, images are just a collection of pixels. Directing how they move around is complicated. One of my professors said it's like a marionette with seven hundred strings."

We added her deficiency in math to the profile we were developing of Betsy and let Kyle get to the animation lab for a tutorial.

By the time Ray and I were ready to leave HAC, neither of us felt like we'd made much progress. "The key is going to be her phone records," I said, as we walked to the visitors' lot where we had parked. "We need to know who she was texting with before she left her room."

"Although she might have been texting with someone other than the person she was going out to meet," Ray said. "I wouldn't be surprised if Betsy had several guys dancing attendance on her."

"We'll have to come back here later this evening to hit the dorms after the students have been to dinner," I said. "You okay with that?"

"Fine with me. Julie isn't teaching today, so she can pick up Vinnie at Punahou and feed him. How about you?"

"Nobody to go home to," I said. "Mike is practicing every evening for the 10 K run his department is sponsoring. And you know about Roby."

"Then we know what we need to do," Ray said.

As we drove back to headquarters, we laid out our plans. "I'll figure out who Betsy's cell carrier was and put together a subpoena for her phone records," he said. "You think you can transcribe the interviews?"

"I can."

As soon as we got to headquarters, I went to Lieutenant Sampson's office. "You were out at HAC," he said, when I rapped on the side of his open door. "Accident or homicide?"

"Too early to tell. Ryan Kainoa spotted a big bruise on the back of her head, which might have been caused by a blunt object. That would account for the large amount of blood on the stone, and the traces leading to the cliffside. No indication from her roommate or her belongings that she was suicidal. And she didn't tell her roommate she was going out late last night."

"Meeting a boy? Or a girl?"

Sampson's stepdaughter Kitty was a lesbian, so he was always open to LGBT angles on a case. "Most likely a boy, because she had a half-empty package of birth control pills in her drawer. But we'll keep our eyes open."

"Let me know when you hear from the ME. If he rules this accidental you can move on. I've got a terroristic threat case that needs a detective when you're free."

"Will do."

By the time I returned to my desk Ray had a cell and office number for Betsy Lawrence's mother in San Francisco. "Rock, paper, scissors?" I asked him.

We both made fists, then swung our hands open. I had two fingers closed together to make a pair of scissors, but Ray handed me a fist. Rock.

"You make the call," he said.

I blew out a long breath and sat down at my desk. It was late afternoon in San Francisco. I dialed the office number.

A woman answered. "Interim Solutions."

"I'm trying to reach Kerry Lawrence," I said.

"Who may I say is calling?"

"Detective Kimo Kanapa'aka, from the Honolulu Police Department."

"Can you spell that, please?"

I did, and she put me on hold. A moment later, a woman picked up. "This is Kerry Lawrence. Is something wrong with Betsy?"

"I'm afraid there's no easy way to say this," I said. "Your daughter fell down a hillside behind the Honolulu Arts College. She didn't survive the fall."

There was a sudden intake of breath, and Kerry said, "You're sure it's Betsy?"

"We had her neighbor at the dorm identify her."

"When did this happen?"

"Last night, sometime after ten PM. That's when her roommate went to sleep. We'll have a better idea after the autopsy."

"Do you have to do that? Cut my little girl open?"

"I'm afraid the Medical Examiner has to perform an autopsy every time there's a suspicious death. But Doc Takayama and his staff will make sure she looks as beautiful as you remember her."

Kerry Lawrence was crying by then, so I waited to ask, "When was the last time you spoke to Betsy?"

"Sunday evening."

"She was happy? Not upset about anything, or depressed?"

"She loved the school and her classes and the tropical climate. It can get chilly here in the Bay Area. She liked her roommate and she'd met a few other girls."

"Did she ever say anything about someone who she didn't get along with? I've got several nieces, and when they were that age they were in and out of arguments with other girls – one day best friends, another day mortal enemies. Was there anyone like that in Betsy's life?"

Kerry hesitated long enough that I thought there was something there. "My daughter could be mean, detective. I tried my best to raise her properly, but her father left us when she was five, and I guess I spoiled her. At school she hung out with a clique of pretty young women, and I heard reports that they were nasty to some of the less attractive girls. She was very susceptible to male attention, too, because her father wasn't part of her life."

"Did she mention any girl in particular she'd had a fight with?"

"No."

"Any boy she was interested in?"

"She said she was chatting with boys online, but she hadn't met any of them yet."

"One more thing. Her phone and computer are password-protected. Do you know her passwords?"

"I don't. Until she turned eighteen, one condition of her having a phone and a computer was that I had to have her passwords. I never had to use them—if I asked her, she showed me what she was looking at, or her phone contact list. But after that birthday she announced I had no right to spy on her anymore."

I thanked Kerry Lawrence, gave her my phone number, and told her I'd be in touch when she would be able to make arrangements to bring Betsy home.

I hung up, feeling like crap. Notifying next of kin was the worst part of my job, especially when I couldn't tell them definitively what had happened. I knew that left them open to imagining horrible things, as I would if anything happened to Addie or Owen. Each death was like a bruise on my soul, and I wondered how long I could continue sustaining them.

Chapter 6
Suicide, Accident or Murder?

Ray prepared the subpoena for Betsy's cell phone records, and left the office to get it signed by a judge and hand-deliver it to the T-Mobile office. We'd had to wait sometimes up to forty-five days for such records, but with a sympathetic ear we could get them earlier, particularly if they were important in the early stages of an investigation.

While he was gone, I went through the tedious process of uploading the audio files for transcription. The department subscribed to a clunky web app that we used for that purpose. I had to use my phone to email the recording, and a speech-to-text program converted it to something we could review. I also sent the recording to my work email, and uploaded the file to our database, so we had both the original recording and the transcription in case they were needed by attorneys.

I began the endless round of paperwork that accompanied a homicide investigation. I began by entering the information that had come in via Simon Aquino's 911 call and moved forward, adding everything we did and everyone we talked to.

I had made some headway, but not a lot, by the time Ray returned. It was dinnertime, and we'd only eaten snacks at the HAC cafeteria, so we stopped at a Zippy's on the way up to Manoa. I knew that I should eat something healthy, but I've loved their loco moco since I was a teenager. It's a hamburger patty on top of rice, smothered with brown gravy and topped with two eggs. I ordered a Sprunch, an island mix of Sprite and fruit punch, to wash it all down.

Ray had long ago fallen under the spell of Korean fried chicken, prepared by Mike's mother, and ordered it whenever he could. The Zippy's version couldn't compare to hers, but it did come with two scoops of rice and one scoop of macaroni salad.

As we ate, I asked, "What's your gut feeling about Betsy Lawrence? Murder, suicide, or accident?"

"I doubt it's suicide. There's no way she could have banged her own head on the stone and flung herself off the cliff. And we didn't get any indication she was unhappy or stressed by the move to Hawai'i or starting college."

I ate too fast, stopping frequently to wipe gravy from my mouth. "I agree. No evidence of prescription drug use or suicidal ideation either."

"Which leaves us with accident or murder," Ray said. "She hadn't been at HAC long, so it's possible she was walking along the edge of the cliff in the dark. She might have stumbled and hit her head on the pavement, which would account for the bruise and the blood. She might have stood up, wobbling from the concussion, and gone too close to the edge."

"True. But why did she leave her room at ten o'clock at night, after her roommate had already gone to bed? She had classes the next day."

"That's the real question, isn't it?" I asked.

A young man whose name tag identified him as Justin was behind the desk at Mizushima Hall when we arrived, and once again I had to hold my badge up to the glass. He stepped out from behind the half-round desk and came over to the glass window. He peered at my badge as if translating it from English into something his brain could process.

He went back to the desk and buzzed us in. "Are you here about the girl who died?" he asked.

"We are," I said. "Did you know her?"

He shook his head. "She was a first-year, and I'm in my fourth year. We wouldn't have any classes in common."

"But you'd see her going in and out, wouldn't you?" Ray asked.

Justin shrugged. "I don't usually look up at who comes and goes. As long as you have an ID, you can get in. And you don't need to badge your way out." He held up a thick textbook with a maroon binding, which I recognized as a newer edition of the art history text I'd used decades before at UC Santa Cruz, and still had somewhere on my bookshelves. "I mostly study."

"Any security cameras in the area?" Ray asked, looking around.

"Not as far as I know," Justin said. "We're pretty isolated up here. Only students and faculty and the occasional hiker ever come this far up the mountain."

We thanked him and rode the elevator to the third floor. Ray started at the suite closest to the elevator, while I walked to the far end of the hall and knocked on the door on the opposite side of the hall.

We repeated the process we had done that morning, showing our IDs, verifying we could record the conversation, then asking questions about Betsy Lawrence and life at HAC. I asked the young women about security and safety, and they all said that they'd felt safe until they heard about Betsy.

No one answered at a couple of the doors on Ray's side of the hall. I got the side with Kyle Goodman, but he hadn't remembered anything new. "You have a roommate?" I asked, looking around behind where he stood in the doorway.

"I did, but he dropped out after the first week of classes," he said. "He was a heavy-duty gamer and he was in the game design program with me, but he didn't realize all the work required for the major. The art, the programming, the math. He was totally overwhelmed and got on a plane for home. They haven't given me a new roommate yet."

He smiled. "Maybe I'll get lucky and get a single for the year."

"Maybe." I thanked him and moved on. Kimora's room was a couple of doors down, but she wouldn't open the door very widely because she had some kind of mud mask on her face. She hadn't thought of anything else about Betsy.

"This was a big waste of time," I said to Ray as we rode down in the elevator. "Did you get anything?"

"Not about Betsy. This student named Lee…"

I interrupted. "Personal pronouns they and their?"

He laughed. "You spoke to them earlier?"

"I did. What did they have to say?"

"There's a guy on the floor named Chris who goes out a lot at night," he said. "Lee wondered about him. Of course, he wasn't in his room, so I'll have to track him down. He might have been outside at the same time as Betsy."

"Or he might be the person Betsy was meeting," I said.

He frowned. "If they lived on the same floor, why go downstairs to meet? When I was in college my friends and I—male and female—were in and out of each other's rooms all the time. Talking, listening to music, playing backgammon."

I looked at him. "Backgammon?"

"It was a thing when I was in college. For the kids who weren't smart enough to play chess. You probably played chess, didn't you?"

"Are you kidding? I was always either surfing, sleeping, or studying. In that order."

I yawned. It had been a long day, and I was eager to get home. I hoped that Mike would be there. We'd exchanged texts earlier and it wasn't clear which of us would get home first.

Not that it mattered. The house would still seem empty.

As it happened, I got home first, and because I was feeling lonely and neglected, I went into our bedroom and picked up the book I was reading, *Hard Dick Failure*. It was a gay romance novel full of sexy images, and I had to admit I was addicted. I'd already read three others in the series: *Dick Drive, Compact Dick,* and *Floppy Dick.* They were all about guys working in high-tech industries and their romantic adventures.

I was glad they were on my Kindle so no one else could see what I was reading. It was a bit embarrassing to be almost fifty years old and getting a hard-on from the sexual exploits of twenty-something tech bros, and I was doubly worried because Dakota was dating one of those guys and I didn't want him to think I was perving on their relationship.

But by the time Mike came home I was horny, and when he came out of the shower wrapped only in a towel, I pounced on him, pulling down the towel to expose his body. He wasn't as well-built as he'd been when we met. I ignored the bit of dad tummy and focused on his dick, which still got hard as soon as I began to lick it.

"Have you been reading porn again?" Mike asked, as I went down on him. "Because if you have been I'm all for it."

I didn't answer. Quickly we moved to the bed, and we worked on satisfying each other. It took longer than it had when we were younger, but I didn't mind, and neither did he. He was still handsome, and I hoped I never got tired of looking at his face or his body.

His mother was Korean and his father Italian, and Mike had inherited features from both of them. Dark, wavy hair, a narrow face, broad shoulders. I teased him sometimes that if he was younger he could have fronted a K-Pop band—but of course, when we were that age we would have thought K-Pop was a kind of soda.

He was nearly three inches taller than I was, which I liked because it made me feel safe in his arms. And the height difference didn't matter when we were in bed.

When we were finished and cleaned up, we sat in bed and shared the news of our days. "We caught a case this morning," I said. "Student at HAC. Looks like murder."

"HAC? Isn't that where Apikela goes?"

"Yeah, I tried to reach her today but couldn't. I'll have to try her again."

"You don't think anything's wrong with her, do you?"

I looked at him. "I didn't, until now. What makes you say that?"

"Well, you just said a student was murdered at her college, and you couldn't get a hold of her. I just put two and two together."

I leaned over and grabbed my phone. A pair of text messages had come in from Api while Mike and I were engaged. The first read simply "Uncle K?"

When I didn't respond, she'd added, "Sorry I missed U. Talk to U tomorrow."

That was a relief. But I had to remember that a young woman had died on that campus, and I had to make sure Api knew to stay safe.

Chapter 7
Semantics

Tuesday morning Ray and I finished as much paperwork as we could while we waited for the autopsy report on Betsy Lawrence and her cell phone records. When we couldn't delay any longer, we picked up the information on the terroristic threat case Lieutenant Sampson had on the docket. Brandon Paikai had been arrested outside a popular Waikiki bar for throwing eggs and tomatoes at couples going in or out.

"I didn't realize throwing tomatoes counts as terrorism," I said.

"You're the one who's always mentioning semantics," Ray said. "I think there's a difference between terrorism and terroristic threatening."

He turned to his computer and looked up the relevant statute. "A person commits the offense of terroristic threatening if the person threatens, by word or conduct, to cause bodily injury to another person or serious damage or harm to property, including their pets or livestock."

"So if someone says, 'I'm going to kill your cow if it keeps grazing on my land,' that's terroristic threatening?" I asked. "Somehow doesn't mean what I thought it would."

"It's still not something the tourist board wants to brag about,"

Ray said. "Come to Waikiki with your sweetheart and have eggs thrown at you."

"His address is on Mekia Street in Waimanalo," I said. "Paikai is a Hawaiian name. I wonder if that's homestead land." I turned to my own computer and punched in the address. Brandon Paikai was listed as the owner of a 1,000 square foot home, which was impressive for an unemployed twenty-six-year-old in our high-priced housing market. When I looked closer and I discovered that the property had been transferred to him by will two years before from someone called Mickey Paikai.

Hunting farther back, I found that Mickey had inherited the property from Noa Paikai twenty years before. So even if it wasn't homestead land, it had been in the Paikai family for a long time.

"What was the father's name?" Ray asked.

"Mickey. But could also be under Michael."

"I'm hunting for an obituary. Here it is. Ah, Mickey was his mother, short for Michelle. Daughter of Noa and Kalea. Survived by son Brandon. No record of a husband."

He read on further. "Donations can be made to the American Diabetes Association or the Waimanalo Seventh-Day Adventist Church."

I pushed back from my desk. "Suppose we drive up to Waimanalo and look for Brandon, see what he has to say."

We took the Pali Highway over the mountains and headed for a Kope Bean coffee shop in Kailua to caffeinate for what was probably going to be a weird morning.

Traffic on the Pali was light and we zoomed along winding roads carved out of steep tree-lined hillsides. I loved the moments when the road curved along the edge of a hill and we got a panoramic view of the valley and Kailua Bay. No rockslides blocked the road or the tunnels so we made good time up to Kailua Road, where we detoured. "Another name definition for you," I said to Ray. "In Hawaiian, pai means to urge or to rouse, while kai means ocean. So Paikai must mean something like making waves."

The Virgin Homicides

"Thank you, Mr. Surfer," Ray said. "There's the coffee shop."

It was fancier than many Kope Beans we'd visited, with stone walls, arched windows, and Greek columns along the front. "Did this place use to be a Greek diner or something?" I asked the barista while he poured my café mocha and added raspberry syrup.

"The Skyline Diner," he said. "Owned by Mr. Pappas. When he died his kids sold the place to the Kope Bean and the chain kept the décor."

Ray and I sat by the window in a red vinyl booth and sipped our coffee and I told him more about Apikela and her career as an influencer. "It kills me to know I've worked as a cop for twenty-five years, and she's nineteen and earning more than I do. And all she does is sit in front of a camera and talk about makeup."

"Different strokes for different folks," Ray said, between sips of his coffee.

"I didn't spend much time with my nieces and nephews when they became teenagers," I said. "They don't need me to teach them surfing anymore, and even at family luaus they cluster together in the corner. It's like they have a special language of slang terms and music references, and anyone over twenty-five isn't cool. So I wonder if this obsession with beauty is recent."

Ray shrugged. "Kids have always focused on externals. When I was a teenager it was all about leather jackets and Doc Marten boots. We wore plaid shirts and listened to Nirvana. The girls painted their nails and used heavy eye makeup, but that might have just been South Philly."

He took a sip of his coffee, a cold brew with hazelnut syrup. "If you didn't dress the way everyone else did you were an outcast. Personally I hated Doc Martens but they were what all the guys wore."

Once we were fortified, we drove over to Waimanalo and found Brandon Paikai's house, a nondescript bungalow with peeling paint and an overgrown front yard. A beat-up Toyota sedan in the driveway had plates that were registered to him, so we figured he was home.

The guy who answered the door was at least a hundred pounds heavier than he should have been, with stringy black hair and a missing front tooth. "Brandon Paikai?" I asked, holding up my badge.

"What do you want?"

"A little conversation," I said. "Can we come in?"

He frowned, but shrugged. "Wasn't expecting visitors."

He led us into a dim living room, with curtains drawn over the front window. It smelled like burnt pizza and dirty underwear. A computer on the desk in the corner was playing a violent video, a brutal fight between two groups of men. He hurried over and shut it down, then walked over to a rickety wooden table with three chairs, and we all sat down.

"Tell us about Sailor's Rest," Ray said.

Brandon sneered. "Yuppie bar."

I hadn't heard that term in a while. "That's why you were throwing eggs and tomatoes at people? Because they're yuppies?" I asked.

"They flaunt their ability to get mates, just because they're good-looking," Brandon said. "The women are whores riding a cock carnival."

I had to resist the urge to laugh at that phrase. During the time after I came out of the closet and before I met Mike, I took a few rides on that cock carnival myself.

"It's the women you're unhappy with?" Ray asked.

"Them, and the guys with them. If it has a pussy, some guy will be desperate enough to fuck it. Men are lining up to fuck pigs, hippos, and ogres."

Brandon was a hippo himself, though not as cute as the ones in the zoo. "What about you? You willing to fuck a pig or a hippo?"

"Not on your life. I deserve a beautiful woman."

"So that's why you were pelting those people with produce. Because you deserve what they have?"

"Why shouldn't I? I'm a man. Because I've got a dick I'm superior to anything with a pussy. Those women ought to be lining up to fuck me."

"But they're not, are they, Brandon?" Ray asked.

Brandon didn't answer, just sneered.

"Look, you can't go around tossing stuff at people you don't like," I said. "For one thing, it's fucking rude. And for another, it's against the law. You don't want to go to jail, do you?"

"Why should I go to jail? I'm expressing my opinion. I'm just doing it with eggs and tomatoes. The first amendment protects my freedom of speech."

I shook my head. "Freedom of speech does not extend to throwing shit at people. You want to stand outside the bar and politely engage people coming out about your views, you're free to do that. But what you're doing is called terroristic threatening, and the constitution of the State of Hawai'i makes that a felony."

"This was your first arrest, right?" Ray asked.

Brandon nodded.

"If you agree not to keep harassing people, we'll talk to the Prosecuting Attorney, see if his office can go easy on you. Bringing you in for a felony makes a lot of paperwork for us, and trouble for you. You want to get a girlfriend? There's better ways to direct your energy. Lose some weight, brush up your conversational skills. Maybe lower your standards."

"I don't need to do all that."

I blew out a breath. "No, Brandon, you don't. But if you keep harassing people you're going to get arrested again. You have money for bail? The average bail amount in Honolulu for the lowest level felony can be up to $20,000."

"No way."

"Yes way," I said, and realized I was parroting Dakota. Funny the influence your kids can have on you when you're trying to influence them. "And if you don't have the money and you have to go to a bail bondsman, you pay that company ten percent. So even if the judge throws out your case, you're still out two grand."

Ray waved his hand around the dilapidated house. "I get the feeling you can't afford to lose two grand, Brandon. So why don't you give this quest of yours a rest. You want to do that?"

He frowned, but he nodded. "I ain't got two grand to waste."

Ray and I both stood up. "Good man," I said. "You listen to what my fellow detective here suggested. And when you speak to whoever's handling your case at the Prosecuting Attorney's office, you tell them you're sorry for your mistake and you're going to turn things around, find yourself a good woman."

He didn't say anything, so we walked outside and got into my SUV. "I need a shower after spending time in that house," I said.

"You think he's going to stop what he's doing?"

"I can't see him joining a gym and cleaning up the house," I said. "So I doubt he's going to start dating soon. But I hope we scared him enough so that he stops harassing people."

"Scared straight," Ray said, and he laughed. "Who knows, maybe he'll go over to your side. Big guy like that probably has a fat dick, right? I'm sure there are gay guys who would blow him."

"You are way too gay friendly sometimes," I said, as I backed out of the driveway.

Chapter 8
Autopsy

When we got back to headquarters, I called the Prosecuting Attorney's office and spoke to Daniel Francois, the Assistant Prosecuting Attorney in charge of Brandon's case and relayed what we had learned. "What are you going to do about him?" I asked.

"Honestly, I think the arresting officer was too aggressive," he said. "Sometimes the beat cops get a phrase in their head like terroristic threatening and they want to use it. I don't think we have much of a case, but of course the city fathers and mothers don't like to see anyone throwing produce at tourists."

"Let me know if you need anything more from us," I said.

Soon after that, the Medical Examiner's office notified us that they had completed Betsy Lawrence's autopsy, and we drove out to the medical examiner's office on Iwilei Road, just off the Nimitz Highway. It was in a two-story concrete building with a slight roof overhang. The paint on the building was peeling and the landscaping was overgrown— after all, the dead don't vote.

The building was between the Salvation Army and a homeless center— something I always thought was an ironic comment, but maybe was intended as an object lesson to those less fortunate. You never know what the city fathers are really thinking, after all.

We pulled into the small parking area in front of the building, and walked in the glass block entrance. The always cheerful receptionist, Alice Kanamura, directed us to Doc's office.

Even twenty years into his tenure, Doc Takayama still looked young, though he had gained lines in his face and a few gray hairs. After greeting us, he got down to it. "Initial examination was correct. Miss Lawrence was hit in the back of the head with a heavy blunt object, resulting in a contusion which caused severe traumatic brain injury. The impact would have resulted in an immediate loss of consciousness."

He looked up at us. "This was followed by an intracranial hemorrhage – bleeding between the brain tissue and skull. When a hemorrhage interrupts blood flow around or inside the brain, depriving it of oxygen for more than three or four minutes, the brain cells die. I'd say Miss Lawrence died within ten to fifteen minutes of the assault."

"Is there any indication whether she fell down the hillside after the assault or was thrown?" I asked.

"There is some abrasion on the backs of her calves consistent with her body being dragged over the ground immediately after death."

"So no chance this was an accident," Ray said.

Doc nodded. "An accidental death would not be consistent with my findings."

"Any idea what she was hit with?" I asked.

"We identified some fibers in the area of the wound," he said. "That implies that she was hit with something heavy that was covered with canvas. I've already forwarded the samples to the crime scene team to see if they can match them to anything."

"How about direction or force of the blow?" Ray asked.

"The blow hit her head straight on, which implies that the assailant was at least a few inches taller. Detective, if I may?"

"Sure."

He positioned Ray, then picked up his cloth laptop bag—empty at the moment. He grabbed the edge of the bag with two hands and pivoted toward Ray's head. "See, I'm several inches shorter than you are, so it would be harder for me to raise the implement high enough to hit with the right force and the right angle."

He turned to me. "You give it a try."

I was about three inches taller than Ray. When I swung toward him, I was able to keep the laptop bag flat, and come right up close to the edge of his head in the correct position.

"Excellent demonstration," Doc said, taking the bag from me.

"No indication if the killer was right or left-handed?" Ray asked.

Doc shook his head. "To obtain the right amount of force the killer had to use both hands."

"Did she fall forward?" I asked.

"I don't think so. There were no abrasions on her palms or forehead that would be consistent with that. Instead I think her knees crumpled and absorbed the force of the blow. Then she would have fallen backwards, allowing the killer to grab her legs and drag her to the edge of the cliff."

"How about indications of sexual activity?" Ray asked.

"Nothing recent. No evidence of sperm or semen in the mouth, vagina or anus. As far as I can tell there was no sexual activity that evening. I also detected a layer of lip primer beneath her lipstick, which would have prevented the lipstick from smudging if kissed. So I can't even tell you if she kissed her assailant."

"Any defensive marks? Could she have pushed him away before being hit?"

"Again, nothing decisive. No material under her nails. By the way, she used a silicone-based nail polish which had a distinctive vinegar odor, and the aroma was still present, which means she polished her nails shortly before her death. Similarly she used a product in her hair which had a honeysuckle scent."

"So she was possibly primping before a date?" Ray asked.

"Given the circumstances, I think that's a reasonable hypothesis."

We asked as many questions as we could, but got nothing further.

As Ray drove us back to headquarters, we began to build a theory. "According to Kimora, shortly before her death Betsy was texting with someone on her phone, possibly a guy," I said. "So let's start with that. Then Betsy washes her hair and paints her nails, as if she's getting ready for a date. Kimora's already on her way to bed so she doesn't see Betsy leave."

"Betsy meets someone outside her dorm," Ray continued. "Given the evidence we found in her room, we can say that person is male. She was ready for a date with the lip primer and nail polish. But there's no indication that they carried through."

"Maybe they argue, and he hits Betsy and drags her body to the cliff, hoping her injuries will look like the result of a fall," I said.

When we got back to the office Ray documented our conversation with Doc and wrote down our speculations as I reported to Lieutenant Sampson. He was wearing another one of his jewel-tone polo shirts, this one an emerald green, and he motioned me to a seat while he finished a call.

"What's up?" he asked, after he put the phone down.

I ran through our meeting with Brandon Paikai. "I don't know if we got through to him, but I'll keep an eye out in case his name comes up again. I spoke to Daniel Francois at the Prosecuting Attorney's office and he doesn't think they have much of a case against Brandon, so they're not inclined to prosecute. And the death of the young woman at HAC has been classified a homicide, based on Doc's autopsy."

"Any suspects?"

I shook my head. "Her mother called her a mean girl, and so did the young woman who works the desk in the lobby of the dorm. Very pretty, liked to hang out with others who were good-looking. We've talked to a lot of students about Betsy and we're starting to put together a profile. My niece is a student up there, and I've been trying to get hold of her to see what she can tell us about the victim and the general atmosphere of the college."

The Virgin Homicides

"Keep me in the loop."

I realized I hadn't heard from Apikela yet, so I called her. I got her voice mail. "Sorry, I'm probably filming one of my awesome TikTok videos right now, so I can't get to the phone. Leave me a message and don't forget to follow me @Apikela!"

"Api, it's Uncle K. I need to talk to you as soon as possible about the girl who died at HAC."

Then I went downstairs to the crime lab on the lower level, where I found Ryan Kainoa. "Autopsy indicates Betsy Lawrence is a homicide victim," I said. "Did you find her phone on the hillside?"

"We found several pieces of a gold iPhone 14 on the rocks below where we found the body. That model uses eSIM technology and isn't compatible with physical SIM cards, so there isn't a physical SIM card. Because of the damage, you can't use what we found or even see the call log."

"That matches the kind of phone her roommate said she had," I said. "How about her emails? Can we read those?"

"Sure. If you want to sign off on the computer, I'll give it to you, and write down the password for you."

"That would be great."

I carried the laptop upstairs and Ray and I sat at my desk to start looking through it. We began with her recent history and I was surprised at how many dating sites she visited. "Isn't that weird?" I asked. "She's a college student. She should be doing her homework, not trolling every dating site."

Ray shrugged. "She'd only been in Honolulu for less than a month. Probably checking out the dating scene."

We discovered that she had identities on six different sites and had been chatting with as many as a dozen boys. "Or people who pretend to be boys," Ray said. "Who knows who's behind those profiles?"

"She used her real picture in her profile," I said. "And real information, about being a student at HAC, interested in animation and so on."

"I'm not surprised she got so much interest. Fresh meat, pretty face, something to chat about that would interest boys."

"We keep using the terms boys and girls," I said. "But Betsy was eighteen, which makes her a young woman. And these people she's chatting with might be grown men."

We made a list of all the profiles who had contact with her, but that was all we could get without a subpoena to each online site. And even then, some of those profiles could have been set up with false information.

I was surprised to look up and see Lieutenant Sampson's large frame looming over my desk. "In my office," he said, glaring at me.

He turned and stalked off. "What did you do now?" Ray asked.

I opened my hands and shrugged my shoulders. "Beats me."

I stood up and followed Sampson to his office, where he motioned me to a chair across from him. That did not bode well.

"Milton Medeiros," he said.

"Dean of Students at HAC," I said.

"You know I like to take a hands-off approach to your investigations," he said. "That includes avoiding calls from peripheral figures, like Mr. Medeiros."

"Why did he call you?"

"He was less than impressed with your people skills," Sampson said. "He called the mayor, whom he knows through the Honolulu Rotary Club, to complain about you. The mayor called the chief of police. Who gave him my number."

"I know. Shit rolls downhill."

"What exactly did you do to upset Mr. Medeiros?"

I thought back to our encounter. "I was standing in front of a group of students watching Betsy Lawrence's body be winched up from the cliffside," I said. "I asked anyone who knew her or had anything to share to step up and talk to me."

Sampson nodded.

"No one volunteered. So I might have used somewhat stronger

language. I didn't curse at them but I did ask if any of them cared that one of their classmates had just been brutally murdered."

"Did you know at that time this was a murder case?" Sampson asked.

"No, we did not," I said. "We didn't know that until after Doc's autopsy."

"So you tossed the word 'murder' around among a group of impressionable young people," Sampson said. "Did you think that was wise?"

We didn't often get dressed down by Sampson for the way we handled cases, but when he dished it out he was merciless.

"No, sir."

"I understand that Mr. Medeiros offered you space in his office to conduct interviews, and that you didn't accept."

I looked up at him. He played minor league baseball for a couple of years before joining the police force, so that meant he had been a good player in college as well. I took a gamble on my approach to his statement.

"I'm sure that as a college athlete, you were focused on your studies and your workouts, so you didn't get called into the Dean's office," I said, with only a hint of sarcasm. "In my experience, being asked to visit that area is not usually pleasant. So I thought students would be more willing to talk to us in a neutral location, like the café."

A hint of a smile danced on the edge of his lips. "I was indeed focused on athletics in college," he said. "But I was called to the Dean's office once, and I did not enjoy it. So I understand your choice. But I want you to speak with Mr. Medeiros and keep him apprised of your progress on the investigation. A pleasant word from him to his friend the mayor would be welcome."

"I understand."

He nodded toward the door. "You can go."

Suitably chastised, I returned to my desk. "We have to go back to HAC," I said to Ray. "I have to make nice with the Dean of Students.

And we need a better picture of Betsy Lawrence." I picked up my phone. "I know who to start with."

I tried Apikela again, but once again I got her voice mail. "Api, it's Uncle K. I'm investigating Betsy Lawrence's death and I need to talk to you. I'm coming up to HAC in a few minutes. Call me as soon as you get this so we can meet up."

I stood up and grabbed my iPad. "I will put out an APB on Apikela if I need to," I said. "I have a feeling she knew Betsy, and she'll have an opinion about her, even if it's only about her personal grooming products."

Chapter 9
Green Monster

Ray volunteered to stay at headquarters and work on paperwork while he waited for Betsy's phone records. It was a bright, sunny day, but the air inside the parking garage was dark and humid. Sweat began to trickle down my back as I walked to my SUV, and I turned the air conditioning to full blast as soon as I got in.

I was heading up Oahu Avenue toward HAC when Apikela's call came through. I always felt like I needed to lean toward the speakers when I answered a call through Bluetooth. "Hey, Api."

"Sorry I didn't call you back right away yesterday, Uncle K. Things are cra-a-zy right now. I'm talking to a major lipstick brand about endorsements. I can't say anything yet but it could be huge."

"That's good. But I need to talk to you about Betsy Lawrence. Did you know her?"

"For sure. I met her like on her second day of school. She had awesome nail work."

"I'm on my way up to HAC now. Can I buy you a coffee or a smoothie or whatever you drink?"

"Sure, there's a terrific café in the lobby of Manoa Hall. That's the student affairs building."

"I'll be there in ten," I said.

"Oh, I have to put on my face. I might be a few minutes longer than that."

I wanted to point out that I had known what her face looked like since she was a baby, but I knew that wasn't what she meant. "See you when I see you."

"Unless I see you first," she said, and she hung up before I could laugh.

I parked in a space marked for visitors and looked around before I got out. There were tall streetlights around the perimeter of the lot and along a pathway that led to the complex of buildings. The area looked well-lit, but I didn't see any cameras, and there was no fence or gate to enter the campus.

I knew Api would take longer than ten minutes, so I walked up to the center of the green between the four buildings and stood there watching the ebb and flow of students. There was a mix of ethnicities, though it tended toward the Asian and Pacific Islander. A couple of big guys who were probably Samoan, lots of Japanese and Korean and combinations.

As immigrants to Hawai'i left their ethnic enclaves and mixed with others, it was harder for me to slot people into boxes. Sure, I could tell there were a lot of very pretty Korean boys and girls, but many of those who passed me defied easy classification, kind of like Mike and me. You could tell that both of us had haole features as well as Asian heritage, but you couldn't immediately say what our ancestry was.

Most of the boys looked grungy, in t-shirts with smart-aleck slogans like "My opinion offended you? You should hear what I keep to myself." And "I hope you step on a Lego."

A few of them looked either preppy or gay—it was hard to tell. Pink polo shirts, white shorts, pristine sneakers. The colored streaks in their hair were probably the dividing line, but then, I didn't hang out with many young, straight guys beyond my nephews.

There was a similar dichotomy between the girls. Many of

them wore lipstick, mascara and nail polish like battle emblems. Their appearance was carefully calculated for maximum curb appeal. On the other end of the scale were girls like Su-Kim, who wore camouflage colors, cargo shorts and t-shirts spattered with paint.

It was an art college, so I expected the students to be artsy. I gave up my surveillance and walked over to Manoa Hall, where there was still no evidence of my niece. I walked up to the café and perused the menu. They leaned heavily toward Generation Z drinks, like boba tea and smoothies that resembled the green slime that accumulated in the sewer drain near our house.

But I wasn't judging. I was about to order myself a café mocha when Apikela bounced up beside me. "Aloha kakahiaka," she said, and she kissed my cheek.

"Good morning to you too. What can I get you?"

She put her arm in mine, but turned her full attention on the pierced young man behind the counter. "Hi, Brian," she said.

"Hey Api. You want your regular green monster?"

"Api-solutely," she said and she smiled brightly at him.

He responded with a shy smile. "And I'll have a café mocha," I said. I handed him my credit card.

He looked from Api to me. "My niece," I said. "For real."

He looked relieved and took my card. "What's in a green monster?" I asked Api.

"Kale, spinach, mango, banana, pineapple, and coconut water. It's a real pick-me-up and great for the skin, too."

"I'll take your word for it."

"I'll bring your drinks over when they're ready," Brian said, as he handed me back my credit card.

Api led me to a table in a nook by the window. It was a great choice, because we could talk without being overheard.

In the past, we'd only spoken occasionally, usually at family luaus or other celebrations. I had the opinion that she was a beautiful airhead, but that was changing quickly. It was clear there was a sharp brain operating behind that makeup. You didn't make a hundred grand from computer videos without some savvy.

And she knew that we'd be talking about something sensitive, and wanted privacy for us. Impressive.

"How did you know Betsy Lawrence?" I asked.

"She was in my social media class," she said. "And we had to sit alphabetically, so she was next to me. I worried that the class would be boring because I already know so much but we started with historical stuff like the origins of the Internet, and I didn't know that. Betsy wasn't digging it, though. I looked over a couple of times and saw her doodling in her notebook instead of paying attention."

"What kind of doodles?" I asked, hoping for hearts and initials.

"The professor's head, mostly. I couldn't tell if she was crushing on him or practicing for a class." She fiddled with a silver ring on her finger, a leaping dolphin. The dolphin was my aumakua, or spirit animal, and I wondered if it was hers as well. But that was a conversation for another time.

"He is kind of cute," she continued. "Though he's way old. At least forty. And after our first exam, she went up to talk to him, like maybe she was hoping to flirt her way to a better grade."

I winced as Brian the barista arrived with our drinks. Api's looked vile, but I resisted saying anything.

When he was gone, after another adoring look at my niece, she said, "I saw her answer sheet and she had missed a lot of simple questions. Like, do you know the name of the government agency that developed the Internet?"

"DARPA?" I asked.

She nodded. "And do you know what those initials stand for?"

She had me there, but I tried. I knew DARPA was part of the Defense Department, so I started there. "Defense Agency for Research Projects... I have no idea what the last A could be for."

"Defense Advanced Research Projects Agency," she said. "I mean, I don't know why we had to memorize that, but Betsy didn't get it right."

"What's the professor's name?" I asked. "I might stop by his office hours and talk to him."

"Professor Hong," she said. "He goes by Hong Xiuquan, with his last name first. He's Chinese, from Guangdong." She pronounced his first name as shu-quan.

"What did you think of her beyond class?" I asked.

"Very pretty, of course, and she knew it. Perfect skin—I never saw a pimple or a blemish, so she probably only used a simple cleanser. Very light hand on blush and mascara, and she used a lot of product on her hair to get the perfect waves."

She looked at me and laughed. "Sorry, you don't want to hear about her makeup. You probably want to know if anyone hated her enough to want to kill her."

I said, "Yeah, that's pretty much what I want to know."

"I thought about it the whole time I was getting made up this morning. The problem is she just got here a month ago. I mean, people make rash judgments about others right away. But I can't think of anyone she made enough of an impression on to generate real hatred."

"How about jealousy? That can be a strong motivation."

She frowned. "Some of the girls she was mean to were jealous of her. Like the dorm manager, Su-Kim. She's really sweet, but you could see when she looked at Betsy or her roommate Kimora, she was wishing she was as pretty as they were. But really, would you kill a girl just because she was prettier than you were, even if she was mean to you?"

She shivered. "I hope nobody feels that way about me."

"Su-Kim thinks you're very nice," I said.

"You talked to her?"

"She was on duty Monday morning when we came up here." I felt myself blushing a little, and didn't know why. "She said some of the pretty girls were mean, and I asked about you."

She laughed. "You wanted to know if she thought I was mean?"

"Yeah. I was hoping you weren't, and she said something about how you gave her a lipstick."

"That's sweet," she said. "But you saw how our parents raised us. We were always making rubber wristbands for charity or cleaning up the beach. I'm really into 'do no harm' when it comes to life, and my videos. I talk about inner beauty as much as outer beauty. And there are so many little things you can do to improve your appearance that will make you feel better about yourself."

I couldn't resist. "What about me? I'm older than Professor Hong. What can I do to improve my outer appearance and feel better?"

It was clear from how quickly she responded that she'd thought about this before. "You need to get your hair cut more frequently," she said. "How we take care of ourselves says a lot. And the other thing I would suggest is eye cream."

I frowned. "Dakota uses that."

"And he should. The skin around your eyes is the thinnest on your body, and the most fragile as well. If you don't get enough sleep, you rub your eyes, and that damages the skin and causes dark patches."

She sat back. "You're lucky that your skin takes a tan so easily, like mine, but that can camouflage some problems, like dark spots under your eyes. You take care of your hair and your skin, and I guarantee you'll have guys looking at you." She smiled. "Though I don't know if Uncle Mike would appreciate that."

I laughed. "Who knows, maybe it's Uncle Mike I want to look at me."

She shook her head. "You two are totally in love," she said, emphasizing the last word. "Anybody who looks at you can see that. But it's nice to have people appreciate your looks, as long as it's not pervy."

We were swimming in dangerous waters, and I had to bring the conversation back to my purpose. "Was Betsy the kind to sneak out late to meet a boy—or a girl?"

"Boy, certainly. She was not into girls at all. I don't know, maybe?

She was very sure of herself. I don't think she would have thought it dangerous to go meet a boy after dark. I mean, we're isolated up here." She waved her hand to encompass the campus. "It's not like we're downtown, where creepazoids are around every corner. And she was from the suburbs, right? Not a city girl."

"From the Bay Area," I said. "Not sure what kind of neighborhood."

"Some pretty girls, they wear their faces as a kind of armor, you know?" she asked. "Like 'I'm beautiful so no one can touch me.'"

"Was Betsy that kind of girl?"

Api sucked on her green drink and nodded. "Yeah, I think she was." She looked up. "But someone touched her all right."

Chapter 10
Empty House

Api had to go to class, so she left, carrying her evil-looking drink with her, and I saw her wave to the barista as she passed him. I felt sorry for any boy who had a crush on her. She was a force to be reckoned with, on many levels. I bet Brian comped her drinks regularly, not knowing she had a six-figure income.

I walked over to Reese Hall, the administration building. The ground floor offices were clustered around a central atrium —admissions, registration, student services. I walked into the last of those and asked where I could find Dean Medeiros.

A young student worker pointed me through a glass doorway into an executive suite, where a Chinese woman in late middle age sat at a broad koa wood desk. Her features were delicately sculpted and her skin was flawless. She had a couple of ivory combs in her lustrous black hair, and I could see her as an empress ruling this tiny dynasty.

I introduced myself and asked if I could make an appointment to see Dean Medeiros. My initial impression of the man had been that he wouldn't welcome drop-in visitors, but she said, "He's been expecting you to stop by. I'll let him know you're here."

She turned her face away from me so I couldn't hear what she said on the phone, but when she hung up, she said, "You can go right in," and she pointed me toward a wooden door.

I knocked lightly and walked in. Medeiros was behind a desk even more magnificent than his secretary's, the wood polished to a high shine. And like hers, his was nearly empty except for a phone and name plate. As exemplars of a bureaucracy I knew was founded on paperwork, I wondered how these people got anything done.

"Come in, Detective. Please sit down." Up close I could see lines in his face that I hadn't noticed when we were outside, and his large frame radiated a sense of self-confidence that I was sure helped him manage the faculty and student body.

He motioned me to a large leather armchair, one that I was sure was designed to make visitors feel small. But I wasn't a lecturer groveling before a superior, or a frightened student about to receive punishment, so I sat comfortably and leaned forward. "I wanted to update you on the status of our investigation."

"Excellent. Have you found the person responsible yet?"

"I'm afraid not. We have the autopsy results, which indicate that Ms. Lawrence was indeed murdered. We have interviewed many students who knew her and begun to draw a picture of her, which will guide us in determining a motive for this terrible crime."

I found myself speaking as if I was one of Lui's reporters for KVOL, but I couldn't help it. "We've spoken with her roommate and her mother, and established that she left her room about ten o'clock on Sunday night, following a series of text messages. Unfortunately her phone is missing, and we are waiting for T-Mobile to respond to a subpoena for her records."

He laced his fingers together and stared at me. "Isn't it true that most deaths of this kind are solved within the first forty-eight hours?"

"The key word there is most," I said. "In my twenty years on the force, most of the murders I've seen or investigated were committed by someone close to the victim. Many are domestic and it's clear almost from the start who is responsible."

I stopped to swallow. "On the other end of the spectrum are incidents like thrill crimes or serial killers, where there's little or no connection between victim and perpetrator. Right now we're treating Ms. Lawrence's killing as somewhere in the middle. It's going to take us time and shoe leather to figure it out, but we will do our best."

Medeiros frowned. "I can't say I'm happy that our campus is still under a dark shadow, but I understand you have your procedures."

He leaned forward. "Once you have established what happened, I would appreciate hearing the news before you release it to the public. I'm sure you will understand that my staff will need to find a way to communicate that news to our academic community."

"I don't have a problem with that, sir," I said. Time to put Medeiros on the defensive, before he could ask more favors of me. "From what we've seen, there aren't many security cameras on campus—certainly not compared to the number, say, at UH, just down the hill. Is there a reason for that?"

Medeiros backed away, and looked like he'd swallowed something nasty. "Every academic institution has its priorities," he said. "And there are always demands for more funds than we have available to allocate. I can assure you that the security of our students, faculty and staff is of utmost importance, and I have staff members revisiting the issue as we speak."

I stood up. "Thank you for your help, Dean Medeiros. I'll be in touch when we have more news."

I turned and walked out before he could ask anything more.

Once out of the administrative offices, I climbed a circular ramp to the second floor, where I found four office suites: Computer Applications, Sciences, Fine Arts, and Humanities. Apikela had mentioned Betsy's flirtation with the professor of their social media class, Hong Xiuquan. I wasn't sure where that fit in the four departments, so I began with Humanities.

A young woman who had to be barely older than the student body sat at a reception desk cluttered with flyers for upcoming events, information on registration, and a stacked plastic display of business cards for faculty members. While I waited for her to finish on a phone call, I spotted a card for Professor Xiuquan Hong, so I knew I was in the right place.

"How can I help you?" the young woman asked when she finished her call. I plucked one of Professor Hong's cards from the display. "Can you tell me when Professor Hong has office hours?"

"He's in his office now," she said. "Down the hall on the right."

I thanked her and followed her directions. There was a large poster on the wall outside Professor Hong's office, advertising a competition for student internships in New Media. His door was open and I knocked on the jamb.

As he looked up, I recalled what Su-Kim had said about good looks among Asians. Professor Hong was in his late thirties or early forties, with a slim face and clear skin and an androgenous rather than muscular physique. I could see that Betsy would find him handsome.

I showed him my badge and introduced myself. "Could I speak with you about your student, Betsy Lawrence?"

"Please, come in," he said. Behind him, a big picture window on the far wall looked toward downtown Honolulu, the ocean a blue strip on the far horizon. Bookshelves lined both side walls, stacked haphazardly with books thin and thick. Papers flowed over piles on the floor and the desk. A placard on the desk, nearly buried by debris, said his name was Xiuquan Hong, in English and beneath it in three Chinese ideographs.

I guessed the department preferred to use the English way of putting given name first, followed by family name.

I sat across from him. "I understand Ms. Lawrence was in your social media class. Can you tell me anything about her?"

He had a smooth, clear voice without a hint of an accent. "Not a very good student, I'm afraid," he said. "As a professor, very quickly I get to know the smart, dedicated students, because they speak up in class and do well on their first exam. Unfortunately I am also able to identify the slackers. And Betsy was much more interested in consuming social media than in learning about it."

"Was she bright and undisciplined? Or perhaps less qualified than some other students?"

"Oh, she was bright," he said. "And very well-spoken, when we discussed something of interest to her. She had a very deep knowledge of Korean boy bands, for example. And she was a big fan of Studio Ghibli, one of the Japanese animation studios. I was looking forward to hearing her thoughts when we reached our unit on Asian influences on social media."

"Did you notice any conflicts between her and other members of the class?"

He shook his head. "Mine is a very sociable discipline, as you might gather from the title, social media. So we have very enthusiastic discussions where students are happy to introduce others to their particular passions. I can't recall any negative situations."

"Thank you," I said. "It's important to get to know Ms. Lawrence in as many dimensions as possible."

I was about to get up when he said, "May I ask you a question?"

"Sure." I wondered if he would bring up the way Api had noticed Betsy flirting with him.

"You have a very distinctive last name," he said. "Hawaiian, of course?"

I nodded. I saw where this was going. "Api is my niece."

He looked confused for a moment. "Oh, of course. Apikela. She's in my social media class as well. Did you know that she already has a very sizeable YouTube audience?"

"I've just learned that recently. I'm not really a fan of makeup."

"Ah, but Api does so much more than that. She's very sharply differentiated herself by including her Hawaiian heritage, and she has learned to use her equipment to create very polished content." He smiled. "I'm looking forward to her class project. I think she'll outshine her classmates."

"That's very good to know," I said. "We're a close family and we take a lot of pride in the accomplishments of our keikis."

"I recognized your name as soon as you showed me your badge," he said. "I moved to Honolulu three years ago, to take this job, and I began to investigate the local gay community. Your name came up more than once, as an influencer within the police department."

Oh. "I'm flattered, Professor. But I hardly think of myself as an influencer. I don't have a YouTube channel like my niece does."

"But influence comes in so many dimensions," he said. "You may think of yourself as an ordinary police officer. But because of the visibility you've had within a traditionally macho environment and the way you have stood up for LGBT individuals and organizations, you have a larger profile than you probably know."

I didn't know what to say. Sure, when I came out of the closet many people knew about me, had seen me on TV or in the newspapers. And I had spent time on pride floats and as a guest speaker in schools and at events. But I had thought all my notoriety was behind me.

"I don't want to seem like a stalker," Professor Hong said. "But many younger gay men in the community look up to you as a role model. You have a handsome husband and two kids, and that's the life that many of us aspire to."

I felt myself blushing, and was glad my darker skin wouldn't show so clearly. It took me a minute to put my thoughts together. "Thank you, Professor. I have gone through some difficult times in my life, and I believe that I've come through them stronger. I hope that just by being myself I can make the path smoother for those who follow."

"And you have." He stood up and reached out to shake my hand. "Thank you."

I stood, shook his hand and smiled back at him. I might not have learned much about Betsy Lawrence but I'd learned something about myself.

As I drove back to headquarters, I thought about my own dating history. I hadn't been monogamous until I got serious with Mike. Back when I was young and confused, I'd never committed to a single girl, and often never had more than a couple of dates with anyone.

Then I came out, and the gay world at that time was all about hookups. I'd meet a guy somewhere like the Rod and Reel Club, a gay bar on Waikiki where I hung out, and end up in a back room with him. Once in a while, I'd get a guy's phone number and follow up with drinks, maybe dinner, then a horizontal mambo.

Mike and I had dated for a while, under a spell of mutual attraction. But I was his first serious relationship of any sort, and looking back, both of us needed more experience to know that we were right for each other. Once we reconnected, in a fireworks display of mutual lust, neither of us looked anywhere else.

Traffic slowed to a stop-and-go on the H1 where it met up with the H201. The near-vertical swale beside us was full of the modified purple leaves of bougainvillea. A billboard advertising wide-body flights on Hawaiian airlines showed the arms and shoulders of a male hula dancer.

Things were different for young people now. Dakota had dated a lot as a teen and young man. Mike and I listened to impassioned declarations that he had found the one—followed later by the agonies of breakups. Dakota was one hundred percent Italian, handsome and vain, passionate and intense. You had to be a special kind of guy to hold onto Dakota Gianelli—and the jury was still out on his current boyfriend.

When I got back, Ray and I still had a couple of hours to kill before the end of our shift, so we focused on cleaning up paperwork. Even cases we had cleared months before still required following up. On a bad day, we could spend three hours or more on our own incident reports as well as requests from attorneys for follow-up documentation.

By the time we finished, I was exhausted. Ray and I were commuting together that day, so I dropped him at his house and drove up the hill to ours. It was dusk, and while Mike's parents' house next door was lit up, ours was dark.

Mike was at work, and the house was empty. I walked around

turning lights on, even as I remembered my father complaining that he was supporting Hawaiian Electric because of all of us.

I meandered around the house for a few minutes, feeling bereft, and finally decided to go next door.

"Hey, Kimo, come on in," Mike's dad said when he opened the door. "What do you need?"

I shrugged. "Just checking in."

I followed Dominic into the living room. Mike's mom, Soon-O, was on the sofa watching the evening news. "Have you eaten?" she asked. "I have a macaroni and cheese casserole in the oven. There's plenty for you and Mike."

My stomach grumbled. Soon-O was a terrific cook, and though her specialties were the Korean food she had grown up with, she'd learned to make Dom's favorite Italian dishes. "I could eat," I said.

The three of us trooped into the kitchen, and I sat at the table with Dom as Soon-O opened the oven and the rich aroma of melted cheese blew out. "What's new with the Five-O?" Dom asked.

"Same old, same old," I said. I told them about Betsy Lawrence and Brandon Paikai as we ate.

"I worry about young men today," Dom said. "They're falling behind academically, failing to attach to mates, and trading potential for addiction. They're twice as likely to overdose and 3.5 times more likely to commit suicide than women."

Dom had retired after decades as an emergency room physician at Tripler Army Medical Center, so I knew he'd seen his share of suicides and overdoses.

"It's a problem," I admitted. "There are more American men behind bars than serving in the military or working as full-time cops and firemen. And there are nearly twice as many prisoners in the U.S. as there are lawyers."

"I don't think we're talking about this enough," Dom said. "We need to do a better job of helping young men find their way. Did I tell you I started volunteering with Boys to Men?"

"The music group?"

Dom laughed. "No, it's a non-profit that mentors young men. We help them with academics and social skills. Nearly three-quarters of the boys we work with are in single-parent homes and they live at or below poverty level. I try to be a positive role model for them. We talk about school and bullying and money."

"That's great. I bet Brandon Paikai could have used that kind of help when he was younger."

"There are so many ways for boys to get into trouble these days," Dom continued. "They watch violent video games and movies that give them all kinds of skewed ideas about how to make money, how to treat women. And if they don't have someone to point them in the right direction, they end up in trouble."

Mike walked in a few minutes later. "There was nobody home in our house but all the lights are on," he said.

"My bad. It was kind of spooky in the dark, and I forgot to turn the lights off before I came over here."

His mother got up and dished out a plate of mac and cheese for him, and I wondered if she'd made so much knowing that we'd gravitate over there. Now that Dakota had moved out and Roby was gone, Mike and I felt like less of a family, and we often ate with his parents, or climbed the hill to Cathy and the keikis. With Sandra in Washington so much, we felt like we were filling a void in their lives.

We ate and talked and laughed. "Do you know that Lui's dog Lilo is sixteen?" Mike asked. "Those little dogs last forever."

"Remember that dog you tried to adopt when you were a boy?" Dom asked. "Back on Long Island."

"You tried to adopt a dog?" I asked Mike. "What happened?"

"I thought he was a stray," Mike said. "He followed me home one day from school and I asked if I could keep him."

"I was worried that he would have all kinds of diseases from living on the street," Dom said. "I argued that he was better off on his own, and when Michael resisted I gave in and we took the dog to the vet."

Soon-O picked up the story. "He wasn't a stray at all," she said.

"The vet recognized him because someone else had brought him in the week before. He was just a dog who wanted to run free. So the vet called the owner and we left the dog there."

"And we left Long Island soon after that to move here," Dom said. "So a dog wouldn't have worked out."

Eventually Mike and I went back next door. "My parents left out part of the story about that dog," he said. "I was getting bullied a lot for being mixed-race and I was so unhappy. I just wanted a friend. That incident was what triggered my dad to ask the VA for a transfer to Tripler."

"I always wondered how that came about," I said. "Was he always set on staying with the VA?"

Mike shrugged. "I eventually put the numbers together when I was a teenager. He was born in 1947, and graduated from Long Island University in 1969. That was the middle of the Vietnam conflict, and he didn't want to get drafted and sent over there. So he enrolled in medical school at Hofstra and got a deferment. By the time he graduated, the war was still going on but he got lucky and was assigned to an Army base in South Korea instead."

"That was lucky."

"Especially since that's where he met my mom. He did his two years and they got married, and she moved to Long Island with him. He got into a three-year ER residency and my mom got a job as a nurse. They had me while he was still in his residency. When he graduated, he signed up with the VA because they still have a couple of hospitals in South Korea, and they wanted the flexibility to go back there at some point."

I sat back against the arm of the sofa, still facing him.

"Then I was born, and they were settled near my grandparents. But I was really miserable, and they thought about transferring to South Korea, but they were worried I'd have the same kind of problems fitting in, only in reverse. So they settled on Tripler, figuring Honolulu would be more tolerant."

"Your dad is a good man. I remember being so worried about

moving in here with your parents on the other side of the wall. But now I'm glad to have them so close."

"Did you see how my dad had trouble standing up?" Mike asked. "He had to hold onto the table for a minute."

"Probably just a little dizziness."

Mike shook his head. "I've been watching him. He's getting old. So is my mom. I'm glad that we're right here if they need anything."

For years, Dom and Soon-O had been there for us, so it was time for us to be there for them.

Chapter 11
Mean Kids

After we walked back to our own house, I talked the case over with Mike. "I feel like we're in a holding pattern," I said. "We know someone killed Betsy Lawrence, but we don't know who or why."

"But you're making progress. You know what kind of person she was. She was a mean girl, right? People get angry at mean girls. Maybe somebody from her past trailed her to Hawai'i and contacted her."

"A boy? Someone who had a crush on her?"

"Could be. Or a girl she was mean to in high school. It's not that expensive to fly here from San Francisco. And if you think she wasn't at HAC long enough to make enemies, you could look farther back."

"Her mother did say that she was mean to other girls at her high school," I said. "Interesting."

Wednesday morning Ray and I drove to work together again. It was a gloomy morning, rain clouds threatening and a strong trade wind tossing the tops of the palm trees like the skirts of hula dancers.

As we crept toward downtown on the highway, we talked about the interviews we had conducted so far. Official HPD policy was to let witnesses or other interviewees recount what they had seen, or what they knew, in their own words.

After the initial statement, we could ask questions to clarify understandings, correct discrepancies, establish elements of the crime and identities of the persons involved. We also had to document the behavior, apparent mental condition, and physical appearance of the interviewee in the police report.

If we were interviewing a suspect, we had to get them to write a statement and sign it. That wasn't necessary when we were talking with people about a victim, as we had been doing with Betsy. But it was still important to create a written record to go along with the recordings of our conversations.

When we had a conversation with someone at a police facility, we were to use the HPD-252 statement form; and if we had more to say than could fit on a single page, we added the HPD-252A Statement Continuation Page. When we spoke to someone off-site, as we had done the day before, it was important to get the transcript of the conversation, as well as our opinions and other data, into those forms.

As we approached downtown, Ray announced that he wanted to go through all our interviews. "I still have more paperwork to go over. While we're waiting for Betsy's cell phone records, I want to do more with the HPD-252s and see if anything jumps out."

"That works for me," I said. Ray and I were excellent partners in many respects, and one of those was his OCD approach toward paperwork. While I was often willing to let it slide while I dug into the specifics of a case, he was slow and methodical and hated to have forms hanging over his head.

I settled in at my desk and went online to look for information on the dynamics of being a high school girl, and I found an interesting source in a self-help book about the social cliques of female high school students, how they related to bullying, and the damaging effects those cliques can have on students. That led me down a rabbit hole of research, mostly about teen girls and their self-images, and how bullying could lead to suicide.

Sampson had finally gotten fed up with the crappy coffee the department provided, and he splurged on one of those capsule machines. We could buy the pods for whatever flavor we liked. I kept café mocha pods in my desk, and I grabbed one and asked Ray if he wanted a coffee, and he handed me a hazelnut pod of his own.

I made the coffees for us and brought them back to our desks. "Mike gave me an idea last night," I said. "Suppose the motive for Betsy's death isn't here in Hawai'i at all, but back in the Bay Area?"

He took the coffee. "What are you thinking?"

"I've been reading about teenaged bullying, particularly of young girls," I said. "It can be very damaging to them. Even causing suicide."

He nodded. "I've heard about that."

"Suppose Betsy bullied someone back home. And they eventually got to a boiling point. As Mike said, it's cheap enough to fly here from San Francisco. The person Betsy went out to meet at night might have been someone from home."

"Someone she was embarrassed to be seen talking to at HAC," Ray said. "Interesting."

He turned to his computer and began typing. "The registrar at HAC sent me Betsy's application yesterday. She went to a private high school in Santa Clara called the Edgemont Academy." He typed for another minute while I sipped my coffee.

"Wow," he said. "There were two suicides last year of girls from Edgemont. Both from Betsy's class."

"You take one name and give me the other."

"I'll do Vicky Benjamin, and you look up Ana Luisa Rodriguez," he said.

I turned to my keyboard. The first thing that came up was the poor girl's obituary, Her survivors included an older brother called Juan Bosco. That had to be a typo—I couldn't imagine anyone naming their child after a chocolate milk brand.

But Juan Bosco might have held a grudge against Betsy Lawrence, if he felt she was responsible for his sister's suicide. I started digging more, applying a bunch of different search terms, and ended up at Juan Bosco's Facebook page, where he had posted a tribute to his sister.

"*Mi hermosa hermana*," he wrote. "You were beautiful inside and out, no matter what anyone else told you. I'm sorry I did not know how much pain you were suffering or I would have offered to share it with you. You listened too much to the other girls at your school, who told you terrible things and made you feel less than they were. I hope they all rot in hell for what they did to you."

I also found an editorial in the school's newspaper about online bullying, which cited a chilling statistic. "59% of U.S. teens have been bullied or harassed online, and a similar percent say it's a major problem for people their age. This is happening even here in the hallowed halls of Edgemont Academy, and it has to stop. We are calling on parents, teachers, and politicians to save our lives."

Ray finished his coffee and tossed the cup into the trash with a rim shot. "Found anything?" he asked me.

"Ana Luisa Rodriguez had a brother who hopes her bullies rot in hell," I said. Ray scooted over to look.

"Saint John Bosco, also known as Don Bosco, was an Italian Catholic priest," he said. "He dedicated his life to educating and helping street kids and juvenile delinquents."

I didn't want to admit I'd thought of chocolate milk. "I'll see if his name turns up on any flights into Honolulu," I said. "Should be unique enough to track. You find anything?"

He shook his head. "Vicky Benjamin was an only child of a single mom, a cleaning lady at one of the tech companies. I'll send you the mom's name so you can check for her, too. But I don't expect she'd have the resources to track Betsy down and fly over here. And her daughter died at the beginning of senior year. If she was going to do anything she'd have done it while Betsy was still in Santa Clara."

"Agreed. Ana Lucia died in March of this year, and it might have taken Juan Bosco a while for his anger to fester into something."

It took a while, but I couldn't find any record of either Juan Bosco Rodriguez or Vicky Benjamin's mom flying to Honolulu. I did find that Juan Bosco was in his third year at the University of California Merced, over two hours east of San Francisco in the mountains. That made it even more difficult for him to get to Honolulu.

T-Mobile hadn't turned over Betsy's cell phone records, so we didn't have any new leads to pursue. I was stewing at my desk when Cathy Selkirk called me.

I met Cathy soon after I was dragged out of the closet. I was desperate to do something to validate my self-worth after all the ugly news stories and the negative reactions I'd gotten at work, so I sought out a gay teen youth group that met at a church in Waikiki. At the time, Cathy volunteered there, coordinating a range of activities. Through her, I met her partner, Sandra Guarino, a prominent attorney in Honolulu who was the volunteer director of the Hawai'i Gay Marriage Project, back in the dark days before the Supreme Court decision in Obergefell v. Hodges allowed same sex couples to marry.

When I met Mike, we'd become a foursome, and one day the gals asked us to donate sperm so that they could start a family. We agreed, and we'd all become even closer after that. Sandra, Cathy and the keikis were incorporated into our ohana, and Addie and Owen were following in my footsteps at Punahou.

"Hey, Cathy, what's up?"

"Can you meet me at Punahou? Like, now?"

"Is someone sick?"

"Owen will be hurting when I get hold of him," she said. "He's in the principal's office after a fight."

"Owen?" He was my sweetheart, my happy good boy. Addie was the stronger of the two and the more likely to get into trouble.

"Yes. Owen. Listen, how soon can you get there?"

"Ten minutes. Less if I use the blue light."

"It'll take me at least fifteen, so you can skip the light. See you there." I let Ray and Lieutenant Sampson know I had to run a personal errand and hurried down to my SUV. Fortunately it was nearly a straight run down South Beretania Street, and I coasted through a few yellow lights.

Set against the backdrop of Mount Tantalus, Punahou was a complex of low-rise buildings of white stone and green roofs that combined architectural beauty with natural charm. My favorite spot as a student had been the iconic banyan tree, where I'd often lounged in the shade to read novels assigned by teachers.

My family had a long history with the school. Lui had begun there in kindergarten, after a judge who had mentored my father suggested it. My parents weren't wealthy; my father had just begun his own construction business, and money was tight, but Judge Fong paid Lui's tuition until my father could afford it.

Two years later, Haoa followed. Lui was the scholar, and Haoa the athlete, and when I entered Punahou eight years later my brothers were already enshrined in various school records. I was an athlete like Haoa but surfing wasn't a recognized school sport. It was only through the efforts of my best friends, Harry Ho and Terri Clark, that I was able to graduate with a decent GPA.

All of Lui's and Haoa's kids had gone to Punahou. Mike and I had managed, through some intensive tutoring, to bring Dakota up to the school's standards after patchy schooling while living with his drug-addicted mother. By the time we fostered him, there was an established gay-straight alliance at Punahou and he quickly found friends there. He also fell roughly in the middle of his cousins age-wise, so he'd been able to rely on them for social and academic help.

None of us had been troublemakers, though. My brothers and I were under our mother's thumb—she was a stalwart of the Parent-Teacher Association and we were too scared of her to misbehave. The worst I'd been accused of was skipping school a few times to go surfing with Harry, but we'd been sure never to miss an exam so the consequences had been minor.

Addie and Owen were in fifth grade, and this was the first time one of us had been called to the school for a discipline problem. As I turned up Punahou Street I wondered what in the world Owen had done.

I parked in the visitor lot and walked up to the Sullivan Administration Building, spying the towers of downtown Honolulu across Chamberlain Field. The school secretary, Hannah Howe, had been there in my years and she recognized me right away. Though that was probably because my son was sitting on a plastic chair across from her desk.

"Good afternoon, Kimo," she said. "It's nice to see you again. You've certainly grown up well."

"Thank you, Mrs. Howe. It's a pleasure to see you again." I looked over to Owen, who was staring down at the floor. "Owen's mom should be here soon."

"I'll let the principal know when she gets here."

I went over to sit next to Owen, and I put my arm around his shoulder and pulled him close to me. I leaned down and kissed the top of his head and whispered, "It's OK, buddy."

He used his fist to push a tear away from his eye.

"Want to tell me what happened?"

He wouldn't look at me. "Johnny Cruz said my dads were a pair of fags. I told him to take it back and he wouldn't. He said fudge-packers shouldn't have kids." He looked up. "So I punched him in the stomach and he fell down."

I couldn't help but feel a surge of pride for my boy. He was sticking up for his principles. But fighting was never the right answer.

"Was there something else you could have done?" I asked. "Instead of punching him?"

In a very small voice, he said, "I could have told the teacher. He violated the code of conduct by using mean words."

"That's true. Did you violate that code yourself?"

He nodded. "By hitting him."

"And do two wrongs make a right?"

He shook his head. "No."

I took his hand and squeezed it. "You're going to face some tough times because of who your parents are," I said. "You can't remember your Tutu Al, my dad. He died when you were little. But he had a hard time when he was your age because his father was a Hawaiian man and his mother was a haole woman. A lot of haole people were mean to her because she married a native man, and my dad met a lot of prejudice for being what they called a half-breed, or hapa haole."

I remembered the stories I had heard as a kid. "Your Tutu Lokelani had problems growing up, too," I said. "She was half-Hawaiian and half-Japanese and never felt like she fit in with either group. And her family was poor, too, so a lot of people looked down on them for that."

"That's not nice," Owen said.

"No, it isn't. Your Grandpa Dom and Grandma Soon-O had problems too, because they were a mixed marriage. And before your Daddy moved to Hawai'i with them, he got the same kind of comments that Tutu Al got, because Grandma Soon-O is from Korea."

"What did Daddy do?"

I didn't want to tell Owen that Mike had gotten into the same kind of schoolyard scraps that Owen had, because that wasn't going to solve anything. "The point is that our ohana has faced these problems in the past, and we always rely on each other. Where was your sister when this was happening?"

"She was off with the girls on the other side of the field."

"How about the next time this happens, you talk to her first, before you do anything?" I asked. I wasn't sure that would solve anything, but it might give my boy's temper a chance to cool down. "And if anyone calls you names, or calls anybody in your family a bad name, I want you to stand up proud and say, so what? My dads are good people who help others. What does your dad do?"

He smiled. "I like that."

Cathy came in, and we went into the principal's office. He'd already heard the story from the teacher, and he asked Owen what he thought.

"I was wrong to use violence to solve a problem," Owen said. "I should have used my words. To talk to Johnny, or to Miss Gresham."

The principal looked up at Cathy and me. "You've raised this young man well." Then back at Owen. "We all get angry, don't we?"

Owen nodded.

"But part of being a good citizen is learning how to control that anger. Have your parents taught you anything about that?"

"That I shouldn't fight with my sister," Owen said promptly. "And that when someone says something mean or something that makes me mad, I should stop and think about how to answer. To count to ten and take deep breaths."

"Very good. Why do you think you didn't do that today?"

"Because I love my daddy and my papa, and nobody should say anything mean about them."

He looked down. "I'm sorry I didn't do what I was trained to do. I promise to try harder in the future."

"That's very good, Owen."

The principal looked at us. "I'm going to have a conversation with Johnny's mother about language, and I hope this will be the end of it." He smiled. "And Miss Gresham has promised to put Owen and Johnny on the same team the next time they have in-class games."

Owen mewed something, and I laughed. "I think that's a great punishment for both of them. Hopefully that will teach them to work together."

Owen was sent back to class, and Cathy and I walked out. "I had a talk with Owen before you got there," I said. I explained what I had said about how many members of his ohana had been criticized about their parentage.

"Did you mention me?"

I shook my head. "Didn't think of you. But of course you would have gotten the same thing, growing up." Cathy's mother was Japanese, her father haole.

"I did. I think it'll be a good topic of conversation at dinner tonight."

"Let me know if you want Mike or me, or Dom and Soon-O, to chip in."

"I will." Cathy leaned up to kiss my cheek. "With Sandy spending so much time in Washington, I'm really grateful to have you and your ohana around."

"And Mike and I, and our whole ohana, will always be grateful that you and Sandy brought us Addie and Owen."

Chapter 12
Fatherhood

I drove back to headquarters, and thinking about being a father sparked me to remember something that Kerry Lawrence had mentioned in passing. "Do we know anything about Betsy's father?" I asked Ray when I got to my desk.

"Should we?" he asked.

"It seems like one of those side threads we ought to pull on," I said.

He joined me at my desk as I pulled up the birth certificate for Elizabeth Cady Lawrence, born at San Francisco General Hospital to Leopold and Kerry Lawrence. "Leopold Lawrence," I said. "That's a mouthful."

Divorce records showed that he and Kerry had ended their marriage when Elizabeth was four. After that, it took some searching to find the right Leo Lawrence. Through a combination of social media sites, we pieced together what had happened to him. He'd ditched a career as an emergency medical physician and moved to Maui, where he worked at a beachfront bar and took people on snorkeling trips.

His driver's license record showed he was still living in Kihei.

Ray found him listed as a guide for tours to Molokini, a crescent-shaped, partially submerged volcanic crater off the coast of Maui.

"Do you think that's why Betsy wanted to come to Honolulu?" Ray asked. "To reconnect with her father?"

I shrugged. "We didn't find any emails between them. When her phone records come in we can see if they had contact that way."

Ray turned back to his computer. "I'll see if Leo flew to Honolulu sometime before Betsy was killed," he said. "It makes sense that she would sneak out to meet him if she didn't want her mother to know."

"But why would he kill her?" I asked. "Maybe they argued, and she said some mean things, and he hit her."

"And then dragged her body over to the cliff to camouflage what he did," Ray said. I could tell by the tone of his voice that he was excited by this clue.

Unfortunately, we couldn't find any record that he'd flown to Honolulu, and we found on a review website that he had taken a tour out the day Betsy was killed, and another the next day. "At least we tried," I said. "Another suspect to cross off the list."

Before we signed out that day, we had to report to Lieutenant Sampson with our discouraging results. "We're waiting for Betsy Lawrence's phone records," Ray said. "With luck it will only take another day or so."

"Any other leads?" Sampson asked, looking at me.

"Nothing that has panned out." I explained about looking into Betsy's past, about speaking with her professor and other students, and our look at her father.

"So we have a beautiful young woman, only here in Honolulu for a month to go to school, and someone murdered her, and you have no leads?"

"That sums it up," I said.

"You guys are better than that. I want something more specific tomorrow."

"We'll do our best," Ray said.

That evening, I told Mike about Owen's visit to the principal's office. "Ten years old, and kids are using terms like fudge packer," he said. "I doubt they even know what that means."

"I wasn't about to explain it to Owen. Though eventually we are going to have to have the talk with him. I saw him in the pool the other day and he doesn't have any hair under his arms yet. But puberty could kick in any time."

"I remember my father having that talk with me," he said. "Full of medical terms that I didn't understand, but I was afraid to ask about them. And of course it was all about preventing pregnancy, and I already knew I wasn't interested in girls that way." He looked at me. "What about you?"

"I had two older brothers, remember. I was always eavesdropping on them. I'd hear them talk about petting, and getting to first base, and all that stuff. Lui bought Haoa his first package of condoms when he was about sixteen and Lui was eighteen. And I wanted to be like them, so I did everything they did. My father must have figured out that I had learned from them, and he and I never talked about it."

I laughed. "That is, not until I made the news. That was a very uncomfortable conversation. But he said that he loved me and supported me in anything I wanted. Dom wasn't quite as good with you, was he?"

"Oh, he was okay with me. It was you he didn't like. He thought you seduced me and dumped me and that caused all my problems with alcohol. It took a while to convince him that it was my fault, not yours."

When Mike and I began dating, we were both fresh out of the closet, without a lot of experience behind us. Though we hadn't discussed monogamy, I was angry that he had sex with a stranger while he was at a conference, and broke up with him. It took us having to cooperate on a joint fire-homicide investigation for us to get back together, and it took Dom a long time to accept that I was the right guy for his son.

After dinner, Mike and I went running, though I began to struggle after the second mile. But the evil man had plotted out a 5K run for us that circled around back to our house, so I had no choice but to suck it up for the next mile.

Mike showered first, while I caught my breath and massaged my aching calves. Then I cleaned up and joined him in bed, where we did nothing more strenuous than watch the latest iterations of our favorite reality programs. Neither of us cared for the ones where an arrogant chef hurled insults at line cooks, or where spoiled rich women fought with each other over first-world problems.

Instead we watched people sewing, or baking, or making pottery. It was soothing to see them scramble to create something beautiful and getting gentle criticism that could help them improve. It was a pleasant antidote to my daily life, when many of the victims and villains I ran into had gotten into their situations by the exchange of angry words.

The next morning, Ray and I drove in separately. When I got to work he was sitting at his desk, looking like that guy in the old comic strip who walked around with a rain cloud over his head.

"What's up?" I asked, as I slid into my chair and dropped my phone and my iPad on my desk.

"Do you ever feel kind of useless?"

I looked over at him. "What do you mean?"

He shrugged. "Julie loves her job, and she's at UH all the time. Running her research project, meeting with her assistants, teaching her classes, speaking to groups. And Vinnie loves Punahou. He's involved with a bunch of clubs, and he's always staying late at school for meetings. At night he's doing his homework or volunteer projects."

"And you feel left out?"

"I do, sometimes. Don't get me wrong, I appreciate that things are going well. When we were back in Philadelphia it was always a struggle. Who's picking up dinner? Who can take Vinnie for new shoes or a dentist visit? What are we doing with him after school? He hated school so one of us had to monitor his homework. And we were always worried about him making friends."

Around us, other officers and staff members were coming in, taking to their desks, settling in.

"And now?" I asked Ray.

"I usually have enough time after work to hit the grocery store and make dinner for us. The late bus from Punahou brings Vinnie back around the time Julie gets home. We eat together and we encourage Vinnie to talk about what happened at school. He goes up to his room to do his homework, and Julie and I talk about our days. She reads and I watch TV."

"You've just described the way a lot of households work, and the way a lot more wish they could."

"I know, I know. It's a first world problem. We're paying our mortgage, we have enough to eat, Vinnie's happy and doing well in school. But I don't know what my role is anymore other than earning money and cooking dinner."

"What do you do for you?" I asked. "Mike runs, I surf, and I read."

He shrugged. "Maybe that's the problem. I don't do anything for me."

"You want to learn how to surf? I can teach you."

"No offense, but we already spend too much time together. And I've never been a very strong swimmer."

He shrugged. "I'll survive. Anyway, the records from Betsy Lawrence's phone haven't come in yet, so I don't know what we should do next.

"Uh-oh," I said, as I saw Lieutenant Sampson approach us.

"Any new leads?" he asked.

I wanted to protest we'd only been in the office a half hour, but I've learned to hold my tongue—though both Mike and Ray might disagree. "Nope," I said.

"Good. Then you can pick up another case while you wait. Head out to Kapiolani Park. Dispatch can give you the details."

I wanted to protest. How could we keep on top of Betsy Lawrence's murder if we had another case to investigate? With luck it would be something simple like a flasher or a robbery.

But luck wasn't with us that morning. Or with the woman whose body was hidden behind the Waikiki Shell.

Chapter 13
When Your Day Ends

Dispatch directed us to the backstage parking area behind the Waikiki Shell, a performance venue in Kapiolani Park, near the intersection of Monsarrat and Paki Avenues. I pulled into the parking lot beside three blue-and-whites with lights flashing.

Lidia Portuondo stepped up to meet us. She was a beat cop in Waikiki, and also the wife of Doc Takayama. "Appears to be one stab wound to the heart," she said. "The crime scene techs are on their way."

"And Paul?" I asked. He usually came to crime scenes where his wife was a responder.

She blushed slightly, which was humorous on her well-tanned face. She was a stocky brunette and the only thing that embarrassed her was any reference to her husband and her marriage. She was the only one who ever called him by his first name—the rest of us called him Doc.

"He'll be here in a half hour," she said. "I already have two officers searching for the weapon."

"This is what's awesome about working with an officer who knows her job," Ray said. "Thanks. Any ID?"

She shook her head. "No purse or wallet, but she had a Fichet key in her pocket. Probably lived in one of the high-rises nearby."

We pulled on blue rubber gloves and put rubber booties over our shoes and walked over to the crime scene. It was secluded, the kind of place you might pull a lover to for a clandestine kiss—or something more.

But there was no sign of sexual assault. The woman's low-cut bright blue blouse and short black skirt appeared intact. "Working girl?" I asked Ray.

He shook his head. "I don't think so. The clothes are too fine. That blouse looks like one that Julie has, although not so revealing. She calls the fabric silk slub. Have to check the label but I bet it's designer. Probably the skirt, too."

"Maybe she was walking home from dinner and someone assaulted her, trying to steal her purse," I said. "Stabbed her when she wouldn't give it up."

"Sounds possible," Ray said. "But that would mean she'd probably have hand wounds if she was struggling to hold onto something. We'll have to ask Doc to check."

"Look at her shoes," I said. "They don't look like they go with her outfit, do they?"

We both looked down. The woman was wearing very casual slip-ons in a dusty rose color. "Wrong style, wrong color," Ray said. "Julie would never go out of the house on a date like that."

"Interesting." We both stood up as the ME's van pulled into the parking lot. Ray said he'd check with the uniforms, and I walked over to the passenger door as Doc Takayama got out. "Hey, Paul," I said.

He grimaced at me. "I take an interest in any homicide involving my wife," he said. "Sue me."

"It's okay, doc. We like to have you around." I wanted to tell him about our purse-snatching theory, but I decided to wait for his initial observation.

I watched as he put on his gloves and booties, then leaned over to examine the woman on the ground. She was face up, as if the killer had pulled the knife out and she'd fallen backwards. He checked her eyes for signs of petechial hemorrhage, which might have indicated strangulation, but there were none, and no marks around her neck.

Her hands were similarly clean. "She doesn't have a purse or any ID other than a key in her pocket," I said, as Ray joined us. "Ray and I wondered if this was a purse snatching gone bad."

Doc shook his head. "If she tried to hold onto a purse strap, there'd be some marking on her hands, and I don't see any."

"First impression?"

"Single stab wound to the chest, probably from a long-bladed knife or something similar. That in itself would not cause death, but endobronchial bleeding in victims with blunt chest trauma can lead to death by suffocation."

"In layman's terms, doc?" I asked.

"The bronchus is a branch of the trachea that goes to the lung. Filling the lung with blood—through the bronchus—means the patient can't get air that way."

He looked up at us. "Clear enough?"

We nodded, and he continued. "There is a bit of a scrape on the right palm, as if she fell on that."

"Time of death?"

He looked up at the sky. "Warm day, but her body was in the shade. My guess right now is sometime between ten PM and two AM. But I'll try and narrow that for you once I have her on the table."

The uniforms hadn't found a knife anywhere, so Ray and I assigned them to survey the high-rises within a few block radius, to see if any of the concierges recognized the kind of key the woman had in her pocket.

I called my brother Lui. "Hey, brah, howzit?" I asked.

"Good, good. What's up?"

"I need a favor from you. Woman's body found this morning behind the Waikiki Shell. No identification. You think you can get a picture of her on the noon and evening news?"

"I'll get a crew out there right away."

"Thanks, brah."

Doc took a few still photos of the woman for Lui to use, and emailed them to me, before he and his crew took the body away. A truck from Lui's station pulled up and a petite Hawaiian woman stepped out. She had the same China doll beauty my mother did, and I thought she was probably as strong as my mother was, to have achieved a reporter job while still in her twenties.

She smiled at both of us but addressed me directly. "You're Detective Kanapa'aka?"

"I am."

"Any relation to our station's general manager?"

"He's my brother."

She looked at me appraisingly. "You're better looking than he is." Her mouth popped open. "But don't tell him I said that."

"It's already common knowledge in our family," I said, and Ray laughed. I introduced him. "We don't know much about the victim," I said. "Probably a local resident, body discovered early this morning. I can forward you a photograph to use with the plea for identification."

"That would be great." She gave me her email address, and I hit a couple of buttons on my phone. By then the cameraman was ready for us. I almost had to bend down to get in the shot with the reporter, and I worried I was looming above her like some kind of pervert.

I gave the standard spiel—did anyone in the community recognize this woman? Call the Crime Stoppers hotline, either the regular number or *crime from your cell phone. Help us identify her and bring her killer to justice.

While that was happening, the crime scene team combed the area looking for the woman's purse, or any sign of a struggle. I saw the cameraman framing the shot to include them in the background.

By the time the TV crew left, Ryan Kainoa reported back to us. "Couldn't find anything. So far it looks like she was stabbed where she fell."

I thanked him and turned back to Ray. "Great. Another female victim without much to go on. At least we were able to identify Betsy Lawrence at the scene."

"Maybe your brother's viewers will come through," Ray said.

It was hot and humid and both Ray and I were soaked with sweat by the time we crawled back into my SUV and turned the AC on full blast. The drive back to the Alapai Headquarters wasn't long enough to cool us down, though, and I caught a glimpse of myself in a first-floor window as we headed toward the entrance.

I looked like I'd stepped out of the surf fully clothed. My black hair, already thinning with age, was plastered down to my scalp, and my aloha shirt clung to me uncomfortably. "I wish I could go home, take a shower and put on clean clothes, and start this day over again."

"I wish we could adopt that slogan from the Chicago homicide cops," Ray said. "Our day starts when yours ends."

Chapter 14
Ravenna Cannon

We got back upstairs in time to watch my appearance on the KVOL noon news. Fortunately the makeup woman had done some magic on me before I was filmed, so I didn't look completely like a drowned rat—but I was sure I wasn't as handsome as my mother would have preferred. I imagined her calling Lui to complain, and that made me smile.

Ray and I were eating sandwiches from the commissary downstairs when Lidia Portuondo called. "The crime scene techs called off the search," she said. "Couldn't find the victim's purse or cell phone, or any knife." She paused. "But I did some canvassing, and I found the building where the victim lived. Canal Point Tower."

She read out the street address, on Ala Wai Boulevard, only blocks away from where the woman's body was found. "Good work, Lidia," I said.

"That's not all. I took a picture of the deceased with my cell phone and showed it to the concierge, and he recognized her right away. Her name is Ravenna Cannon, resident of unit 16E." She spelled the name.

"Tell me again why you aren't a detective?" I asked.

"Because it's more fun showing you guys up," she said, and ended the call.

Ray and I finished our sandwiches quickly and drove over to Canal Point Tower. It was a relatively new addition to the skyline, twenty floors of glass and balconies, angled to provide maximum views of the ocean from one side and the Ko'olaus from the other.

The concierge was an older Chinese man named Alexander Moo Kau. He shook his head after we showed him our IDs. "Very sad," he said. "Ms. Cannon, she was a very nice lady. Always have a friendly word for me, and give me a nice tip at Christmas."

"Were you on duty last night?" I asked.

"No, my shift is from 8 AM until 4 PM. Another guy, he comes on when I leave, stays until midnight. We have a security guard on duty midnight until eight."

We got the names and phone numbers of the other two.

"Ms. Cannon, I think maybe she don't work anymore, or she's on a long vacation. Because maybe for the last two weeks, she don't go out in the morning like she used to."

"How about visitors?" Ray asked.

Moo Kau looked like he had smelled something nasty. "A couple of times she has men come over. Always younger, even look like maybe college students."

"They stay long?"

He shook his head. "Maybe one hour. They always look happy when they leave."

He didn't have much more to say about Ravenna Cannon, because she had been at work most days when he was on duty, and there was a separate staff for the weekend, mostly security guards.

He took us upstairs and used his master key to open Ravenna's apartment, and left us to sort through everything and see if we could figure out what had drawn her out to the bandshell.

Once he was gone, I said, "Gentlemen callers in the middle of the day. They could have been work colleagues, but I doubt it."

As we put on our blue rubber gloves, I noticed, "Purse on the table by the door. Either she was in a hurry and left it behind or deliberately didn't take it."

It was a shoulder bag of the kind that my sister-in-law Liliha carried, with the Gucci logo imprinted on the fabric, and a red and green stripe down the center, with the interlocking Gs in gold. I opened it and looked inside. "No phone. But here's her wallet, with a bunch of credit cards. We'll have to check in case she took one with her."

I took notes and photos on my iPad as Ray walked around the living room, which had floor-to-ceiling windows that looked up toward the mountains. We went carefully through the living room and kitchen, and couldn't find a phone. She did have a high-end Mac book laptop, which we bagged as evidence, along with the purse and its contents.

I took the bathroom, where she had a similar range of beauty products to the ones Betsy Lawrence used, though hers included a remover for bags under the eyes, facial treatment essence, brush-on sunblock, and eyebrow razors. Exfoliating gel, vitamin C serum, and even masks to put on your butt to make the skin there smoother.

Clearly a woman who wanted to look her best, and defy the effects of aging. It was sad to think she'd put all that effort into staying young, but her life had been cut short so tragically.

But there was nothing in the bathroom that told me about her murder, so I joined Ray in the bedroom. "Lots of La Perla lingerie," he said. "Low-cut blouses, skirts with high slits. This is a woman who liked her beauty."

"That's what I got from the bathroom, too," I said.

Though we hunted, we couldn't find her cell, and the phone on the wall was only a direct line to the concierge desk.

"Sampson is not going to like this," I said, as we prepared to leave. "Two dead women, no clues."

"And nothing to link them together," he said. "Different ages, location, and cause of death. The only thing that links them is that we caught both their cases."

"Don't forget the missing cell phones," I said. "We'll have to figure out who her cell carrier was and prepare another subpoena."

"Oh, joy."

When we got back to headquarters, Sampson was out at a meeting. We dove into research on Ravenna Cannon. Ray had already drafted the subpoena for Betsy's phone records, so he changed the name, date and circumstances and took it over to Judge Yamanaka's chambers.

While he was gone, I checked with the credit bureau. None of her cards was missing, and there hadn't been any charges to her account since the night before. Then I moved on to Facebook, Instagram, Pinterest, and TikTok. She didn't have accounts on any of them, but I found a profile of her on LinkedIn.

She was the vice president of human resources for a company called Uila Tech, which developed climate change software. I called the company's phone number and gave them my name. "I'd like to speak with someone about Ravenna Cannon."

"I've been given instructions that all questions about Ms. Cannon should be referred to our attorneys," she said.

That was strange. How did they know she was dead so soon after we'd discovered her identity? Had someone seen her on the noon news?

"Do you know that she's dead?"

She caught her breath. "I didn't know that."

"So in light of that information, who can I speak with?"

"Hold on, please."

Instead of hold music, I listened to a spiel about global warming and how it was already affecting the Hawaiian islands, and how Uila Tech could help companies reduce their carbon footprint. Finally the receptionist returned. "I'm afraid the best I can do is give you the name of our attorney. You'll have to speak with her, and she'll direct any communication from us."

I sighed. "Fine. What's her name?"

"Sarah Byrne. She's with Fields and Yamato."

Great. I knew Sarah, and she was a paralegal with the firm, not an attorney. I thanked the receptionist and put in a call to Sarah. She was in court, but the guy who answered the phone at the law firm said he'd have her call as soon as she was free.

Ray returned after getting the subpoena signed and delivered. "Your old singing friend is involved in this case," I said to him as he sat down.

I had discovered years before that my partner had a great singing voice, and so did Sarah. They both liked a singer called Dave Frishberg, too.

"That's great. I haven't seen her since we moved back to Honolulu."

I told him what I'd learned so far, and while I continued looking into Ravenna's professional life, he looked her up in government records. After an hour, we shared information. "Driver's license and Lexus convertible registered to her at Canal Point Tower," he said. "She bought the apartment two years ago, and has a big mortgage on it."

"I looked through the bank account records we found at her apartment," I said. "Nothing unusual. Salary deposits every two weeks, including one last Friday. Mortgage, car payments, credit cards. Nothing that jumps out as unusual."

"The only other data I could find was that she belonged to the Society for Human Resource Management and the Aloha Chapter of Business Network International," Ray said. "None of that unusual."

It was early afternoon and we still had a couple of hours to go on our shift, but Sampson was out and I was fidgety. "I'm going to take some personal time," I said. "I'll pick you up tomorrow morning, regular time."

"Going surfing?"

"If I can. I need to clear my head." I usually kept a short board in the back of the SUV, along with board shorts and a wet suit, depending on the weather. In September, the surf temperature was ideal, an average of 81 degrees, so I drove over to Waikiki and parked in the garage on Seaside Avenue. I used the handicapped stall in the garage restroom to change into board shorts and an old t-shirt Mike had bought me that read "I'm not trying to be difficult – it just comes naturally."

I hadn't been surfing for a while, and my conversation with Ray that morning, along with the frustrations of two cases, probably drove me there that afternoon. But I still knew a lot of guys who hung out there, surfers and workers, and I was able to leave my car key safely with one of the valets who knew me.

I toted my board down Waikiki Surf Alley, an access lane beside the Royal Hawaiian Center. When I reached the sand of Kuhio Beach Park, I ditched my rubber slippers next to a catamaran stand and waded out into the water. The break ahead of me was called Canoes, and though it wasn't my favorite it was good enough for my purposes.

I duck-dived through the incoming surf, then waited out beyond the breakers for the right wave. I let other guys who'd been out there longer take the first ones, and finally scrambled onto my board and stood up.

The sun and the spray were glorious, and I loved the feeling that the city of my birth was rushing toward me, welcoming me inside. I managed a couple of short turns, then hopped off into the water. My body immediately rang with "Again!"

That was the great thing about surfing. I was able to push away all the evil I saw on the street and focus on the water. All thoughts of murder, rape, robbery, or all the other bad things one human can do to another washed away.

I surfed for two hours, until my legs began to feel rubbery. I dried off and stepped into my slippers. I felt that endorphin rush that comes from playing in the waves, happy I'd taken the afternoon off.

My problems would still be there once the surfing adrenaline wore off, but I hoped I'd have new energy to focus on them.

Chapter 15
Broken Jaw

I got dressed again in the same disabled stall of the men's room in the parking garage and as I fastened my watch I realized it was barely five o'clock. I knew I'd have to face rush hour traffic to get home, and since I was in Waikiki it was almost criminal not to visit my mother.

During my father's last illness, my parents had sold our house in St. Louis Heights and moved into a high-rise condo on Kalia Road, near Fort DeRussy. He had only lived there for a year or two before he passed away, but my mother had remained. A few months before, she'd suffered a stroke, and after hospitalization and a stint in rehab my brothers and I had decided that she was too frail to live alone.

Through some of her charity work, Lui's wife Liliha had found a sweet Nisei woman in her fifties, a widow whose children had moved to the mainland. Reiko became a companion to my mother, making sure she took her pills, driving her to doctor appointments, and chatting with her in Japanese—which was all my mother had spoken for the first five or six years of her life.

She was 78, and she had worked her whole life, so she deserved a little pampering. She had toiled in her family's kitchen garden as a child, then gone to secretarial school. She had met my father and worked beside him for decades, keeping the books for his small construction business while raising three rambunctious boys.

I drove over there, pulled up in a guest spot in the small parking lot, and rode up in the elevator. Reiko answered my knock. "Kimo! Your mother will be so pleased to see you."

Reiko's hair was gray but her face was unlined, and she bowed a little as she ushered me inside. I returned the bow the way I had done with my mother's father when he was still alive.

My mother was in an easy chair by the sliding glass doors that led to the patio. The vast swath of the Pacific stretched out beside her. Though I knew about her hospitalization, and the very slow recovery, it was still surprising to see how frail she was. She had always been short, but she seemed to have shrunk into herself. When I took her hand it was cold, barely skin and bones. I leaned down to kiss her cheek.

"My baby boy," she said, as I pulled up a chair to sit beside her. "You know I wanted you so much."

"So I've been told," I said.

"When Lui and Haoa weren't in school they were playing in the yard or the woods," she said. "My heart ached at how fast they were growing up. Your father thought I was foolish to want another child. But you know how kind he was. He gave me everything I ever wanted."

Yes, my father was kind and loving. But he was also stubborn and quick to anger, and I'd tested his boundaries constantly as a child. In his last years, my brothers and I had come to rely on his strength and wisdom, and I'd done my best to wash away the times he had chased me with a belt, or called me names.

Reiko brought us both cups of special green tea Haoa had imported from Japan, and I sat with my mother and sipped the tea and we talked about my childhood. I realized once again how lucky I was to have parents who had valued me and encouraged me. They were so proud when I graduated from UC Santa Cruz, and though my father thought it was a waste of time, they'd supported me when I spent a year trying to succeed on the surf circuit.

My mother had been frightened when I decided to attend the police academy, but my father had calmed her, telling her how strong and smart I was, and that I'd have nothing to fear in my job.

That hadn't been quite correct, but for the most part I'd shielded my parents from the dangers I faced as a patrolman and a detective. And most importantly, they had accepted me when I came out of the closet, though it was a rocky time for a while.

"How are my *mago*?" my mother asked, using the Japanese word for grandchildren. She looked into space for a moment, as if trying to remember their names.

"She goes back into Japanese more and more," Reiko whispered to me.

"Addie is turning into a real beauty, like her grandmother," I said. "Sleek black hair and an oval face. Mike and I will have our hands full when she's ready to date."

She smiled. "Addie Lokelani," she said. "After me."

"Indeed. And Owen has a real talent for surfing. I'm trying to take him out at least once a month."

"Owen," she said. "Owen Albert?"

I shook my head. "Owen Dominic, after Mike's father."

She nodded. "But Dominic doesn't surf. Your father was such a handsome man, so athletic. Sometimes I would sit on the shore and watch him surfing and be so proud." She reached for my hand again. "He would be so pleased that all you boys are happy."

I sat with her for a while, and left when Reiko announced it was time for my mother's dinner. I was still restless, though, and knew there was no one waiting for me at home. So I called Apikela, and was surprised when she answered her phone.

"Hey, Uncle K," she said. "I was thinking of you because I'm near your office."

"Really? What are you doing down there?"

"Meeting with a beauty company. I'm just waiting for my Uber to show up to get back to school."

"How about if you cancel the Uber and I pick you up and take you to dinner?" I asked. "I have more questions I want to ask you."

"I can do that," she said. "My homework's all done for tomorrow."

She told me where she was—on South King Street, in the neighborhood we'd called the Forest as kids because the streets were named Alder, Birch and Cedar. It only took me about ten minutes to get there, and I was struck as I pulled up at how beautiful and professional she looked. Her hair and makeup were perfect, despite the heat and humidity, and she wore an oversized man's aloha shirt over calf-length pink slacks my mother would have called pedal pushers back in the fifties and sixties.

She jumped in and kissed my cheek. "This is cool," she said. "Where are we going for dinner?"

"Any ideas?"

"There's this little place I've been dying to try on the edge of Chinatown," she said. "Kind of half-Brooklyn, half-Honolulu."

"A hapa haole," I said. "Like us."

"Exactly."

Even though I had been driving around Honolulu since before she was born, she directed me to Hotel Street where I snagged an on-street parking spot, and we walked over to the restaurant. It was housed in an old brick building that had probably once welcomed GIs on R&R from Vietnam, with brick walls and pendant light fixtures. A few TVs hung high on the walls played a retro mix of music videos from the eighties and nineties. Probably stuff the folks around us watched in elementary school.

I ordered a cocktail with gin, elderflower, and Prosecco, and because Api looked so grown-up the server let her order a Campari and soda without asking for ID.

The crowd was a real mix of Young Honolulu—pony-tailed hipsters fresh from their ad agency jobs, pale-faced nerds accustomed to hunching over computers, and well-dressed young men and women of all ethnicities who looked like real estate agents. I felt old, and it was only the fact that I'd been surfing that afternoon that let me hold my head up high.

"So what's the occasion?" Api asked me, as we perused the menu.

"I wanted to talk to you about guys," I said. "Specifically straight guys looking for women like you."

"Oh, my god, I could write you a dissertation," she said. The server, who was tall and slim as a greyhound, dropped off our cocktails but disappeared before we could order.

We sipped our cocktails. "Where do I start?" Api said. "How about all the straight guys who bomb my YouTube channel with nasty comments?"

"Really? You have straight guys watching you?"

She shook her head, and her earrings, which were cobalt blue rubber slippers encrusted with tiny diamonds, moved behind her hair, which she pushed back behind her ears. "I don't think they watch at all. I tried blocking comments from anyone who doesn't subscribe, but that just encouraged them to provide fake email addresses. On the one hand, that pushed my numbers up, but I've had to hire a virtual assistant to monitor the comments and delete the horrible ones."

"What are they saying?"

"Mostly they're incels and they're just parroting the nonsense they find in Reddit forums. That women are all whores who are more interested in looking pretty than in finding husbands."

The greyhound returned and deigned to take our order. A grilled zucchini and fried eggplant parmesan for Api and a grass-fed burger for me, with a cheese and toast appetizer to share.

"That was a lot to process," I said to her after he left. "Incels?"

"It's short for involuntary celibates," she said. "Guys who want to have girlfriends but can't get them because they feel they don't have enough money or aren't handsome enough."

I nodded. "And Reddit?"

"It's a social media site where a lot of these guys hang out in forums. They complain and commiserate. They share websites and YouTube videos and other places they can gang up on. I know a couple of influencers who have been reduced to tears by what these guys have said."

I thought of Betsy Lawrence. "Do they make any physical threats?"

"Oh sure. How they want to beat us up and give us black eyes and rape us." She caught her breath. "It's why I hired my assistant. I can't read them anymore. It's too upsetting."

"Is there anyone you can report this to?"

She shrugged. "You can report them to the company that provides the platform, and even have them banned, but they're like cockroaches. They just pop up again with a different fake email address. But you can tell it's the same guys, or at least that they're hearing the same stuff, because sometimes the language is an exact match."

She picked up her drink and sipped. "The thing that worries me is that I've heard from other influencers that you can't engage with these guys at all because it's a quick jump from nasty words to violence."

Suddenly a group near the front door jumped up and began miming the movies of Michael Jackson as his "Thriller" video played on one of the monitors. It was creepy to see these prosperous twenty-somethings suddenly turn into zombies. I watched, open-mouthed, until the song ended and they went back to their conversations.

Apikela finished her drink and pushed the glass aside. "There are other guys who take on all this baggage and decide to do something about it. They're almost as bad."

"How so?"

"There's this friend of Jeffrey's who had his jaw broken," Api said.

"In a fight?" I asked.

"No, by a surgeon. He had this pointy chin that made his whole face look pinched, and he was obsessed by the idea of having plastic surgery. Jeffrey asked me to meet him and give him my opinion."

"Which was?"

"That there are plenty of men out there who aren't conventionally handsome but make up for it by being charming, empathetic, or wealthy. But he didn't listen, and I have to say, after all the surgery healed he has a much more manly chin line."

"Really? And is more successful with girls now?"

She shrugged. "He has a girlfriend, but she's an airhead totally obsessed with looks."

Her mouth opened. "OMG, I could be describing myself."

"I think you're more than that," I said. "Your videos are helping other girls look better, and I love the way you bring in native Hawaiian material."

"Well, thank you," she said, as the server brought our appetizer.

"This is our Pohaku Tomme, a low-fat goat's milk cheese originally made in the Swiss Alps," he said, speaking as if he had memorized the whole thing. "The pohaku are ancient Hawaiian stone artifacts which have inspired the cheese's round shape. It's produced in Wailua by Sweet Land Farm, and that's our home-made bread and banana jam. Enjoy."

"Wow," I said when he'd left. "That was a mouthful."

"I know. How cool is that? Goat milk contains fatty acids that help repair the skin barrier, probiotics to encourage the growth of normal skin flora, and vitamin A to help gently exfoliate." She looked embarrassed at how technical her language was, and added "I did a series of videos on goat's milk products last month."

I wanted to get back on track. "So Jeffrey's friend had his jaw broken to look more masculine," I said.

She nodded as she slathered some cheese on a slice of toast. "There's this whole thing going on about how certain facial shapes and structures are the best for attracting girls. That if you are better-looking, you have a greater chance of getting laid."

"Which is true," I said.

"But these guys take it to extremes. Did you ever see the movie *The Matrix*?"

"Sure, with Keanu Reeves," I said. "People have told me I look like him."

"You do. Do you remember the point when he had to choose between a red pill and a blue pill, and the red pill was the one that showed him the way the world really is?"

I nodded.

"These guys use that analogy for the realization that, if they're homely their life is going to suck unless they do something about it."

I ate some cheese myself and it was really good. Maybe it would have an effect on my skin, too.

"It sounds like a very dark path to go down," I said.

Our entrees arrived and they were delicious. "How do these guys approach girls like you, if they're so obsessed with the fact that they don't look good?"

"They either have an oversized ego—maybe because they work out, maybe because they make money—and they come on strong. Or they don't talk to girls at all. You should see some of the nerds at HAC. They look at girls like we're lionesses on the Serengeti and they're prey."

I laughed. "What about you? Are you dating anyone?"

"I had a boyfriend at Punahou, but he went to Pepperdine and we decided to break up. Right now I'm focused on my business."

It was great talking to Apikela, and I was sorry that I had missed spending that kind of quality time with her siblings and her cousins. By the time we finished dinner I had a much better idea of what motivated guys like Brandon Paikai, and how young men might be interacting with women like Betsy Lawrence and Ravenna Cannon.

Chapter 16
Sexual Harassment

Friday morning, Ray and I put together a plan as we drove to work. "Whenever we come up with a suspect to talk to, we have to see if we can connect him to both women," I said. "The more I think about these two crimes, the more I see connections between them, and they come back to horny guys looking for sex."

I turned to Ray. "Can I ask you a personal question?"

He laughed. "Since when do you have to get permission?"

"What did you do for sex before you met Julie?"

I looked straight ahead, allowing him some privacy to collect his thoughts. "I was younger and more studly then," he said. "My height was a problem sometimes, but if I put on a tight-fitting shirt and low-hanging jeans I could go to bars and meet women. I didn't have it as easy as some guys, and it usually took a couple of dates to get a girl into bed."

He turned to me. "Was it like that for you, when you were dating women?"

"I think there was more of an element of desperation, if I want to be honest," I said. Traffic slowed to a crawl and we had to talk over the sound of a motorcycle beside us. "I knew that I was attracted to guys, but I could have sex with women, too. I kept hoping I'd meet the one woman who would shift me down the Kinsey Scale and hold me there."

"When you jerked off, was it to images of men or women?"

Fortunately I'd spent enough time with Ray, and felt close enough to him, to be able to answer that honestly. "At first it was pictures and videos of men and women together," I said. "That's what was easily available to a teenager. When I was at a used bookstore and I stumbled on this magazine aimed at women, lots of shots of naked men."

Traffic began to inch forward. "You know how they talk about marijuana as a gateway drug to harder stuff? That magazine—it was called *Viva*, I remember it like yesterday, that was my gateway drug to gay porn."

"Does this conversation have any relevance to our investigation?" Ray asked. "Or are we just sharing?"

I laughed. "I was thinking last night about guys like Brandon Paikai. What chance does he have of getting laid? Not much, as far as I can tell. If he was gay, he could find a guy to suck his dick in the dark somewhere. But you don't find straight women hanging out at glory holes."

It was Ray's turn to laugh. "True that," he said. "It does seem like there's sexual motivation behind both these murders, even though the specifics are so different."

"Ravenna Cannon seems to be the opposite of Betsy Lawrence, though. From what the doorman said, she was having guys come over to her apartment for nooners. It doesn't sound like she would have turned someone down."

"You'd be surprised," Ray said. "Back in high school, there was this girl who everybody said was loose. The football players bragged about her. But this friend of mine who was chubby and wore glasses tried to ask her out to dinner, and she turned him down."

"We have to speak to Sarah Byrne," I said. "She's the key to talking with people Ravenna worked with, who might know more about her behaviors."

"And boyfriends," Ray said. "Maybe one of her male visitors was more than transitory and got jealous of the others."

When we got to headquarters, I tried Sarah Byrne at Fields and Yamato again.

"I gave her your message last night," the receptionist said. "She told me if you called again that she hoped to get back to you by lunch."

I thanked him. In the past, Sarah had been eager to help us, but perhaps she was tied up in a case with a demanding attorney and she couldn't get away.

Sampson came by my desk and I filled him in on our progress on Ravenna Cannon.

"You don't have much, do you?" he asked.

"No. But we're exploring several avenues."

"Don't let the young woman at the arts college slip by," he said.

"We won't. I hope we'll get her cell phone records today."

Ray said, "The supervisor at the Mint Mobile store faxed the subpoena for Ms. Cannon's records to the main office while I waited," he said. "He says we can expect the results by Monday morning."

"That's better than average," Sampson said. As he left, my phone rang.

"Good morning, detective. It's Sarah Byrne."

"Sarah! Thanks for calling back. Your firm is representing a company called Uila Tech?"

"We are. I was watching the news last night when I saw the picture of Ravenna Cannon, so I was expecting you to call. But I had to be in court this morning to wrap up a case."

"I figured the attorney you were working with was keeping you busy. Uila Tech won't let anyone talk to us without approval from you, or whatever attorney is handling the company's business."

"Oh. You should know I'm no longer a paralegal here. I graduated from law school last year so I've been promoted to associate. Though sometimes it doesn't seem like a promotion."

"That's great. Is Uila Tech your client?"

"It's complicated. Can you come over here and talk?"

"Sure. What time is good for you?"

"Say two o'clock?"

"Congratulations on your new job. Ray and I will be there at two."

I hung up the phone and turned to Ray. "That was Sarah." I explained her new role at Fields and Yamato.

"She didn't say if Ravenna was a client?"

"Just that it's complicated."

Ray settled into paperwork on the status of both cases, while I did some more research on Uila Tech. I discovered that the word *uila* meant lightning in Hawaiian, and the company had been started by two undergrads studying at UH's Manoa campus.

Kai Gronedahl and Arlo Schultz had become friends through a shared passion for surfing, which led them both to care about the environment. Gronedahl had a BS degree in Global Environmental Science from the Oceanography Department in the School of Ocean and Earth Science and Technology. Schultz had been in the interdisciplinary program in the Institute for Sustainability and Resilience and both were concerned with the social and environmental implications of sustainability.

At least that's what the website said. It wasn't clear to me what they actually did, but they had a roster of local and national clients. I switched over to help Ray with paperwork. At one o'clock we left the office to get lunch at a Chinese hole-in-the-wall café that had great dumplings. When we were finished, we walked over to the gleaming office tower that housed Fields and Yamato.

We arrived at the office promptly at two, and Sarah came out to greet us. I was pleased to see that she had retained the purple streak in her hair even after getting her law degree.

"Congratulations on law school," I said, as she led us down the hall. "I didn't know you were going."

"I kept it quiet. The partners were very supportive, and UH has a good part-time program. All the classes are offered after 5:30, and I took three each term, so I was able to finish in four years."

"That's great." We followed as she led us into a conference room, where she set up her laptop on the polished koa wood table.

"You said your relationship with Ravenna Cannon was complicated," I said, as we sat down. "Can you elaborate?"

"You're probably familiar with the bro culture that's developed around high-tech industries," she said. "In general, it's dominated by over-confident, arrogant, obnoxious men. The dark side of that is the gender pay gap and sexual harassment at work."

"Was Ravenna harassed at work?" Ray asked.

Sarah shook her head. "She was part of the problem, not the solution. Uila Tech has had issues with bro culture in the past. Most of the employees are young men, many of whom come out of the surfing world, which I'm sure you know has its own issues."

"My niece Ashley is on the world circuit, and she's complained about a lot of problems," I said. "It's hard for some men to take her seriously as an athlete because she's beautiful. And the men get jealous when the women get media attention."

"Exactly. It's hard for some men to accept women as equals and avoid sexualizing them. So two years ago Kai and Arlo hired Ravenna Cannon as their director of HR. Unfortunately, that was like putting the fox in the henhouse."

She looked at her computer. "Ms. Cannon jumped right into the position, and she was very supportive when women brought claims of sexual harassment to her desk. Unfortunately she had an innovative and unprofessional way of handling them." She pursed her lips. "She turned around and harassed the harassers."

"In what way?" Ray asked.

"She used a lot of the same behaviors on them, and on young men in the company. Unwanted sexual gestures, inappropriate touching, innuendo in language."

"Really?" I asked. "And the men complained?" I found that hard to believe.

"At first they thought she was just, as one of the men put it, a brassy dame. But she started requesting sexual favors in exchange for ignoring complaints. Her attitude was "You wanted it, now come and get it.""

I looked at Ray and he raised his eyebrows. "Did the men accept?" he asked.

"In a few cases. But in many others, the men were married or dating seriously and they weren't interested in the complications of sex with a coworker. And they didn't like having the shoe put on the other foot."

"How did this end up with Fields and Yamato?" I asked.

"Arlo approached us. He recognized that Ravenna had become a liability to the company, but she also had a lot of dirt on his best friend, Kai, as well as some other members of senior leadership, so we were hired to negotiate a settlement with her. The case was assigned to me."

"Did they fire her?"

"We were in the middle of negotiations," she said. "I was drafting a final settlement when I heard Ravenna died. No money was going to transfer between the parties, and Arlo said that if she agreed to enter treatment for her sex addiction, they wouldn't press charges or tell anyone the reason why she was leaving Uila."

Out of the big picture window, I saw a Hawaiian Airlines jet take off gracefully from the reef runway. People were always coming to Hawai'i to vacation or to relocate, and they brought their problems with them, even though they might have felt our tropical paradise offered a chance to escape them.

"Do you think maybe someone at Uila Tech might have had a motive to kill her?"

She shook her head. "That's not what I'm suggesting, at all. Ravenna ... well, she confided in me. And I've already spoken to Arlo to understand what part of our conversations was protected, and what was what you might call girl talk."

Once again, I looked at Ray. Neither of us seemed to know what to ask.

"Ravenna was a sexual compulsive," Sarah said suddenly. "We had a lot of conversations, some of them over wine, and she told me that she had been sexually assaulted when she was younger, back in Maine, where she grew up. She felt that her sexual compulsions were a way of getting back her agency when it comes to men."

"Wow. That's a lot to confess."

"You bet. We had a strange relationship, because in a way, both she and the company were my clients. I tried to rein her in, but she insisted that I had to know everything."

She sat back. "Apparently she came out of the womb with jet-black hair. Her mother was an enrolled member of the Penobscot tribe, and she named her baby Raven, because of the hair. Her mother had some problems of her own, moving from man to man, and one of those men began sexual acts with Raven when she was about nine or ten. That went on until she was fourteen, when she killed him."

I sat up straight. "Ravenna Cannon killed a man back in Maine?"

Sarah nodded. "But it was ruled justifiable homicide, and she spent a couple of years in juvenile detention. She says she was a model prisoner there, got her GED and attended the University of Maine after her release."

"Were you able to verify any of that?" Ray asked.

"She showed me her court records, and her college transcript. She changed her name from Raven to Ravenna, graduated with a bachelor's in business administration and management, and started working her way west. She spent a couple of years in Chicago, and a few more in San Francisco, before she ended up in Honolulu."

"Any problems with employers in those cities?" I asked.

"She wouldn't tell me about any if there were. She worked at another firm briefly here in Honolulu in HR before getting the job at Uila Tech."

"We're still going to need to speak with Mr. Schultz," I said. "And

Mr. Gronedahl, and anyone else who made claims against Ms. Cannon."

"I understand. I cleared all that with Arlo. I can send you the names of the men involved, but I'm not allowed to reveal the nature of their complaints against Ms. Cannon."

"I presume her juvenile record in Maine is sealed. But did Ravenna ever say anything about blowback from the man she killed? Does he have any survivors, for example, who might be out for revenge?"

"Not to me. But I think she told me the name of the man who molested her. I'll hunt through my notes and look for it."

"That'll do for a start," I said.

Chapter 17
Free Drink

We walked back to headquarters under gray skies, the trade winds tossing the palm fronds restlessly. "At least we have some leads to follow up while we wait for the cell phone records for both women," Ray said.

"I'll call Uila and schedule appointments for Monday," I said.

The records didn't come in on Betsy's cell phone, though they were promised for Monday morning. Doc called about the autopsy on Ravenna Cannon. "You're in luck, detective," he said. "Ms. Cannon was wearing a cheap flea market watch on her right wrist. The dial must have smashed as she hit the ground. So I can time her fall at 10:35 PM."

"You're sure the watch broke when she fell?"

"Occam's razor. The most reasonable explanation is usually the correct one. Yes, it's possible she was wearing a broken watch that had stopped at 10:35 on a different day. But unlikely. Plus the crime scene team picked up some shards of plastic near her body which match the watch."

"Thank you, doc. You always provide the best explanations."

"Flattery will get you everywhere. However, just because the watch smashed at 10:35 doesn't mean that's her time of death. My calculations indicate it probably took about a half hour for suffocation to occur."

"That's grim. If her assailant didn't mean to kill her, he could have called an ambulance and saved her life."

"Deep stab wounds to the chest of this sort are rarely accidental," Doc said.

I thanked him and hung up, then communicated that information to Ray. We heard back from Sarah Byrne later that afternoon. "I dug into the man who molested Ravenna when she was a girl," she said. "He died in prison, and left no close survivors."

"So no one is coming after her because of him," I said.

"No, I don't think so. Can you tell me when exactly Ravenna was killed on Thursday night?"

"She was wearing a watch that cracked at 10:35 PM. Doc posits that the damage happened when her arm hit the ground, but that death might have taken another half hour."

"There was a meeting of the Honolulu Environmental Council that evening at a hotel in Pearl City. Arlo was the keynote speaker, and the whole company showed up to support him," Sarah said. "The event broke up at about ten o'clock, but Arlo and Kai invited all the staff to drinks at the bar, where they had a server take several group photos with Arlo's phone. They're all time and date-stamped."

"Let me guess. After 10:35."

"You got it. All of the guys who had problems with Ravenna, including Arlo, are in the photos. So none of them could have been in Waikiki at that time."

My shoulders sagged. Another dead end.

"But I did find two cases where Ravenna testified against men accused of sexual harassment at the companies where she worked," Sarah said. "I'll send those names over to you."

I thanked her, and told Ray the news. I watched my email inbox until her message appeared. "Divide and conquer?" I asked. "I'll take Zach Petrosian and you take Oliver Bart."

"Works for me," he said.

I found Zach's bio easily, on a website for a charity on behalf of Armenian refugees in Turkey. His father's grandparents had died in the Turkish genocide of 1915 to 1916 and he had started a foundation in their memory ten years before.

Further digging uncovered that he had funded that foundation after the sale of his plastics manufacturing business, based in Chicago. The sale was tied to a civil suit for sexual harassment brought by four women who had worked for him. One of those was Ravenna Cannon. She and the other three women shared a fat settlement.

Petrosian had landed on his feet, though; he had sold the business, of which he had sole ownership, for approximately twenty million dollars.

He and his third wife now lived in Palm Beach, Florida, where they had a very active social life. That didn't give him much reason to disrupt his life by tracking down Ravenna Cannon and taking revenge against her.

When Ray finished his research we shared notes. "Oliver Bart was a British wunderkind who graduated with a PhD in biochemistry from Oxford," Ray said. "He moved to Silicon Valley and founded a startup to capitalize on some technology he developed as part of his PhD thesis."

"A tech bro," I said.

"Indeed. His problem was that he couldn't keep it in his pants. He put the moves on every woman he encountered, including those who worked for him."

"Ravenna?"

"She was an HR assistant there, and she's the one who blew the whistle on him. But that was the least of his problems. I didn't dig too deep into the science, but it looks like he was trying to develop a drug that would reduce resistance to antibiotics. However, he fudged some of the clinical trials, so when Ravenna called him out, his whole empire crumbled."

"That would give him a motive," I said.

"It would, wouldn't it? Except he committed suicide while in pre-trial custody."

"Any survivors to exact revenge?"

"Not that I can find."

"So we're back to square one," I said. "No motive and no suspects."

"Yes, Eeyore, that's correct," he said, and I laughed.

Lieutenant Sampson stopped by our desks and told us that if we didn't have any strong leads, there was no need for us to work overtime during the weekend. "Just jump in with both feet on Monday," he said.

We agreed. Mike texted me that he was going to run that evening with some of the guys from the fire department, and would get something to eat with them afterward.

I was faced with the prospect of going back to an empty house again, so I texted Gunter to see if he was free for a drink.

He replied quickly. "Free drink? Always up for that." He also included an eggplant emoticon after the word up. He was almost fifty and still horny, god bless him.

A flurry of messages later, we agreed to meet at our old standby, the Rod and Reel Club on Waikiki, at 4:30, in time for happy hour.

I had met Gunter at that very club when I was on my first steps out of the closet. I was on a police stakeout so I was dressed like a moke, our name for island criminals. I can't remember what I wore, but I must have been tough-looking, because on one of my restless circuits around the bar Gunter leaned in close to me and whispered, "I like it rough," into my ear.

I didn't know what I liked back then, and that overture freaked me out. It sent me careening out of the club, into the back driveway, where I spotted two men dragging what turned out to be a dead body.

Even so, I had good memories of drinking and dancing at the Rod and Reel during my single gay years, and for a few years after that. There was an outdoor patio with a bar and a dance floor, the towering palm trees overhead decked out with fairy lights. The area conveyed a sense of tropical abandon, evidence by the bar's logo, a fishing rod stylized to look like an erect penis, with a pair of balls in place of a reel.

The indoors was decorated like an old fishing retreat, with rustic wood and photos of deep-sea fishermen and their catches. Some of those catches included half-naked guys dressed as mermen, but the tourists never seemed to notice or care.

I must have been seized by a fit of nostalgia, or perhaps it was reading all that gay erotica, but as soon as I spotted Gunter by the bar I marched up to him, grabbed him by the shoulders, and kissed him deeply on the mouth, our tongues dancing.

My dick swelled and I knew I was on dangerous ground, so I backed away. "Well, that's special." Gunter reached over and palmed my dick through my khakis. "Someone is very glad to see me."

I swatted away his hand. "Just a friendly hello," I said, already embarrassed.

He turned to the bartender. "My gentleman friend here is buying. I'll have a dirty Absolut martini with two olives."

"I'll have a Big Wave Golden Ale." I didn't drink much anymore but when I did I liked to support local breweries, and I'd been to the Kona Brewing Company brewpub on the Big Island.

We got our drinks and walked over to a small table in the corner as the Cheeky Monkey Club sang "Hula Lula" on the speakers. "So, the ball and chain let you off tonight?" Gunter asked.

Gunter and Mike maintained a low level of hostility toward each other, but it was generally all in fun. Mike knew that I had fooled around with Gunter before we met, and he could be jealous, but so far I'd given him little to worry about.

"My darling partner is preparing for a 10K run this weekend," I said. "And with Dakota on his own and Roby gone, I've found that I don't like going home to an empty house."

"I'm sure there's someone here who could assuage your loneliness," Gunter said, waving his hand around the bar. The crowd at the Rod and Reel skewed young, men in their twenties and thirties, like we were once upon a time. There were a few old lizards prowling around, hoping to score some young booty.

Now I realized we were probably close to the age of those old lizards, while the rest of the men around us were still young and in their prime. Another depressing thought.

Gunter looked closely at me. "You're unusually dour today. A case bothering you?"

I nodded. "Two dead women. A student at Honolulu Arts College hit over the head and pushed down a cliff, and yesterday morning a business executive stabbed behind the Waikiki Shell."

"I saw the police lights as I was going to work." Gunter lived in a ranch house a few blocks from the murder scene, and usually walked down Ala Wai Boulevard to get to his job, where he was a concierge at a fancy high-rise on the other end of Waikiki.

"No real clues in either case, though the second woman has been called a sexual compulsive, and it's possible she went out to the park to meet a man. But her clothes hadn't been disturbed."

"She could have been providing a service." Gunter formed his mouth into an O and made a sucking sound.

"I suppose. Didn't think of that."

"Been a while since you've had lips around your lizard?" Gunter asked.

"Gunter. Why do you have to make everything about sex?"

"You're the one who brought it up." He sipped his martini. "Seriously. Think about the position of her body. Could she have been blowing a guy? If I recall correctly there's a gravel surface back there. Any marks on her knees?"

"Now you're the detective," I said. "But you're right. She was stabbed in the heart from above, by someone taller than she was. So she could have been below him."

"Harsh way to thank someone," Gunter said. "Or maybe she bit down and he didn't like that."

"And just happened to have a knife handy? When you go out on the prowl, you carry a weapon with you?"

"Just this." He pulled a hot pink gizmo about six inches long from his pocket, which was attached to his key chain. "Pepper spray. Boy's best friend."

"You're hardly a boy," I said. "You ever have to use it?"

He shook his head. "These days I make it clear to anyone I bring home what I'm willing to do and what I'm not. This is more for protection from strangers."

I raised my eyebrows and he said, "Not intimate ones. Assholes on the street."

I nodded. "Good for you. Take care of yourself."

"Because the police won't?"

"Gunter. When was the last incident you heard of?"

"People coming out of the Sailor's Rest got eggs and tomatoes thrown at them," he said. "One of my residents was there and saw it."

"Those were straight couples," I said. "I know, because Ray and I investigated."

"Really? And what was this guy's reason? Couldn't get a date?"

"Something like that. Fat, homely, missing a tooth. And he still thinks women should be falling over themselves to have sex with him."

"An incel," Gunter said, repeating the term Apikela had used. "You know there are gay incels, too."

"I didn't know that. Haven't they ever heard of glory holes and anonymous sex?"

"Oh, they have," he said. "I was having a bad day and I needed to feel good about myself. So I posted a photo on a website. This boy came at me with a vengeance. Called me a shallow empty fuckboy who wouldn't be caught dead with anyone below pornboy looks."

"You're not a shallow empty fuckboy," I said. "You're too old to be called a boy."

He held up three fingers to me and said, "Read between the lines."

I laughed. "I'm sorry, Gunter. That was mean. Both what I said and what he said."

"At least you were telling the truth. I am not a boy anymore, no matter how much I feel like one inside. Fortunately I still have my looks, so I'm not desperate for male attention. But this boy – man, I shouldn't have engaged him, but I did."

"Did you offer to blow him out of the goodness of your heart?"

"Well, I asked him to send me a picture first. An honest one. And I sent him a picture one of my exes took. I had a pimple on my chin, my hair was a mess, and the way I was posed on the bed made it look like I had a tummy." He held up his hand. "Well, more of a tummy than I have."

Gunter had always been on the scrawny side of skinny. Eventually his metabolism began to change, and his workouts shifted to keeping the weight off instead of building up muscles. Even so, he was still slim, and the way his aloha shirt hung over his belt camouflaged anything in the stomach area.

"Did he answer you?"

He nodded. "Sent me a nude he took in the bathroom mirror. He was pear-shaped and had man-titties and his belly hung over his dick. But he had a nice smile and a good haircut. I'd have done him in a pinch."

"Did you?"

"No, he was somewhere in the Midwest. And the more we traded messages, the nuttier he got. I could tell he had a bad self-image, but he wasn't willing to admit that any of it was his fault. He was working two jobs because his father was sick and he had to pay all the bills. He didn't have the time or the money to go out to bars often. When he did, no one would talk to him."

"Probably because he radiated that image, beyond his body. I've had sex with guys who didn't have model-quality bodies. But they had personality."

"You're preaching to the choir, brother," Gunter said. "But it was his sense of entitlement that really got to me. Not just for sex, but for everything. His bosses didn't recognize his potential. He wasn't being paid what he was worth. And he shot down every idea I gave him. I finally had to ghost him because he was messing with my own self-image."

"That sounds a lot like the guy who was arrested at Sailor's Rest," I said. "Although I think he's straight. He was jealous of people who looked better than he did, who had more money or the sexual cachet to attract dates."

"And that's your incel in a nutshell," Gunter said. "Now from what I've read online, they're expanding their resentment to business and politics. They're jealous of anybody who looks like they've got their shit together."

We talked for a while longer, and then Gunter had to get home to meet a date. "Aren't you tired of this constant merry-go-round?" I asked him. "You don't want to go home to the same guy every night?"

"And where is your guy? Not home waiting for you, right?"

"You know what I mean."

"Tell me honestly, Kimo. When was the last time you and lover boy did the horizontal mambo?"

I counted back the days. "Monday. He went out for a run, and I was reading some porn, and when he came home I jumped him."

Gunter nodded approvingly. "And how was it?" He put his hand on his heart. "Tell the truth."

"I think there's a lot to be said for knowing your partner and what turns him on. It's not always exciting, not like meeting a stranger in an alley and dropping your pants."

Gunter's eyebrows rose.

"Not that I've done that for a long time. But I still remember. Mike is—he's the man I love. It makes me feel good to give him pleasure. And when he turns to me, my heart races and I get this out-of-body feeling, like we're riding a wave together."

"Trust you to use a surfing metaphor." Gunter leaned down and kissed me, though without the passion I'd kissed him with. "Don't stay here too long. Lover boy might get jealous."

"I won't."

I finished my beer and considered ordering another. But they were playing Kui Lee's "Ain't No Big Thing" and guys had begun to dance, and I felt self-conscious there in the corner, watching the passing parade of men exchanging glances. I didn't want anyone to think I was a lonely old lizard, and I didn't want to have to parry anyone's advances, though I wondered if I could get any if I tried.

Chapter 18
Holding Hands

Saturday morning Mike and I were eating papaya and pineapple chunks for breakfast when he said, "I want a new dog."

"Okay."

He looked up at me. "That's it? No argument?"

"I miss Roby. And so do the keikis. You want another golden?"

He nodded. "If we can get one. I'd like to try the Humane Society first."

"You want to take Addie and Owen with us?"

"Sure. They should get a chance to decide on the dog, too."

"As long as they don't want to adopt every dog in the place," I said.

While Mike showered and dressed, I called Cathy and made sure she was okay with us getting a new dog. It would live with us, but I knew the keikis would want to have visits, and it wasn't fair to make a decision without her input.

"As long as I don't have to pick up after it," she said. "I have enough trouble with a pair of ten-year-olds."

"No, it's going to be Mike's dog. Addie and Owen will be lucky if he lets them play with it."

I arranged to pick up the keikis in an hour, then showered and dressed.

"Can we get a dog, too?" Owen asked, as he and his sister climbed into the back of my SUV.

"You can help us pick one out, but it's going to be Daddy's dog," I said.

"But we can play with it, right?" Addie asked.

"Absolutely. Every time you come to our house."

The Hawaiian Humane Society was in a modern building on Waialae Avenue just off the H1 highway. We walked inside to the smell of clean dogs and a cacophony of barking. We were quickly led to several rows of cages. We didn't see a dog that looked like Roby, but the closest was a big white dog with a square head and a fluffy tail. The tag on his cage read "Griffin" and said that he was 92 pounds and a golden retriever.

"How can he be a golden retriever if he's not gold?" Owen asked.

Mike shrugged. "I don't know. Want to take him out?"

"Yes, please," both kids chorused.

The attendant opened the crate and hooked up the leash, and Griffin tried to dash out. Mike took the leash and said, "Whoa, boy."

The dog looked up at him and I saw love at first sight, on both parts. Griffin walked obediently by Mike's side until we got out into the fenced yard, when he tugged forward and peed copiously on a bush.

The kids played with him for a few minutes, but the decision had already been made. Griffin was coming home with us.

Owen took the leash to lead Griffin back inside. We walked up to the desk to complete the paperwork when a short woman in a dress that would have been fashionable when my mother was young came over to us. "That's Griffin, isn't it?"

"It is," I said.

"I'm taking him," she said. "I already put my name in."

Owen stood protectively by the dog. "We were told he was available for adoption," I said. "My partner and I are adopting him."

She looked from me to Mike and it looked like she'd swallowed something sour. "No," she said. "I represent Golden Friends, and we have priority for every golden retriever or golden mix that comes to the shelter. We make sure that the dogs will get good homes."

"That doesn't work for us," I said. "We have a big yard, we walked our last golden regularly, and he'll have our keikis to play with, too."

"They can't be your children," she said.

"This conversation is over," I said. Mike was already at the desk, filling out the paperwork. I turned away from her.

Suddenly I heard Owen yelp, and I turned back. The woman had one hand on Owen's shoulder, and the other on Griffin's leash.

"Let go of my brother!" Addie said, and she kicked the woman in the leg.

"Take your hand off my son or you will be in serious trouble," I said. Owen cowered under her hand and my heart raced.

I reached into my pocket and brought out my badge holder. "I'm a sworn officer with Honolulu PD. Take your hand off my son or I will arrest you."

She let go of Owen, and he and Addie closed protectively over Griffin. "People like you don't deserve to have dogs," she said, and she turned and stalked out.

I knelt down beside Owen. "Are you okay, buddy?"

He nodded. "That lady was mean. I'm glad she couldn't get Griffin."

"She was mean," I said. "How's your shoulder?"

He raised and lowered his shoulders. "It's okay."

"What did she mean?" Addie said. "That people like us didn't deserve dogs."

Our daughter was already a beauty at ten years old. The genetic mix that made her shone in a slim face, almond eyes, and fair skin. "Because we don't look like her?"

What should I say? She and her brother were smart enough to know when either Mike or I tried to sugarcoat the truth to them. I stayed on one knee so I was at eye level with both of them. "It's like that boy who said something mean to Owen the other day about him having two dads. Some people don't like that."

Addie shrugged. "When kids say stuff like that to me I tell them we're lucky because we have double the love."

"What a great answer," I said. "I think that lady was unhappy because I called Daddy my partner."

"Why don't you get married?" Owen asked. "Then you can call him your husband. Mommy and Mama are married and they call each other wife."

I laughed. "That's a great question." I stood up. "But that's something we can talk about later. For now, let's focus on Griffin."

Mike had finished the paperwork by then, and paid the fees. Griffin was two years old, had all his shots, and had been neutered. Mike took the leash from Owen and led all of us outside.

Griffin jumped right into the back seat, where he sat between Addie and Owen and got lots of love. I noticed Mike looking back at them. "Jealous?" I asked with a smile.

He shook his head. "It makes me happy to see them happy. Plus, I know Griffin is going home with us."

We spent a couple of hours that afternoon getting Griffin accustomed to his new home. I played with him and the keikis in the back yard while Mike got out all of Roby's toys and food bowls, which we'd hidden away to avoid the memories.

We discovered that Griffin did not know how to fetch. When Addie or Owen threw him a ball, he jumped up and grabbed it in his jaws, then settled down on the grass to chew it. But he was happy to chase them around the yard, and delighted when they sat beside him to rub his belly.

I opened my iPad and did some research. "I think he's what they call an English Cream Golden," I said. "That's why he's mostly white."

"He has a gold streak down his back," Mike said. "But you have to look for it."

"It says here that the English Cream line has less chance of cancer than the American goldens. That's good."

We still had half a bag of Roby's chow hidden away in the cupboard, and while Owen and Addie tossed a ball to each other in the back yard, we tested Griffin on a few bits of it. He chomped it eagerly and we filled a bowl for him.

"Are you happy?" I asked Mike.

"He looks like a sweetheart. I'm not surprised that bitch wanted to swoop him up."

I sat back in my chair and looked at Mike. "Owen said something at the shelter."

"About that woman and what she said?"

"In a way. He asked why you and I don't get married, like Sandra and Cathy."

Mike looked up at me. "Why don't we?"

"Well, for one thing, neither of us have ever asked. Are you asking?"

"I think it's something we should consider. Our life insurance policies are already deeded to each other. But my next-of-kin with the fire department is my father, and yours with the PD is your mother, right?"

I nodded.

"We'd have to fill out a lot of paperwork."

I looked at him. "Is that what you think marriage is about? Paperwork?"

He shrugged. "We've already done all the other stuff. I love you, you love me. We have a life together, two kids and a dog."

I couldn't argue with any of that, but I also couldn't put into words how I thought things would be different if we were married.

"We should both think about this," Mike said.

"I agree."

It was time to take the keikis back up the hill, even though they wanted to stay and play with Griffin. We compromised and the four of us walked up there with the dog so that Addie and Owen could introduce Griffin to their mother and his second home.

On the way, Mike reached out and took my hand.

Chapter 19
Expanding the Ohana

I didn't want to like George Murasaki. He was a beefy, tattooed Nisei who ran a motorcycle repair shop in Kaneohe, and I worried about his criminal record, even though he'd been clean for nearly twenty years. But the real reason I didn't trust him was because he was in love with Angelina Gianelli.

Angelina had been released from the Women's Community Correctional Center in Kailua in January of 2020. She moved to a halfway house in Kaneohe and got a job cleaning office buildings. But she wasn't happy. She wanted a new relationship with Dakota and she wasn't subtle about it. She felt he owed her for the years she had taken care of him, even though in my opinion she'd been a shitty mother, often high on drugs and always teetering on the edge of poverty and homelessness.

Dakota stood up to her and refused to let her move in with him. He started to see her regularly, and he reported back to Mike and me that he thought she was finally changing, taking responsibility for her own life.

Then she met George, and within months she was living with him in a one-bedroom apartment in Kaneohe and running the office for his repair shop. I was sure disaster was in the offing.

But so far, Angelina and George had proved me wrong. That night, after leaving Griffin under the watchful eyes of Dom and Soon-O, Mike and I drove up to Kaneohe to meet them for dinner, accompanied by Dakota and his boyfriend Josh. It was to be Josh's first chance to meet his potential in-laws.

"What are you thinking?" Mike asked me, as we headed into a tunnel along the H3.

"That I'd rather be investigating a serial killer than facing this dinner."

"Kimo. I know you've been angry with Angelina for a long time. But even you have to admit she's turned around."

"I don't want Dakota to get hurt."

"Getting hurt is a part of life," Mike said. "And Dakota is a smart guy. You see how he's been taking it slow with Angelina. He's determined to rebuild his relationship with her, and it's up to us to support him."

"I know. But it doesn't mean I have to like it."

We pulled into the parking lot of a seafood restaurant on Haiku Road and saw George and Angelina standing beside a motorcycle waiting for us. She had let her black hair, now streaked with gray, grow down her back and begun wearing cowboy boots, jeans, and denim shirts studded with rhinestones.

George had his arm around her shoulders and they looked like a happy older couple, as Mike and I might look in ten or fifteen years.

"Remember, be nice," Mike said, as we parked.

We walked over to them and shook hands. Angelina was wearing a clunky turquoise bracelet, and Mike complemented her on it. "George gave it to me for our anniversary," she said proudly.

"A year," I said. "Wow. Congratulations."

"You didn't think we'd make it," Angelina said. "I know, and I don't blame you for thinking that. But George is the man who made it all happen. I know it's not liberated to be a woman who needs someone to take care of her, but I knew that I couldn't make it outside on my own."

I spotted Josh's rented Porsche as it approached the restaurant. He was spending more and more time in Honolulu and the boys had plans for him to relocate permanently. For the time being, he was sharing Dakota's apartment near the hotel.

"I never lived by myself," Angelina continued. "I went right from my parents' house to my first boyfriend's apartment, and I bounced around from man to man until I had Dakota. Then it was him and me against the world."

Josh pulled into the parking lot, and he and Dakota unfolded themselves from the low-slung car.

"I know I didn't do right by him and with George's help I've been trying to make it up to him. You guys have been good to him and I appreciate that. But he needs his momma in his life, too."

Mike and I nodded politely as Dakota and Josh approached. Josh was pure Han Chinese, tall and sallow, with black eyes and black hair, and a short, flat nose. He was as handsome as Dakota, and they fit together well.

Dakota leaned down and kissed Angelina on the cheek, and shook hands with George. "This is my boyfriend, Josh," he said. "My mom, Angie, and George."

Josh shook hands with everyone, and George said "Well, let's go on inside. You like steak, Josh? They do a great New York Strip."

We chatted about the menu and then were led to a table overlooking the valley, with the mountains in the background. "This is lovely," Josh said.

"Ain't it?" George asked. "Angie and I come here at least once a week."

I took a deep breath and looked at the stunning view. For a moment, I was struck by the natural beauty of my island home. Puffy white clouds hung over mountainsides dressed in green trees and gray rock. Down below, a narrow blue river glistened in the dying sunshine. I reminded myself how lucky we were to live in a place other people worked for years to save up for a visit.

My mother had always emphasized the importance of ohana as I was growing up. Not just the family we were born into, but everyone around us who needed connection. Our luaus always included my godfather, Uncle Chin, and his wife Aunt Mei-Mei; my father's UH classmates and the guys who worked for him, and my far-ranging group of cousins and hanai relatives.

Hanai meant adopted family—and gradually we were including Angelina, George and now Josh into our ohana. Sometimes couples divorced, families broke up, or people either moved away or simply lost touch. But they were always welcome, even after drama or tragedy.

It was up to me to continue my mother's tradition. Once I realized that, it was like something opened inside me. I felt a warmth toward Angelina and George I'd never felt before, and I laughed at George's jokes, smiled when Angelina put her hand on her son's arm.

I was glad to see that George and Angelina were completely welcoming to Josh. For a while, Angelina had felt Dakota was gay simply because she'd never provided him with good male role models, or showed him what a heterosexual relationship could be like without loud voices, drugs, and guns.

She was distrustful when Dakota moved in with Mike and me, but gradually she came around. That was mostly Mike's doing. Maybe because he was part Italian, and because he'd lived in New York when he was a kid, he understood her boisterous personality and saw the love underneath it.

"I'm glad to see you boys are so close," Angelina said to Dakota and Josh over dessert. "I don't think I could have made it on the outside without George. A lot of women I knew in prison were released, and offended again just to come back to a place where they were looked after."

She tried to smile, but it didn't reach her eyes. "Not that it was so great, mind you. But every day I knew what was expected of me. I knew how I had to behave. And in exchange I got food and shelter. For a gal like me, that really meant something."

"How did you and George meet?" Josh asked.

"At an NA meeting," George said. "Narcotics Anonymous. I saw this beautiful gal across the room and I couldn't wait to hear her story, get to know her. But she was shy and didn't speak up."

This time, when Angelina smiled, it was genuine. "I saw this Asian cowboy looking at me, and I went all bashful. It wasn't until the third meeting that I told my story, and he come up to me afterward."

"And that was the start of a beautiful relationship," George said. "We both value what we have together and we work to keep each other on the straight and narrow." He turned to Josh. "And what about you two?"

"I have an apartment in Los Gatos," he said. "It's a town in Silicon Valley. I was complaining to my boss about the traffic and he suggested I could work from home for a while if I wanted. But the forecast was for a couple of weeks of rain, so since I could work anywhere, I decided to find someplace with better weather."

He looked over at Dakota and smiled. "I picked the resort where Dakota worked, and when I got to the check-in desk this handsome guy was working. We traded some smiles and I flirted a little, and he flirted back, and so asked him out for a drink after work."

"I had to say no," Dakota said. "I explained that employees weren't permitted to socialize with guests." He looked over at Josh. "I worked hard to get into the training program and I wasn't going to do anything to put my job in danger. Not even for a great-looking guy with a sexy smile."

"But I was determined," Josh said. "I checked out the next day but Dakota wasn't on duty. I moved to a hotel across the street, and came back twice before I caught up with him. I told him that I wasn't a guest anymore, so he didn't have an excuse not to go out to dinner with me."

"That's romantic," Angie said, with a smile.

"What do you do for work, Josh?" Angelina asked.

"I design and program retail shopping sites for corporate clients."

Josh named a couple of corporate clients that I recognized. George talked about buying auto parts from one of them.

We squabbled for a few minutes about the check. I suggested we should split it three ways, but both George and Josh wanted to pay. Finally George won, and he said that Josh could pay next time. "I hope we'll see a lot of you boys in the future."

"It's interesting the different ways that couples meet," I said to Mike as we drove home. "You and I met when we had to work together. Dakota wouldn't date Josh until there wasn't a work relationship between them. And Angelina and George met through let's call it a shared interest."

Mike laughed. "You could call it that."

"I think it's harder for couples to establish a real relationship these days," I said. "At least that's what I'm learning at work and from Apikela. Men and women who have such different expectations are having trouble getting into relationships and making them work."

"Keep in mind that you only see a certain subset of the population," Mike said. "The criminal subset. We know a lot of very happy couples, gay and straight."

"I know. But these two murders are getting to me. I keep feeling that they're linked, and the reason is because it's so hard for men and women, or even for two men, to connect when so much of the world is focused on surface stuff."

By the time we got home, we were both tired, and we settled into bed together.

And that was our life together. I still loved him and I knew he loved me, but we'd moved on. Our love language had gradually changed from physical touch to acts of service. We still had sex, but we showed our affection instead by doing things for each other. I made sure to pick up foods that he liked when I went grocery shopping. He fixed things around the house without asking, and so on.

Gunter protested that we'd become more like roommates, or friends with benefits, than lovers, and I disagreed. Gunter had a bad track record with lovers, discarding them as frequently as used toothbrushes, so I didn't listen to him. I knew from occasional asides that he was secretly jealous of the settled life Mike and I had achieved.

Because it was easier for gay men to have anonymous sex than straight ones, I didn't think there was as much testosterone-fueled desperation. I knew from experience that if you let yourself get too horny without release, you could get into trouble.

Was that what had happened to Betsy Lawrence and Ravenna Cannon? They'd gotten in the way of a horny guy desperate for sex? Both women had gone out after dark, potentially to meet men. Neither had been sexually assaulted, though. Was it because they'd refused advances?

Was there really that simple a line tying the two crimes together?

Chapter 20
Sensorvault

Sunday Mike and I drove down to Kapiolani Park for the Fire Department's 10K run. It was a crisp fall day, sunshine and trade winds. Lots of friends and family of firefighters were running, but I'd chosen to stand on the sidelines and cheer, and donate as one of Mike's supporters. Cathy brought the keikis and we staked out a spot near the finish line.

We cheered him on, and he came in first in his age group. We spent some time in the park with the keikis and Griffin afterward, and by the time we got back to Aiea Heights we were all exhausted.

Ray and I drove separately to the office Monday morning, and Betsy Lawrence's cell phone records arrived by email after we'd gotten our first cups of coffee. We looked at them together.

She had been texting with someone in the hours before she died. Apparently she and the guy, whose name came up on the texts as K, were chatting about classic anime.

She loved the work of Hayao Miyazaki and his Studio Ghibli, particularly *Nausicaä of the Valley of the Wind,* which she called a masterpiece. He was most fond of *The Secret World of Arrietty,* based on a series of books I'd read as a child about a race of tiny people who lived hidden in the houses and landscapes of full-sized humans, and survived by "borrowing" things from them.

I was already bonding with K because I'd loved those books, and even seen the movie. I could see why Betsy would agree to meet him, even if it required sneaking out of her dorm room late at night.

He was explaining the math behind the way a character moved, but she didn't seem to understand. "You have to show me," she wrote. "Now? I can meet you."

His last message came in at 10:05 PM on the night she died, and it was simply a thumbs-up and the word "outside."

I did a quick Google search on that phone number and got the message, "It looks like there aren't many great matches for your search."

I tried it again with parenthesis around the area code, and got a bunch of answers with some part of the phone number, but not all of it.

"Burner phone?" Ray asked.

Something tickled at the back of my mind. "When Dakota came to live with Mike and me, he had a cell phone that he'd bought from someone on the street. It wasn't registered to a carrier, and he just bought minutes for it. He didn't have a fixed address or a credit card to get a regular phone."

"So this means we can't get records for it from anyone," Ray said. "It might be a criminal who wants to hide the number, or it could just be a college student on a budget." He licked his lips. "I have an idea. I was doing some research online yesterday afternoon and I read about this thing called the Sensorvault. Have you ever heard of it?"

I shook my head.

"The way I understand it, Google has been collecting detailed location data from most Android devices for over a decade. Also from iPads and iPhones that have Google Maps installed."

I held up my iPad and my iPhone. "So Google knows where I am as long as I'm carrying one of these."

He nodded. "And they keep all this information in a database called Sensorvault. We can prepare an affidavit for what they call either a geo-fence or reverse location warrant. We state that we know Betsy Lawrence exchanged text messages with someone else immediately before her death. We believe that the person carrying the phone that sent and received messages was present at the time of her death, and we need the phone information to find him or her."

"Why don't we just call the damn number and see who answers?" I asked.

Ray shrugged. "Say we do that. What happens when the person answers? We ask them do you know Betsy Lawrence?"

I pursed my lips. "How about if we pretend to be from HAC and we're doing a student survey."

"Lying to a suspect is never a good idea," Ray said.

"All right. Suppose we hold off on calling the number until we have more evidence. What does your Sensorvault data get us?"

"It can place the person who texted Betsy on the campus, in the area where she died, at the time of her death."

"How precise can we get?" I asked. "For example, if we request data from the whole HAC campus, we could get information on every student in the dorm."

"We use latitude and longitude," he said. "Measure out the immediate area around where her body was found, and include the area where she might have been hit, but avoid the actual dorm buildings. If the CSI team can do that."

"I think they can," I said. "But how accurate is this data? Sometimes I use that "Find My" app on my phone to know where Mike is, and the location is off by a couple of blocks."

"I read an article in the Harvard Law Review that cited a couple of inaccuracies. We have to be careful with whatever data we get."

I pushed back my chair. "Before we spend too much time on this I think we need to bring Lieutenant Sampson into the loop."

We walked over to his office and told him what we were planning. He motioned us to sit across from him. "I've never heard of a geo-fence warrant," he said. "Explain to me what that is."

Ray spoke, since it was his idea. "The warrant is a request for cell phone location data that Google collects. We specify the immediate area where Betsy Lawrence's body was found. We ask them for data about phones in that area an hour before she left her room and end an hour after the window of death Doc establishes. Then Google will tell us whose phones were in the area during that time."

"What if the killer didn't have a phone with them?" Sampson asked.

"Then we wade through a lot of data for no reason," I said. "But we know they exchanged text messages until Betsy left her room. So it's likely the killer had a phone with him. Though it's possible that he drove to HAC and parked at the bottom of the hill, left the phone in the car, and climbed up to meet Betsy."

"That implies either a careless killer who left their phone behind, or one who was very methodical about being noticed," Ray said. "And from what I've read, not a lot of people know about this Sensorvault yet."

"You're going to have to explain this very carefully to Judge Yamanaka," Sampson said. "He's accustomed to rubber-stamping the same kind of warrants and subpoenas every day. And I don't know that's he's that tech-savvy."

"I saw pictures of his grandchildren on his desk the last time I was there," Ray said. "He told me they're living in Japan right now and the only way he can see their faces is by Face Time. So he's at least that knowledgeable."

"Okay. Put something together and let me know."

While Ray started drafting the affidavit, I went downstairs to the B1 level to see if Ryan Kainoa could give me the precise coordinates of the crime scene. I had to explain the Sensorvault concept to him, but he caught on quickly.

"Normally we use landmarks and measurements to identify the area, but we've used latitude and longitude in geocaching exercises we do for CSI students," he said. "I can run up to HAC and get the data you need."

"Stay as far away from the buildings as you can. We don't want to get phone information from every kid in the dorm."

"Will do."

When I got back upstairs, Ray had found a sample geofence warrant and was copying the language used there. "Better to give Google something they've seen before," he said. It took a while for us to get the language right, and we had to wait for Ryan to get us the coordinates. He texted them to us from the HAC campus, and we added them to our affidavit.

Ray and I drove over to the judge's chambers together. His office was in Ali'i Iolani Hale on South King Street, the home of the Hawai'i State Supreme Court. It was an impressive two-story building with a four-story clock tower, and looked in many ways like Iolani Palace. The impressive gold-leaf statue of Kamehameha the Great stood in the center of a grass circle in the front of the building.

"This is a request for a search warrant, detectives?" he asked, as he scanned the paperwork. "For these coordinates? What does Google have to do with that?"

"It's a request to search their database, called Sensorvault, for records of any cell phone found within those coordinates at that time," I said.

"It's a way for us to access location data from devices that were present in the area where Betsy Lawrence was killed, at the time of her murder. We've narrowed our request as much as possible to avoid getting false data," Ray added.

Judge Yamanaka looked up at us, over the rims of his reading glasses. "And how is this different from a fishing expedition?"

Ray said, "Because we have reason to believe that Miss Lawrence's killer was texting her up until a few minutes before her death. Identifying the cell phone will lead us to her killer."

"And you can't just call this number?"

"We don't want to do that without knowing more about the person behind the number," Ray said. "As far as we can tell it's a prepaid cell so there's no other way to track it."

He turned to his computer and began typing. In the meantime, Ray and I sat uncomfortably in his office waiting.

The judge was in his seventies, a portly fellow in a navy suit with a tie loosened at the neck. I saw the pictures Ray had mentioned on his desk, and there were many photos of him with local dignitaries on his walls.

Finally he turned back to us. "I did some preliminary research, and it appears it is within my jurisdiction to grant this warrant, so I'll sign it. But before you bring charges against anyone I want to see corroborating evidence that your suspect made contact with the victim, and that he or she can't be placed anywhere else at the time of the murder."

Ray and I both nodded. "Certainly," Ray said.

When we were outside the judge's chambers, Ray and I high-fived each other. We were excited by our prospects and celebrated by stopping at our favorite malasada stand for some puffy Portuguese donuts. We laughed as we licked our fingers. There's nothing like the high of feeling like you're closing in on the bad guys.

Back at the office, Ray scanned the warrant and dug around until he could find the online system where such requests could be submitted direct to Google.

While he worked on that, I had another idea I wanted to look into.

Of course I'd heard about incels before; there was a time when they were all over the news. But I'd never really investigated what made them tick. And having both Apikela and Gunter mention them in the context of my case made me dig in.

I thought about our victims. Betsy Lawrence was a beauty who used cosmetics, while Ravenna Cannon was an older woman who was open to sexual encounters, perhaps even preying on unwilling men. What did they have in common? We suspected that Betsy had left her dorm room to meet a man, and that Ravenna had either agreed to meet, or run into, a man behind the bandshell.

I was trying to keep an open mind; there was no indication yet that our killer was male. It was possible a woman had killed both Betsy and Ravenna, but I doubted it. Maybe our run-in with Brandon was prejudicing us.

It was possible that K, who had been texting Betsy, was someone who looked like Brandon Paikai, and had his attitude toward women. Betsy might have turned her nose up at him in person, despite their bonding over animation. Maybe Ravenna Cannon had done the same thing.

Could that rejection have led to their deaths?

Chapter 21
The Wrong Things

I started researching incels, if only to wipe out this odd idea. I began with a dictionary definition, and my original ideas were challenged quickly. I thought that incels just wanted to have sex, and were angry that women wouldn't provide it to them because they weren't handsome or charming or wealthy enough. But their philosophy, if you want to call it that, was about more.

These men, who recognized their unattractiveness and often even called themselves subhuman, had developed a violent political ideology that leaned toward white supremacy. They directed hatred at things they thought they desired; they were obsessed with female beauty but despised makeup as a form of fraud. Like Brandon Paikai, they were angry at everybody who had sex. Women who were sexually active were called sluts, or much worse names.

I went online searching for places that incels hung out, hoping to see if there was a local message board Ray and I could investigate. Many incels had clustered around groups on Reddit, but those had been shut down because of their content.

The messages I found were sad, but explained a lot about how the posters felt about their self-image. One guy didn't like to go out with his parents because they were surrounded by couples enjoying themselves, and that reminded him that he was alone.

Another said that his emphasis on earning money and moving ahead in his job had prevented him from spending the time necessary to cultivate relationships. There were still others who were depressed because of their lack of human companionship, even friends and acquaintances.

Some of the ideas were just downright stupid. One poster said that women who had sex with different men retained bits of their DNA, and if you married one of them your kids could be only partially genetically yours. "25% Chad, 25% Tyrone, and 50% yours."

Ray finished uploading our affidavit and warrant to Google and came over to my desk. "What are you working on?"

"Do you think Brandon Paikai is an incel?"

He cocked his head. "I thought we were done with him."

"With him, yeah. But I've been thinking about what Betsy Lawrence and Ravenna Cannon have in common."

"Both women, both attractive," he said. "And both dead."

"But there's another connection. Betsy was trolling dating websites, and Ravenna was a sexual compulsive. They're both the kind of women that incels hate."

"I thought incels hated all women."

I turned my computer screen so he could see what I'd been reading. "I think it's less than that, and more," I said. "They have these demeaning terms. Women are either 'Stacys,' who are hyperfeminine, attractive, and unattainable and who only date 'Chads' – who are muscular, popular men."

He looked closely at the screen. "I've heard that term Beckys," he said. "They're average women."

"Also called femoids—Female Humanoid Organisms. Or foids for short."

"That's chilling," Ray said. "Humanoid. I mean, do they think of their mothers that way?"

I pointed to one poster who complained about "high-tier Beckys" who spent their time harassing, bullying and gaslighting lonely virgin men. "It's like they make themselves the center of the universe, and everything other people do is all about them."

"Which makes them angry," Ray said, nodding. "But angry enough to kill?"

"Self-proclaimed incels have already committed murders in California, Oregon and Canada, among other places, though they don't get much attention unless they kill multiple people at once."

"You think we have a serial killer on our hands?"

I shook my head. "That's not what I meant. The incels who have been accused of murders have killed a bunch of people all at once. I'm wondering if there is enough of an incel community here in Honolulu that they're spurring each other on."

"Like egging Brandon Paikai to go harass people coming out of bars." He realized what he'd said. "Literally with eggs."

"There have always been loners, some of them violent, but our traditional view of them has been men who are socially inept, more comfortable on their own than in groups," I said.

"The kind of guys who preferred to play solo video games than organized sports, because they're clumsy or not team players," Ray said. "But the internet has given them a place to get together and organize."

I nodded. "This incel movement seems darker than a bunch of geeks playing video games. We've seen how social rejection combined with access to weapons has led to many terrible crimes, often mass shootings."

"But we don't know yet if our two murders were connected. They're so different on the surface that I'm having a hard time seeing one person killing both women."

"But what if it's two different killers, both motivated by the same online crap?"

"I think that's a theory we can keep on the back burner."

My computer beeped with an incoming email, a copy of what

was being sent to Ray, containing the records for Ravenna's cell phone.

He brought his chair over and we looked at them together. Sure enough, Ravenna had been texting with someone until shortly before her murder. She had agreed to meet him to "get it on" behind the bandshell.

"Both of our victims were texting right before they were killed," I said.

"But this isn't K," Ray said. "Different handle. Moke_Man." He sat back. "Honestly, I can't see a woman who knows anything about Hawaiian culture agreeing to meet a guy who calls himself a moke."

I shrugged. "Some women are into that, I'm sure. Any word from Google yet on the Sensorvault data from HAC?"

"Not yet." He looked down. "I kind of adjusted the affidavit before I sent it to them."

I looked over at him. "Adjusted how?"

"Like you, I don't believe in coincidence. So I got the coordinates for the Waikiki Shell from Ryan and added a request for the geofence data there around the time of Ravenna's stabbing."

"And you did that after Judge Yamanaka signed the warrant?"

"Well, the warrant only referenced the affidavit," he said. "Google won't know."

I lifted my hand for another high-five, which he accepted. "You've been working with me too long," I said. "You're learning all the wrong things from me."

Chapter 22
Shivers

After Ray went back to his desk, I continued snooping around online for information about incels, and I was surprised to find a Reddit called *Noho maleole*. That Hawaiian phrase, with the addition of an okina, or backwards apostrophe, meant "to remain unmarried."

I clicked through to it. I was asked to sign in through Google, but I didn't want to use my real name or email address, so instead I signed up with Reddit using a Proton Mail account I had created a while before to use for investigations. Proton Mail was very secure and I was confident someone couldn't track the account back to me personally.

Before I could get started, I had to answer some questions. I identified myself as male, and said I was interested in lifehacks, books, and animals. They were close enough to the real me that if anyone asked I'd have something to say. I had to choose a subreddit to subscribe to from a list, so I picked one on books.

I chose an angry-looking young male avatar with a red beanie and skin a few shades darker than my own, though not verging into African-American. I had to verify my email address, so I had to switch over to Proton Mail, find the message from Reddit, and reply to it. I finally was able to join the Noho Male'ole subreddit.

It was called a Subreddit for men in Hawai'i who felt they weren't cut out for relationships. In the box for "about community" there was a link to a suicide prevention hotline, which I thought was sad, but I was glad that whoever set the subreddit up recognized it might be useful.

I began scanning through the messages. One poster began his with "It doesn't get better," about how the longer you remained single the harder it became to find someone. Another was scornful of how casually his coworkers talked about sex, as if it was as easy to obtain as buying a bottle of water at a convenience store.

A third, Waimea_Falls033, was angry that women insulted him by calling him a "kissless virgin."

Did women really talk that way? Or was that all in these guys' heads?

I thought back to the way Betsy Lawrence's mother had called her a mean girl. She'd meant it in terms of the way her daughter treated less attractive young women. But what if girls like her really did demean unattractive men?

It was close to quitting time, and I had to get home and look after our new puppy. Dominic and Soon-O had agreed to let him stay with them during the day, to make sure he got fed and exercised and didn't tear up the house. But I had enough time to talk to someone I thought could help. I called Api, and surprisingly she answered.

"Hey, Api, it's Uncle K. If I swing past HAC on my way home can we meet up for a few minutes?"

"Sure. I'm in my room experimenting with some Halloween makeup for my TikTok. I can't exactly go out like this. You want to pick me up a green monster and bring it to my room?"

"I can do that. I'll be there in about thirty."

I avoided most traffic by taking side roads from downtown up into Manoa, and picked up her drink from a different barista in the student café. Justin, the guy at the front desk in Mizushima Hall, recognized me and buzzed me in, and I rode up to Api's room.

I was startled when the door was answered by a monster with a matte-white face and five extra eyes. Api laughed. "That's just the kind of reaction I want to get. Come on in, my roommate's out studying."

Her room was almost a carbon copy of the one shared by Betsy and Kimora, down to the magazine clippings on the corkboard, though Api's were all of beautiful Asian women.

It was hard to concentrate when I sat down at the round table across from her as she sipped her ugly green drink, but I worked at it. "Tell me honestly, do pretty girls have nasty names for unattractive guys?"

She laughed. "Of course we do. I think all girls, pretty or not, do. Fugly, for sure. Monkeyface, pukeface, toad. Loser or choad."

"Choad?"

She smirked. "Someone with a short dick."

"Did you ever hear someone called a kissless virgin?"

She laughed again. "No, but I love it."

She must have noticed my frown, because she said, "I wouldn't call anyone that. At least not to his face."

"How about serial-killer-type guy?"

"What's this about?" she asked.

Without revealing too many details, I told her about the connection between my two cases and how I wondered if Betsy's mean-girl attitude could have caused someone to want to kill her.

"You're giving me shivers, Uncle K," she said. "I try and be nice to everybody, you know? It's how I was raised. And with my TikTok I'm trying to elevate girls to be their best selves. The idea that someone would hate us for that is awful."

"I'm sorry to upset you, but I'm trying to get a handle on how these guys feel, and that has a lot to do with how girls like you treat guys like that."

I sat back. "There are a lot of terrible people in the world. You keep being nice, but watch out for yourself, all right?" I wanted to kiss her cheek but I didn't want to mess up her makeup, so I settled for a fist bump.

When I got home, Mike had already gotten Griffin from his parents and they were on the floor in the living room, the big dog climbing over Mike and licking his face as Mike laughed.

When I walked in, Griffin jumped up and rushed over to me, nuzzling my hands. But as soon as he'd established who I was, he went back to Mike.

After dinner, Mike settled down with one of the fire investigation journals he'd been ignoring while he practiced for the 10K, with Griffin on the floor beside him. He used his right hand to hold the book and his left to pet the dog.

I went back to the subreddit. It felt weird, as if I was spying on these people's private pain, but there was something magnetic about it, too. Like I was secretly feeling superior to them because I'd found my love.

I responded to a couple of comments, telling guys that they had to hold on, work on themselves, and that love could follow. It was a cliché, but I truly believed that you couldn't convince someone to love you until you loved yourself. And that meant being happy, or at least content, with your personality, your looks, and your station in life.

That didn't mean you couldn't continue to improve. Dakota was using all those beauty products to make himself look better even though he had a boyfriend. Mike and I were exercising to stay fit, but also because we wanted to stay attractive, if only to each other.

God knows I wanted to make more money. I didn't need the outward trappings like expensive jewelry or a fancy car, but I wanted more of the freedom that money gives you, to travel, to buy gifts and experiences for the keikis, and so on.

I read through page after page of posts, many of them desperate cries for help. The responses were a mixture of support and negativity, which was weird. One guy called himself a low-value male; he was overweight and his only good characteristic was his height and posture.

The responders were split. Some told him that he'd hit the genetic lottery with his height and to stop complaining. Another reminded him, "A term like low-value male is demeaning and you shouldn't use it on yourself. Don't let other people get in your head that way."

It wasn't until I'd gotten about three pages in that I found someone who said he was so angry that he'd considered violence as the only way to deal with those feelings. "Sometimes I see couples out there all kissy-face and stuff and I want to grab something and hit them," he wrote. "Like I don't need to see that shit right in front of me to remind me I don't have anything like that."

As with most of the posts, there were a mix of positive and negative comments. Someone told him, "Dude, get a grip. Someone else's happiness shouldn't affect yours."

Another poster wrote, "You don't know what's going on in anyone else's life. Maybe that girl is just using him for fancy dinners and expensive gifts."

A poster called Kane_123, wrote, "Sometimes it can be cathartic to lash out when a foid rejects you. Trust me, it feels great!"

Nobody else picked up on that topic, but I highlighted it and copied it. I doubted I could track Kane_123, not without a subpoena, and that kind of vague comment wasn't something a judge would find actionable.

It was almost bedtime, and Mike wanted me to walk with him and Griffin, so I shut down my laptop, stood up and stretched. I saw the smile on Mike's face as he hooked up Griffin's leash, and knew that I was lucky to have both of them in my life.

Chapter 23
Spectrum

Tuesday morning I got a call from my nephew Keoni, which was unique. I usually only spoke to my nieces and nephews at family parties, or when I reached out.

"Hey, Uncle K. Api called me last night."

I was surprised by that, too. I didn't realize that the cousins were in that close contact.

"She said you're looking for men who hate women."

"Not exactly, but close enough. What's up?"

"You think you could come out to where we're working sometime today? One of the guys who works for us is freaking me out with the things he says."

"Sure. Where are you?"

He gave me an address on Ala Moana Boulevard, near the cruise terminal, and I said I could be there in a half hour. "You want to take a ride?" I asked Ray, after I hung up.

"Still no response from Google to our subpoena for the geocache information on both sites," he said. "So why not?"

It was a cloudy day, and the trade winds were sweeping pieces of newspaper and fast-food wrappers in the gutters along South Beretania Street. Like many names in Honolulu it was a reminder of our colonial past, in this case when Captain Cook "discovered" the islands where my ancestors had been living for centuries. He had unwittingly arrived during a period in the Hawaiian calendar representing Ku, the God of War. An altercation on the beach led to his death, and things didn't pick up again until Captain George Vancouver arrived in 1792, and trading began between Britain and our islands.

When there was a war scare in in 1843, Kamehameha III asked the British for protection, and the British flag was raised over each island, and all Hawaiian flags were destroyed. Hawai'i was welcoming for the next half-century, and the British consul's office was located on Beretania Street. Because each syllable in Hawaiian has to end in a vowel, 'Britain' became 'Beretania.'

I remembered as a kid learning the alphabet, and being taken to Kaimuki, where the streets were alphabetically organized with English names: Brokaw, Catherine, Duval, Elizabeth, Francis, George, Hayden, and James.

I was always partial to James Street because that was my middle name. When my older brothers were born, it was illegal to give a child a Hawaiian name, so Lui and Haoa had official English names, Louis, and Howard. My parents chose to give me the best of both worlds, as my mother said, and call me Kimo James – Kimo was the Hawaiian translation of James.

Ray and I turned onto Punchbowl Street to head toward the water, passing Honolulu Hale and the old Kawaiaha'o Church, where my parents had taken my brothers and me occasionally for religious services as kids. With its stone face and round columns, it wouldn't have been out of place in New England, which was where many of the early missionaries had come from.

The address Keoni had given me was where Punchbowl ran into Ala Moana. Two four-story glass office buildings, called the Spectrum, faced each other at a forty-five-degree angle, the best views looking out at Honolulu Harbor over a manicured triangle of grass, bushes, and tree-shaded benches.

Haoa was a proud graduate of UH, as was Keoni, and Kanapa'aka Landscaping workers wore pinneys of dark green and white, the school's colors. Many of the men wore long-sleeved shirts underneath, to protect their skin from the sun's harmful rays, as well as broad-brimmed hats that reminded me of ones my grandfather wore when he came to Hawai'i to work in the sugarcane fields.

As we pulled into the parking lot behind the building, I texted Keoni that we'd arrived. He replied that he was in the building's first-floor coffee shop—an outpost of Ray's and my favorite, the Kope Bean.

When we walked in, I saw him at a corner table, talking on his phone and taking notes on a laptop. I waved hello and Ray and I got our coffees.

By the time we joined him, he'd finished his call. "What's up, Keoni?" I asked. "You said one of your guys has been disruptive?"

"Not so much that as just weird," he said. "I told Api about him the last time we were together, and she called me last night and told me I should talk to you."

I nodded and sipped my coffee.

He looked down. "This is kind of embarrassing to talk about."

I looked at Ray and he shrugged. "You're among family here," I said. "Whatever you tell me won't go any further unless it's relevant to an investigation."

When Keoni looked up, his usually smiling round face was pulled tightly as if he was in pain. Oh, no, I thought. He's going to come out to us.

"It's not very easy for me to get dates," he said, in a strangled voice. "I think I have a low-level version of Asperger's, and it's hard for me to talk to girls. Plus it's hell to get the dirt out of my fingernails and the creases of my skin, and when girls see that they immediately think I'm some loser guy with a manual job."

"You ever go online to talk to other guys about this?" I asked, thinking of the subreddit I'd been reading. Had one of those posts come from my nephew?

"Why would I do that?" he asked. "It's nobody else's problem but my own."

I sipped my coffee, but Keoni didn't seem to have anything more to say. Finally I asked, "What does this have to do with the guy that works for you?"

"He's a jerk," my nephew said definitively. "Sometimes he gets the guys to tease me about not having a girlfriend. Like I'm a loser because I don't have an office job like Jeff and a pretty girl like Chesa. I can't even talk about my brother anymore in front of the guys."

"What's this guy's name?" I asked.

"Ricky. Ricky Kuapi."

I recognized the origin of the last name. "Samoan guy?"

He nodded. "He likes to play video games instead of dating," he said. "He doesn't want a girlfriend now. He's going to wait and marry some fat Samoan girl who can't find a better husband. But I can tell he's bitter that no girl wants to date him."

"You ever heard the term incel?" I asked.

"Involuntary celibate. Yeah, I think that's Ricky. You want to talk to him?"

I looked at Ray, who nodded. We were both thinking the same thing—that Ricky's last name started with K, and along with his yen for video games, which might make him the guy who'd been texting with Betsy Lawrence before her death.

"I think he might be useful for our investigation, but we don't want to scare him off yet," I said. "He's a regular worker?"

Keoni nodded. "I can give you his information."

"That would be great," I said. "Can we walk outside and have you point him out? Without him noticing?"

"Sure. We don't even have to go outside. He's part of the crew trimming the hedges."

He led us over to the broad windows that looked out on the area where his crew was working. "He's the big guy on the end. The one with only a pinney, no shirt."

The guy he pointed out was at least six-four and broad-shouldered, with a big belly that strained across the green pinney. His skin was tanned nut-brown, and his kinky black hair was cut short and tight to his head.

I heard Ray rustling for his cell phone and the click that indicated he'd taken a picture. "Thanks, Keoni," I said. "We'll be in touch."

As we walked back to my SUV, I asked Ray, "What do you think?"

"He's as good a lead as we've got. When we get back we can check him for priors and compare his phone number to the ones the women were texting. But I still think that phone is a burner and won't lead us anywhere."

"However, if the same burner shows up in both geofences, then we know we've got the same killer."

"There's that."

As we rode back to headquarters, Ray said, "We need to start hiring out your family. Seems everyone who has information for us is someone you're related to."

"Oahu is a small island. I have a large family."

I realized, not for the first time, that those little keikis who had clustered around me demanding surfing lessons were all grown up now. My mother was growing increasingly frail, and soon she would not be around to serve as a connector between us. Lui, Haoa and I would remain close, but the next generation was spinning away from us, choosing their own paths.

I hoped that like Keoni and Apikela, they would stay in touch. It would be cool to see them take over the responsibility for family luaus when we couldn't manage it any longer.

I felt bad for Keoni, though. More and more kids I knew were showing signs of Asperger's or some other version of autism, and I wondered if that was just because we'd grown better at diagnosing it.

If my brothers and I were still kids, I wouldn't be surprised if Haoa was diagnosed somewhere on that spectrum. Looking back, he'd never been the best student, preferring to play sports instead of studying, and it was only my mother's perseverance with him, and the football coach's persuasion, that had gotten him through Punahou. At UH he'd taken the path of least resistance, studying agriculture, because he was so comfortable outdoors and had a real connection to the land.

Maybe that was Keoni's situation, too. He loved being out in nature and working with his hands. I hoped that soon he'd find a woman who shared those passions.

In the meantime, though, we had to discover what had motivated the murders of two women—and hopefully prevent more from happening.

Chapter 24
Profile

While we were on our way back to headquarters, I got a call from Alice Kanamura, the receptionist at the ME's office. "Doc wanted me to let you know that he pulled a fingerprint for you from Ravenna Cannon's blouse. Do you want to come over here and have him explain how he did it?"

"Absolutely," I said. "We can be there in a half hour."

Turning toward Iwilei, we were caught in a microburst of rain that had me slapping the windshield wipers rapidly. "Welcome to paradise," Ray said.

Of course, within a mile, the clouds had cleared and the road was bone-dry. That's the truth about the weather in the Aloha State. Don't like it? Drive a mile or wait a few minutes, and it will change.

The heat and humidity were oppressive as we got out of the SUV, so we hurried up to the cool interior. Alice waved us down the hall, intent on something on her computer.

"I've been lobbying for the funds to buy a vacuum metal deposition machine." Doc led us to a room and opened the door. "Gentlemen, meet the VMD1260 from a company out of Scotland."

It looked like a large washing machine, with a front-loading door. "We are one of a relatively small percentage of U.S. law enforcement agencies to have the latest VMD technology," Doc said. "Before this, I'd have to send material to California to get results."

"What does it do?" Ray asked.

"The original technology used gold and zinc to recover the fingerprint marks on plastics, glass, and other smooth surfaces. But the newer machines, like this one, use fine layers of metals to display fingerprints on fabrics." He smiled proudly. "The technique has been around since the 1970s but only recently has been fine-tuned to use on fabrics."

"Impressive," I said.

"Let me show you. It's similar to using photographic negatives, where a color will show up as its opposite. I put Ms. Cannon's shirt in this vacuum chamber, then heated up gold to evaporate it and spread a fine film over the fabric."

Ray and I both nodded.

"Then I heat up the zinc, which attaches to the gold where there are no fingerprint residues. This helps reveal the fingerprint – where contact has been made we see the original fabric, where there was no contact we're left with the grey color of the metal film."

"Have you entered the fingerprint in the IAFIS?" I asked.

The Integrated Automated Fingerprint Identification System is a computerized system maintained by the FBI.

"I normally leave that up to your crime scene techs, but I was curious." He smiled. "I got a partial match on a print. Come back to my office and I'll show you."

We followed him out of the room and back to his office, where he sat at his computer and hit a few keys. Then he turned the monitor toward us.

"Holy shit," I said. "Ricky Kuapi."

"You know him?" Doc asked.

"We were just introduced," I said. "He works for my brother's landscaping company."

I looked at Ray. "This investigation just got a lot more interesting."

"Let's not get too far ahead of ourselves," Ray said, as we drove back to headquarters. "Doc was only able to get a partial print, from her sleeve. That's not enough to convict him."

"I know. It's not even enough to bring him in for interrogation yet. He could say that he was out walking in Waikiki and Ravenna tripped, and he grabbed her arm to steady her."

"If he's smart enough," Ray said.

When we were at our desks, I pulled up Ricky Kuapi's record. Ricky was his real name, not a nickname for Richard. He had a juvenile record that had been sealed, and a handful of arrests on minor charges, including public intoxication and a class D misdemeanor for urinating in public.

But there was nothing more than that. He had a cell phone in his name, but it didn't match the phone number used to text either woman.

Ray said, "I just got the geofence data. Give me a couple of minutes to figure it out and I'll look for Ricky's cell phone there."

I knew something I could do while Ray was looking. I went back to the subreddit and checked the posts again, looking for anything that might connect one of the posters to Ricky Kuapi. Nothing jumped out at me.

"No luck," Ray said, and I looked up at him. "His cell phone number doesn't show up in the geofence data for the time around either murder."

"We need another approach," I said. "I'm going to create a profile on this subreddit for incels in Hawai'i and see if I can draw someone out."

"You can't encourage someone to commit a crime," Ray said.

"I'm not going to do that. Just make some posts and see who responds."

"Are you sure about this?"

"I'll be careful. I'm going to use some real details so I don't trip myself up. I'll be a version of Keoni. Guy who gets his hands dirty, has trouble talking to girls, and so on."

"What if Ricky is on that site and recognizes Keoni? You could be putting him in danger."

"I'll use some of my own details, and I'll keep track of them. I'll be a few years older than Keoni, without a college degree, working for a company on a different part of the island. I'm sure he's not the only landscaper who has trouble getting a date because of his job."

Ray blew out a breath, which was a signal that he didn't approve of what I was going to do, but wasn't going to stop me. "I'll work on analyzing this data," he said. "See if I can find any phone numbers that are in both data sets."

"Sounds like a plan." I set out to create my own profile. As I'd said to Ray, I used some of my own details and some of Keoni's. "I'm thirty-one, about 75% native Hawaiian. Too bad I look more like Kalani Pe'a than Keanu Reeves." I figured those native references would connect me to other Hawaiians. And while I loved Kalani's music, he was bigger than I'd ever want to be.

I also wanted to sound friendly. "My 'aumakua (spirit animal for anyone who doesn't know) is the dolphin," I wrote, "and I have a dolphin tattoo on my ankle." I took a picture of my actual tattoo. I added that to the image section.

There was an NSFW area, but in the instructions for the group the moderator had warned against dick pics, so I skipped that, even though I had a few I wouldn't have minded sharing anonymously. And I was pretending to be a straight guy anyway.

I allowed people to follow me and my content to be visible but I didn't agree to let people see other groups I belonged to, because I didn't want anyone to see this was my only group and get suspicious. I didn't have any social links I wanted to add, either.

I was set, and thought about my first post. I couldn't just jump in and ask if anyone else was interested in killing women. That would immediately send me to moderation, and also be seen as entrapment.

I decided to take a different take from one I'd seen in other posts.

"I took a good look at my paystub the other day and it really pissed me off that I'm forced to pay taxes for schools, welfare, and support for other men's children. The government ought to have a separate category for Chads and Beckys to make them pay for that shit. It sure doesn't look like I'm going to find a woman to marry and have kids with so why should I pay for stuff that doesn't benefit me?"

I looked it over and when I was satisfied I hit the "Post" button. I hoped that would generate some discussion and give me entrée to this group.

Chapter 25
Young Lovers

Ray scoured the Sensorvault data but couldn't identify any cell phones that had been in the area around both murders. "It doesn't mean the same killer isn't involved, because he could have discarded his burner phone after Betsy's death," he said.

"Use of a burner phone implies premeditation," I said. "That whoever went out to meet Betsy and/or Ravenna knew that we could track his phone, and deliberately chose to use one that's not trackable. So even though it didn't pan out, it adds something to what we know."

"Sampson is not going to be happy," Ray grumbled. "And I'm not either."

I knew he was irritated that the new technique he'd pushed hadn't worked out. "What we can do is trace each of the numbers that come up in the data," I said. "There aren't that many of them."

Because we'd narrowed the area, and because of the late hour, there were only about fifty phone numbers present. On our own, we narrowed the range considerably. We knew that someone had texted Betsy at 10:05 the night she died, and from the phone records we'd subpoenaed we saw the message was "Outside."

"So we need someone who was outside Mizushima Hall at

10:05," I said. There were only five numbers that fit that criteria – one of them Betsy's. Too bad it was in pieces and missing the SIM card, so we couldn't compare it to the other numbers.

The first unknown number was one that had gradually moved closer to the building, according to the data. But it kept moving, leaving the area within ten minutes. "I have a hunch," I said. I called the security office at HAC and spoke to the supervisor we'd met that first morning. I asked him for the cell phone number of the officer who'd been on duty that night, without saying why.

A minute later he gave me the number, and it matched the one we'd been looking at. I thanked him and hung up.

The next two numbers had been in the area for an hour before the murder, near the studio building, and moved across the quad to Mizushima Hall, where they disappeared, because our geofence had specifically excluded the building itself, to avoid getting a ton of numbers from students sleeping in the building.

"Hello, young lovers, whoever you are," Ray sang, in his attractive tenor voice.

"You think that's who they are?"

"The way they're together for an hour that late at night? And move to the dorm together? I think so."

"We should still get their names in case they saw or heard anything but haven't come forward."

The final number had all the right signals. It entered the area about five minutes before the text to Betsy, moved around the area where we thought the murder had taken place, and left soon after.

Ray requested further information on those three numbers. I thought we were getting close.

We turned to the geofence information from the area behind the Waikiki Shell. It wasn't unusual to get a lot of traffic in that area on a Thursday night. Parking was always tough on Waikiki, and if you lived in Kapahulu or even on the other side of the H1, you'd probably want to walk to your nightlife location, and walk home if the weather was clear.

So we had a lot more numbers to track, and Ray and I stared with dismay at the long list. "Let's try something," I said. "To get started. Let's find Ravenna's number and track her movements."

It was tedious work, but we saw that she had entered the area we'd erected the geofence around at 9:59 PM. Her phone traveled to the area where she'd been killed, remained there for about ten minutes, and left, heading toward the ocean along Monsarrat Avenue.

"Are we sure that's her number?" I asked Ray.

"Hundred percent."

"Then the killer took her phone away with him. Why?"

"So she couldn't call for help?"

"Or maybe she had taken a picture of him with her phone, or it was just impulse."

We looked for other phones that had been close to Ravenna's at the same time, but the data wasn't that precise, and we still came up with a dozen numbers that we had to get information on from Google.

Ray went to do that, and I looked back at the subreddit I'd joined. I hadn't gotten any responses, but I'd only put my message up a few hours before, and many of the people who belonged to the subreddit might have been at work.

We left headquarters a half-hour later. I dropped Ray at his house and drove up the hill to ours. I was there first, and I got Griffin from Dom and Soon-O and took him for a quick walk. Over dinner, Mike asked about my day, and I debated how much I needed to tell him.

"Keoni called me this morning."

"Keoni your nephew?"

I nodded. Keoni was a popular name among Hawaiians, and we knew a couple of men by that name, including a neighbor down the street.

"He heard from Api about my investigation, and he wanted to tell me about a guy who works with him who he thinks might be an incel."

"Really?"

"Yup. So Ray and I drove out to where they were working, and he pointed the guy out. And on the way back to headquarters, Doc called to say he found a fingerprint on the silk blouse of our second victim."

"Sounds like a busy morning."

"You haven't heard the whole thing. The fingerprint? Belongs to the guy on Keoni's crew."

"Did you pull him in?"

I shook my head. "We don't want to spook him yet, and all we have to connect him to Ravenna Cannon is that partial print. He has a record for minor beefs but nothing serious. And we checked his cell phone number against the Sensorvault data we got from Google. Can't place his phone at the crime scene."

"But you can interrogate him, can't you? See what he tells you?"

"We'll probably do that tomorrow. But we can only connect him to the second murder, and we'd like to get something on the first murder, too."

"Aren't you worried he'll run away? Or kill again?"

"Of course we are, Mike. And ten years ago, I'd have hauled him into an interrogation room and tried to get him to confess. But I like to think I've matured. Slow and steady wins the race, you know."

"Not in my case." He grinned. "I was the fastest one."

"In your age group," I said. "There were a dozen younger guys ahead of you."

"They better watch out next year."

While he kept reading, I opened my iPad to check in on the subreddit. I'd gotten a few responses to my post, all but one agreeing with me. The only objection was a woman who hoped that someday she would meet a man and have children.

I couldn't argue with that. None of the other posters identified themselves in any way that might connect to our murders—but I was just getting started.

Mike stood up and stretched. "I'm going to take Griffin for his bedtime walk."

I watched his butt as he bent over to hook the dog's leash, and walked out the front door, and I felt myself getting hard. I could hurry into the bedroom and be waiting for Mike when he got home.

It was a weeknight, though, and I was tired and I was sure he was, too. But I remembered all the guys I had been reading about on subreddit, who were desperate to have the kind of love I'd found.

I hopped up and hurried to the bedroom, where I stripped down. And because I was over forty and didn't want to lose my erection, I grabbed *Hard Dick Failure* from my bedside drawer and began reading. The hero was a sexy nerd who worked in tech support for a fast-growing company, and he spent his time traveling from office to office setting up computers and troubleshooting problems.

He had just walked into a manager's office with his own laptop and set of tools in a briefcase. "What seems to be the problem?" he asked.

The manager was a DILF, his favorite kind of guy, and he looked stressed. "I turned the computer on this morning and all I got was this blue screen." He shifted the monitor so Randy, the appropriately-named tech, could see.

"The blue screen of death," Randy said.

"Is that bad?" the manager asked.

"It means you've got a hard disk failure," he said. "But don't worry, I can handle that."

He turned his well-toned butt to the manager and bent over his briefcase, sure that his khakis were showing off one of his best features. When he glanced over his shoulder he saw the manager staring.

I was just getting to the good part when Mike walked in. "Someone's excited," he said. I was naked and my dick was as stiff as a flagpole.

He saw the Kindle in my hand and shook his head. "You're living in a fantasy world with that crap," he said.

I tossed the Kindle onto the table and wrapped my right fist around my dick. "Come show me the reality," I said, and smiled.

He quickly shucked his t-shirt, shorts, boxer briefs and rubber slippers and climbed onto the bed beside me. We had just begun kissing when Griffin clambered up, too.

"This is not a threesome," I said, and I pushed against Griffin's side with the flat of my foot. "Down!"

The big dog didn't want to obey. Mike had to get up and grab his collar to get him off the bed. "Stay!" he said, as Griffin sat by the side of the closet.

"He's watching us," I said as Mike got back onto the bed with me. "He thinks I'm going to hurt you."

"Not if I hurt you first," he said, and he grabbed my right nipple and pinched. That sent electric shocks to my groin and I lifted my leg up over Mike's and pulled him close.

Griffin started barking.

"Your dog is a cock-blocker," I said. Roby had occasionally gotten upset when Mike and I became amorous, but over the years he'd gotten accustomed.

"Griffin! Quiet!" Mike said.

"He's going to wake your parents," I said. "They're going to worry something's wrong."

"I'll be back."

Mike jumped up, his dick wagging, and hurried out of the bedroom. Griffin followed eagerly.

I heard the two of them thumping down the stairs and debated picking up my book again. Maybe we should just go back to sleep. It was the middle of the week, after all, and we both had work the next morning.

Mike hurried back up the stairs. "I gave him one of those chew treats," he said. "That should keep him busy for a while. Now, where were we?"

I smiled broadly and told him.

Chapter 26
Three Numbers

Wednesday morning on our way to headquarters, Ray and I talked through the work we had ahead of us. "I was thinking last night," Ray said. "If we're not going to pull Ricky Kuapi in for questioning right away, we should put a tracker on his car. That way we can see if he's getting into trouble."

"You think Judge Yamanaka will sign off on the warrant for that?"

"All I have to do is cite that Supreme Court ruling from 2012 and he'll cave," Ray said. "He doesn't like to go against precedent."

"Good. You handle that, and I'll bring Sampson up to date."

Our lieutenant wasn't wearing one of his jewel-tone polo shirts that morning. Instead he wore a black shirt with the HPD badge over the left breast and gold stars on his epaulets. That wasn't good.

"Meeting this morning with the all the HPD lieutenants to talk about how each of our departments is doing," he said. As I stood in the doorway of his office, he put on his reading glasses and looked down at a printed sheet. "My statistics show we have forty-two cold case homicides department-wide and four open cases in District 1. You have any good news to update me?"

"Sorry, no."

"Get back to me after this meeting. And try and bring some good news, will you?"

"Will do."

By the time I got back to my desk, Ray had left for the judge's chambers. I looked up Ricky's information in the DMV database and found out what he drove.

I called Keoni and verified that Ricky was with his crew that morning. "Did he drive there in his own vehicle? DMV data puts him in a silver 2012 Nissan Altima."

"We're working at the Koa Tree Diamond Head Hotel overlooking Leahi Park so the guys were directed to park in the employee lot. You know where this hotel is?"

"Brah, I was surfing those breaks before you were born," I said.

"Yeah, you were doing a lot of things before I was born, which my parents say we're not allowed to talk about," Keoni said.

"Ouch. Can you ask one of your guys on the QT if Ricky drove?"

"I'll call you back. I'll ask Butch. He's running the tree-trimming operation where Ricky's working."

While I waited for his call, I checked the subreddit again. A few more responses came in during the wee hours of the night, and they all agreed with me. I had begun reading the other posts when Keoni called me back.

"Yeah, he drove," he said. "He lives up near Maunawili and he picked up two other guys on his way in."

I thanked my nephew and hung up. I went to the quartermaster's office and signed out a car tracker with my name and the case number. I was supposed to put the subpoena information on that form too but I wrote TK, for to come, instead.

By the time I got back, Ray had returned with the subpoena for the tracker. Now all we had to do was find his car and attach it. We took Beretania until it met Kalakaua, and headed toward Diamond Head, moving slowly through downtown Waikiki.

We passed the Sailor's Rest. "There haven't been any more incidents reported like the one with Brandon Paikai, have there?" I asked.

"Not that I've heard. But I've got Lidia's cell. If anything's been happening she'll know."

While he called, I drove and observed the usual mix of tourists and locals. A pair of women in head-to-toe burkas, accompanied by two men in dark suits. A group of Japanese tourists following a guide who held up a tiny rising-sun flag. A group of school kids still young enough to hold each other's hands as they crossed the street. A tall man in a gold costume reminiscent of King Kalakaua, handing out fliers for Hawaiian heritage jewelry. A typical day in our island paradise.

Ray put Lidia on speaker so I could hear the conversation. "Sampson sent us out to talk to the guy responsible for the incident at Sailor's Rest last week," he said. "Anything similar happening?"

"Nothing involving an arrest," she said. "But this kind of problem is growing. I've spoken to a number of couples who say that they've been harassed for holding hands, sometimes for kissing. One couple were posing for wedding photos at Kuhio Beach Park and a guy started yelling at them. They thought he was homeless and the photographer shooed him away."

"But nothing violent?" I asked.

"Not specifically. But I got descriptions of the guys causing the problems and it looks like there are at least three or four different ones."

"Can you send those descriptions to us?" Ray asked.

"Sure."

"Uh-oh," I said to Ray. Towards the phone I said, "We've gotta go. Situation on Kalakaua near the aloha shirt outlet. We're responding, but see if you can send someone else."

Ray ended the call and looked toward where I was pointing. A teenaged boy, wearing a black hoodie and carrying a pink purse, was on the run along the pavement beside the beach, heading towards Diamond Head. A uniformed cop was on his tail, but at least a block behind.

"That purse does not match his outfit," I said to Ray. Fortunately there was no one on the sidewalk ahead of me so I was able to steer my SUV over the curb and onto the sidewalk, just as the kid approached.

Ray and I both spilled out at the same time. We unholstered our guns and called out "Stop! HPD!"

The kid tried to feint left, but I was there, and when he went right Ray was in his face. A young uniformed officer I didn't recognize came running up behind the kid. I holstered my gun and pulled out my badge. "We're detectives out of District 1," I said to the cop.

"Thanks," he said. He didn't even seem winded, though his face was red. "I was gaining on him but I had to dart around that group of school kids."

"I'm sure you would have caught him," I said. The officer cuffed the kid and took the purse. A middle-aged haole couple hurried up, waving their hands, and Ray and I got back in the SUV and continued on our way.

"All in a day's work," Ray said.

"Does get the adrenaline running, though. You ever miss patrol?"

He shook his head. "I did my time on the streets in South Philly in all kinds of weather. Snow, sleet, rain. A couple of times I had to pull in guys I went to high school with. Don't miss that at all."

"I used to live on Lili'uokalani Street near Kuhio, and I walked Waikiki on the day shift, and on the overnights I drove a Cushman. I knew all my neighbors and the people who owned the stores and restaurants. I did my fair amount of chasing suspects, but mostly it was just community policing, and I liked that."

"That's a reason why a lot of us join the force," he said. "That was big for me, having the sociology degree. It seemed like a way to put what I learned in school into practice. And the larger sense of doing something to help the world."

"The hero thing has to be part of it, too," I said. "I remember watching *Magnum PI* when I was a teenager, and *Hill Street Blues* and *Miami Vice*. The cops were the good guys."

"Not so much today," Ray said. "At least in the media. But we do our part."

"That we do," I said.

We continued out to Diamond Head. I badged the guy running the gate at the hotel's employee lot, then drove up and down aisles until we found Ricky's car. I parked behind it, blocking anyone from seeing what Ray was doing, as he began securing the tracker in the left rear wheel well.

An elderly couple wearing matching aloha shirts approached and I worried that they'd look too closely at Ray, but the rest of their family, a young father and mother and two kids, came hurrying up to them and they were too busy with each other.

While Ray was working I downloaded the app for the device to my phone, and once he was back in the SUV I verified that it was working.

Ray pulled a plastic baggie of wet wipes from his pocket and wiped his forehead. "Vinnie gets dirty," he said. "I discovered that I can use these, too."

We drove back down Kalakaua to Kapahulu, where we turned inland at the zoo. School buses were parked on both sides of the street, making it slow going, and there were packs of keikis all around us, from the tiniest up to teens.

"Did you come here as a kid?" Ray asked.

"Of course. School visits at least every other year. And sometimes for special events. Focus on indigenous species. The zoo after dark. Event concerts on the great lawn."

"I miss the kind of stuff Julie and I did when we were kids," he said. "In Philly there are so many great museums. I used to go to these special Saturday morning programs at the Franklin Institute. And my parents took us to the Museum of Art and probably every other museum on the Parkway."

"We have museums here," I said. "Not as good as in Philadelphia, but we have other things to make up for it. And you're for sure seeing the aquarium a lot."

"I'm not dissing Honolulu. All three of us missed this place when we went back home."

"There are always vacations," I said. "You want Vinnie to know his grandparents. So you take enough time to show him what you did when you were growing up."

When we got back to headquarters, we had to write up our reports on that morning's purse-snatching. That took us until lunch, and after getting tacos from a truck parked near the Honolulu Museum of Art, we were back at our desks. "I really want to pull Ricky Kuapi in and grill him," I said. "But I know we should hold off until we have more information."

"Where do we get that?" Ray asked. "We've already pulled up his record. We know where he lives and where he works."

"And we know that he makes fun of my nephew for not dating, but he doesn't date himself." Something Ray said rang a bell in my head, and I narrowed my eyes and let my brain run free.

Chapter 27
Tracking

"What?" Ray asked. "I can tell from that look on your face that you're thinking of something. Probably something hare-brained."

"I have to make a phone call." I pulled out my cell and found the number for Karen Gold, who I'd gone to elementary school with. We had reconnected years later when I discovered that she worked for the Social Security Office in Honolulu. I dialed her number.

"Hey, Kimo, it's been a while," she said.

"Yeah, too long. Your kids must be in college now, aren't they?"

"Not quite. I've got a freshman and a junior at Farrington. How old are yours?"

"Ten. They're in fifth grade at Punahou."

"What can I do for you?" she asked.

"Can you run an employment record for me for a suspect?"

"Have his social security number?"

"As a matter of fact I do." I hunted through my paperwork to find the information Keoni had sent me on Ricky Kuapi. I read the number and spelled the name.

I heard her typing. "Got him. You want me to fax this over?"

"That would be great." I gave her the department fax number. It might be old technology but that's the way governments still worked.

I thanked her and hung up. I walked around the corner to the fax machine. All our department emails came with a pre-packaged footer that said any content there was subject to subpoena in a court of law, so I was glad to have used my personal cell and the fax machine to get Ricky's work history. If I hadn't known Karen, I'd have had to get yet another subpoena and wait a few days.

That was the way it worked on a small island. My personal address book was a web of people I had met in my forty-some years of contact, from elementary school, Hawaiian school, Punahou, my family network and their connections, all the way through everyone I'd worked with on the force. And as Ray had pointed out, I used my family contacts frequently.

I waited impatiently by the machine for it to spit out the fax, and had to restrain myself from leaning down to read the lines as they printed out. I finally took the sheet back to my desk.

Ray scooted his chair over as we scanned Ricky's work history. "What are we looking for, specifically?" he asked.

"Somebody he worked with who could tell us more about his attitude toward women," I said. "Keoni's not the best source, because Ricky was making fun of him, and he might be slanting what he told me."

I was dismayed to read through the list of places Ricky had worked and realize that except for Kanapa'aka Landscaping, we had several degrees of separation between us.

"Wait, I know that company," Ray said, pointing to one name on the list. "Regal Crown Apartments. We leased our first apartment through them."

When Ray and Julie first moved to Honolulu, she was a graduate student at UH and they'd lived in McCully, a neighborhood adjacent to both our department and the campus in Manoa.

"Did you know the building manager?"

"Yup. I even did a couple of part-time security gigs for him when Julie and I were scraping along." He picked up his phone. "Let me call him."

The call was brief and I could only hear Ray's side of it. "He has something to say about Ricky," he said. "Let's go talk to him."

"It's funny," I said, as we walked toward the garage. "I'm the one who usually knows people in town but now it's your contact."

"I have been here for a while," he said.

The sky was completely overcast, but there was no smell of rain in the air and no breeze. We drove out South Beretania to McCully Street, and turned toward the water for a block to Algaroba Street. "Algaroba is another name for carob," Ray said. "When I was a teenager I had some acne and a doctor told me to avoid chocolate and eat carob instead. It's in the same family as the kiawe."

I laughed. "And now you're the one lecturing me about Hawai'i," I said. "How the tables have turned."

The Hale McCully was an L-shaped six-story building that looked like an airport motel. Back then, Ray and Julie shared a car, so I'd often stopped for him on the way to or from work. We parked on the street and Ray led the way up to the front door. The area around the building was well-manicured. Low hedges neatly trimmed, the dead husks of palm trunks sliced away, pretty flowers along the pathways.

Since my brother was a landscaper, I'd learned to notice these things.

Ray rang a buzzer marked superintendent, and when the door chimed we walked in. A skinny middle-aged man met us in the hallway.

"Mr. Chow, good to see you again," Ray said.

"And you," Chow said.

Ray introduced me and asked if we could talk in his office. Chow led us to an open door and we walked into a small office with a desk and a couple of chairs and a filing cabinet along the wall.

"We wanted to ask you about a former employee," Ray said. "Ricky Kuapi."

Mr. Chow pursed his lips and narrowed his eyes. "Bad man," he said. "I used to take care of the landscaping myself, but I fell from a ladder and I couldn't do it all. So I put an ad in the *Advertiser* for a yard worker, and he's the only one who answered."

"When was this?" Ray asked.

"Last year. He did a good job, I'll give him that. I'm very particular, as you know, and I want this building to look nice. But tenants started complaining."

"About Ricky?"

Chow nodded. "It started slow. He was calling women by names that weren't theirs."

"Becky and Stacy?" I asked.

Chow looked at me. "How did you know?"

"I can explain later. But please, go on."

"I had to speak to him. That it was his job to take care of the plants, not to speak to the tenants. He denied that he spoke directly to them, but admitted that he might have said things under his breath."

"Anything beyond that?" Ray asked.

"There was one tenant, a very handsome man. He insisted that Ricky had keyed his car, but he didn't have proof. He said that Ricky said nasty things to him about him having sex with women." He shook his head. "That was when I finally had to let him go. It is very hard to get good tenants, and I didn't want to lose any of them because Ricky said bad things to them."

He turned to me. "How did you know the names he called those women?"

I explained briefly about the incel culture and the nicknames they had for women. "Did he by any chance call your male tenant Chad?"

Chow's mouth opened in surprise. "He did!" He looked at Ray. "Is he in trouble for something?"

"We're not at liberty to say right now," Ray said. "We're just gathering information." He stood up and reached out to Mr. Chow's hand. "Thank you very much."

I seconded the thanks and we walked out. "So that puts Ricky directly into incel culture," I said, as we walked back to the SUV. It's one more link."

"He'd really have to lie about himself in a dating profile for Betsy to agree to meet him," Ray said. "Ravenna Cannon seems less picky."

We drove back to headquarters and Ray wrote up our interview. After we spent some time on paperwork, it was time to head for home. I pulled up in our driveway and since Mike's truck wasn't there, I knew that Griffin had to be next door with Dom and Soon-O.

I knocked at the door and Dom opened, and behind him I saw Griffin skidding toward me on the tile floor. I leaned down and let him lick my face, which made me smile. "How's he behaving?" I asked Dom.

"Well, he's more obedient than Michael ever was." He handed me the dog's leash. "He's a love sponge. Every time I sit down he's right beside me, wanting me to pet him."

"I hope he'll be well-behaved enough soon to stay in the house by himself," I said. "Roby was good about that."

"Roby was needy when you first got him, too. But I don't mind. I spend most of the day sitting anyway, and at least he gets me out of my chair to take him out to the back yard."

I hooked up Roby's leash to Griffin. The two dogs were similar in many ways, though Griffin was much lighter than Roby's gold. But they were both happy, sweet, inquisitive boys. We started toward the street, and he immediately had to stop and pee beside a hibiscus loaded with orange flowers.

I was tempted to pick one to put in his collar but when I looked more closely the blossoms were crawling with tiny black aphids. That was a metaphor for life in Hawai'i if there ever was one. Beneath the beauty of our islands there was always something dark and potentially deadly.

Something that had taken down two beautiful women in the last two weeks, and Ray and I were still grasping at straws.

Chapter 28
Vulnerable to Stress

Griffin and I walked up the street in the velvety darkness, the evening illuminated only by security lights on houses and some intermittent streetlights. Roby had been a very placid walker—he stayed by my side, only stopping occasionally to sniff and pee. Griffin was a different dog. He had his nose down to the grass beside the street, sniffing eagerly, pulling ahead to get to the next great scent. I noticed that when he peed, his nostrils twitched and his big black eyes swiveled around. This was a dog who was in love with everything, from Mike and me to the sights and smells around him.

We circled back on the other side of the street, and we were about two houses away from home when Mike's flame-painted truck pulled into the driveway. It had been brand-new when we met, and it was still running well fifteen years later because he had pampered it.

Griffin must have recognized the truck, because he jerked ahead to get home, and I ran behind him, the dog panting and me laughing. I let the leash go a few feet from Mike and Griffin made a mad dash at him.

He was a beautiful dog in many ways, particularly in motion. His body was sleek and the feathers on his tail blew straight back. "Whoa, whoa, easy boy," Mike said as Griffin jumped up on him.

I kissed Mike's cheek when I reached him, and the three of us went inside, where we played with Griffin, fed him, and had dinner ourselves. And then Griffin wanted attention. Mike and I sat in the living room and tried to read, and Griffin bounced back and forth between us for ear scratching and belly rubs.

"Anything new at the cop shop?" Mike asked after a while.

"We're making baby steps forward, but neither case is coming together very well," I said.

"At what point do you give up and move on?"

"It's never that defined," I said. "Eventually we run out of steam, and some other case comes up that takes all our attention. But I don't want either of these deaths to go to the cold case file. I feel like we almost have the answers. We just need one more clue to crack things open."

Thursday morning Ray and I drove in together. "I found a woman who lives in Aiea and gives voice lessons," he said as we got onto the highway. "The only time I ever learned about singing was in choir in high school. This woman says that she can help me with using proper breath support, increasing my vocal range, and learning to project my voice without straining it."

"That's great. What did Julie say?"

"That she expects regular serenades," he said with a smile. "I told her I could manage that. And Vinnie's happy because he wants to audition for the Punahou Choir and he said I can help him."

"He's carrying on your musical tradition."

"We'll see. At least I know he can carry a tune."

As soon as we got in, Ray checked his email and found that he'd gotten the information we'd requested from Google. Of the three numbers we had submitted, they were only able to provide two names: Christopher Mandac and Tyler Morse. The third phone, though it was running the Android operating system, didn't have a name attached.

"Chris," Ray said. "Why does that name sound familiar?" He looked through the reports of his conversations with students at HAC. "Here is. Lee said that there was a guy on the floor named Chris who went out a lot at night."

"Perhaps to meet Tyler," I said. "Maybe they were study buddies. Or something more."

Mandac and Morse were both in a class that Betsy had also been registered for, so we knew where they'd be from 11:00 to 12:15. "We can catch them both as they're leaving class," I said. "If they're both gay, they might have wanted a secluded place to hang out. Or they could have been working on a class project together. Not that it matters either way."

"But they probably recognized Betsy because they were in a class with her," Ray said. "Maybe they spotted something."

We did some basic follow-up on our two cases, still searching for connections between them. I was relieved when it was time to leave for HAC and track down Mandac and Morse.

From the H1 we began climbing to Manoa, passing the UH campus. The students there didn't look any different from the ones we'd seen at Honolulu Arts College except there were fewer instances of brightly colored hair.

I drove in through the two marble plinths that marked the entrance, and up the winding drive, surrounded by trees that had been growing there long before Ray and I were born. We circled around the campus until I spotted the Cushman driven by Zhao, the security guard we'd met the week before.

I parked beside him and Ray and I got out. It was a couple of degrees cooler up there on the mountain than it had been down by the shore.

"Do us a favor?" I asked Zhao. "Can you pull up a couple of photographs from that online pig book you showed us last week?"

He agreed, and I gave him the names of the boys we were looking for. Christopher was blond and skinny, with a pink streak in his hair. Tyler had a rounder face with a brown fringe over his forehead.

We thanked him, drove into the parking lot, and walked toward the classroom building. On our way, we spotted several kids who looked familiar from our questioning, including Kyle Goodman, the boy who'd volunteered to ID Betsy's body and thrown up. He had what looked like a heavy backpack on his shoulder. "Probably math books," I said. "Isn't he the one who said Betsy was asking him for help with math?"

"Yup," Ray said. "But if he had a hope she was going to date him it was a false one. If you looked up geek in the dictionary you'd find his photo."

"He's not that bad," I said. He had a cool haircut, but he wore oversized glasses and his pointy chin reminded me of the friend of Jeffrey's who'd had surgery in that area. "He's got a couple of pimples but he could cover them up with concealer, and he'd do well with contact lenses."

Ray laughed. "Yeah, you go over and introduce him to the concept of concealer."

"Who knows? Maybe Betsy did. And that's why he was willing to identify her."

We continued to Obama Hall, the classroom building which had been named in honor of our former president and one-time Honolulu resident. We waited in the hallway until a classroom door opened and students began to spill out.

Christopher walked out with Tyler, who was unexpectedly tall and gawky. We showed them our badges and asked if there was somewhere we could talk.

The two boys shared a glance and Christopher said, "There's a study room right down the hall." His voice shook.

"Nothing to get worried about," I said. I walked with him, with Ray and Tyler behind us. "We just want to ask you a couple of questions about last Sunday night."

The room was small, with a single round table in the middle and four wooden chairs. We sat to one side, with the boys on the other.

Ray explained about the Sensorvault data. "So we know you guys were outside from about nine-thirty until eleven," he said.

"It's not illegal," Christopher protested. "It's not like we have a curfew or anything."

"We're not interested in what you guys were doing," I said. "You know that Betsy Lawrence was murdered around that time, don't you?"

They looked at each other and both nodded.

"So all we want to know is if you heard anything, or saw anything, around that time."

"We were kind of…" Christopher began.

"Into each other," Tyler finished. "It's hard to find a private place to make out around this campus. It's so small, and even a room like this, anybody could walk in any time."

Ray smiled. "I know what that's like. But you had to break apart to walk back to the dorm, right? You see anybody or hear anything?"

"Oh, that guy," Tyler said. "We figured he was coming from the library because he had a backpack over his shoulder. He was totally in his own mind. Like muttering to himself. He almost knocked into us and didn't even apologize."

"Did you recognize him?" I asked.

Both boys shook their heads. "There are a lot of streetlamps around, so you never feel unsafe, but there are still dark places." Tyler and Christopher shared a sly glance. "This was one of them."

"You're a pretty tall guy," I said. "He was shorter than you?"

"For sure."

I turned to Christopher. "How about you?"

"Maybe my height, but stockier. That's all I remember."

We thanked them both, and they left.

"What do you think?" Ray asked. "They saw the guy who hurt Betsy?"

"They mentioned a backpack," I said. "And remember when we were at Doc's office? The way he used his laptop bag to demonstrate how Betsy was hit?"

"So if we have the right guy, he might have used his backpack to hit Betsy and knock her down. Or maybe he was arguing with her and swung around away from her, and hit her accidentally with his pack."

"And then dragged her body to the hillside? That was no accident."

"But it's a possibility. Remember, these kids are teens. And for boys especially, their brains are still developing. They're especially vulnerable to stress, and they don't always think through the consequences of their actions."

"But what about Ravenna? How does she tie in here?"

He shrugged. "Maybe she doesn't, and your theory about incels is off base. Two random acts, different locations, different weapons, different victim characteristics. We could be wasting our time trying to connect them."

I stood up and pushed back the wooden chair. "Then we need to get back to headquarters and rethink our strategy."

We started to walk back toward where I'd parked. "What if that number we couldn't find an ID for belongs to a student? As long as we're up here, we could dial it."

"What, and ask him who it is?"

I shrugged. "We could explain about the Sensorvault data."

"Or I have another idea," Ray said, as Zhao drove past us in his Cushman. Ray flagged him down. "We need another favor. Can you call this number? Identify yourself and tell whoever answers that you found a textbook with this number inside it. Ask if it's theirs."

Zhao reached back into the Cushman. "I'm taking a course here myself, at night." He pulled out a math book. "I can tell the person it's this book."

"That's awesome," I said. I gave him the number, and he dialed. He put the phone on speaker so we could hear.

"Hello?"

"This is Officer Zhao from campus security," Zhao said. "I found a textbook with this number written in it. *Visualizing Data*, by Fry?"

"Hold on." We heard someone moving what sounded like books around. "I don't have mine with me. Could be mine. Where can I pick it up?"

"I'm in the Cushman. I can bring it over to you."

"I'm sitting on the bench outside Manoa Hall," the guy said. "My name is Kyle Goodman."

Ray and I looked at each other, our eyebrows raised.

"I'll be right there," Zhao said.

Chapter 29
Call My Dad

Ray and I thanked Zhao and walked over to Manoa Hall. As he'd said, Kyle was sitting on a bench in the shade. He'd already put the phone back on the bench beside him and was poring over a math text.

"Hey, Kyle," I said, and he looked up. "Detective Kanapa'aka. We spoke last week when you helped us identify Betsy's body."

"Yeah, that was grim," he said. "I had no idea I was going to upchuck like that."

"Seeing something like that can be really tough." I sat beside him, leaving Ray standing by me. "So we had a couple more questions for you."

He looked at his watch. "I have a class at three o'clock."

"We'll do our best to get you back here by then," I said, and I stood up. "We'd like you to come to our headquarters with us."

His eyes opened wide. "I.. I... don't know anything more than I told you already."

"I think you do, Kyle," I said. "We know that you were outside the dorm when Betsy was killed. We'd just like to talk to you about anything you might have seen or heard."

"I should call my dad," he said.

"How old are you, Kyle?" Ray asked.

"Eighteen."

"We can question you without having an adult present," Ray said. "Why don't you come with us, and after we've had a talk, you can call your dad."

We were on dicey ground. Kyle was still a kid, and if we were being nice, we would have let him make that call. But his dad would probably tell him not to say anything to us without an attorney present.

He shook his head. "No, I'm pretty sure I'm allowed to make a phone call."

"That's if you're in police custody," I said. "Right now we just want to have a talk."

He picked up his phone. "No, I'm going to call my dad." He wouldn't look at us while he waited for the call to connect. "Hi, it's Kyle. Can I talk to my dad, please."

His voice broke when he spoke again. "Dad? The police are here and they want to talk to me."

He listened for a minute, then held the phone out to me. "He wants to talk to you."

I took the phone, which was sweaty from Kyle's grip, but handed it to Ray instead. "I'd flip him out with my name."

Ray nodded. He took the phone and hit the speaker button. "Mr. Goodman? My name is Raymond Donne, and I'm a detective with the Honolulu Police Force. We're investigating the murder of a young woman your son was acquainted with, and we'd like to ask him some questions."

"What kind of questions?" Mr. Goodman asked.

"We received data from Google's Sensorvault program which puts a cell phone in your son's possession in the area where Elizabeth Lawrence was killed, at around the time of her murder. We'd like to ask Kyle if he saw or heard anything at that time."

"My son loses his cell phone the way his sister loses a contact lens. Which is to say at least every few weeks. That phone probably wasn't even in his possession then."

"We have the number, sir, and when we called it a few minutes ago, Kyle answered. So he's definitely in possession of the phone that was in that area at that time."

"Hold on." We heard him pick up another phone, probably a cell, and press a series of buttons. Then we heard a message that said the number he dialed could not be reached.

"Can he hear me?" Mr. Goodman asked.

"Yes, dad," Kyle said.

"What happened to your phone?"

"I'm sorry, dad. I lost it a couple of weeks ago. I bought a new phone but I didn't know how to use my old number."

"And this phone you bought, that's the one these officers are tracking?"

"Yes, sir."

"Is my son in custody?" Goodman asked.

"No, sir," Ray said. "Like I said, we just want to ask him a few questions. But if he won't go willingly with us to our headquarters... well, you can see how that won't look good."

"Give me your phone number," Goodman said.

Ray gave him the main number at headquarters, as well as his personal cell.

"Kyle, go with them, but don't say anything until I can get you a lawyer. Do you understand?"

"Do I have to, dad?"

"I don't know what kind of trouble you're in and it's not like I can run right over to your college and stand beside you. So I'm going to do the next best thing, which is get the best damn lawyer I can find in Honolulu to represent you."

Kyle's voice was a whine. "But I didn't do anything."

"Then you don't have anything to worry about, and I'm being overprotective. I'll have an attorney meet you at the police station."

He hung up.

"I guess you're coming with us," I said, as Ray handed Kyle his phone.

"I really don't want to."

I pulled the handcuffs off the side of my belt and opened one side. "Give me your wrist."

A couple of kids were already watching us, and more were assembling. "You might be completely innocent, Kyle," I said. "You want your classmates to see you walking off in handcuffs?"

He closed his textbook and put it into his backpack, then stood up. "I'm coming."

I put the cuffs back on my belt and we walked toward my SUV, with Kyle between us. "I think at this point we need to Mirandize him, don't you?" Ray asked.

Reading him his rights would probably make Kyle even more nervous, but Ray was right. Even though he wasn't in cuffs, Kyle didn't have the opportunity to walk away from us, which meant that he was in custody, and we had to read him those rights. And since his father had already told him not to speak to us without an attorney present, there wasn't anything more we were going to get out of him.

"Go for it," I said.

Ray pulled a card out of his wallet and started to read as we approached my SUV. Kyle began to shake and cry as he realized the full importance of what was going on. If he'd agreed to answer our questions and come up with a bullshit reason why he'd been in the area, we would have pushed him up on our suspect list but left him alone while we gathered more details.

Now he'd dropped himself into it. We reached the SUV and I grabbed a pair of blue plastic gloves from the back seat, along with a large evidence bag. "I'll take your backpack, Kyle," I said, reaching for it.

By then he was sobbing. "It wasn't my fault. It was an accident."

Ray pulled out his phone. "Do you mind if we record this?" he asked.

Kyle shook his head. We were in a parking lot, with a light

breeze causing the gravel to skitter past and waving the tops of the trees. It wasn't the best place for an interview, but Kyle was vulnerable and if we waited until we got to headquarters he'd probably shut up.

Ray pulled out his phone and hit the record button. He introduced himself and me and stated the date and time and location. "Kyle Goodman. Do you agree that you have already heard and understood your Miranda rights and that you agree to have this conversation recorded?"

He nodded, and Ray said gently, "You have to speak."

"I do."

I took the backpack from him and put it into the evidence bag, careful not to get my prints on it. If we were correct, there might be bloodstains on the fabric, or we might be able to match its fabric to the threads Doc had recovered.

"Walk us through what happened on Sunday night the 11th of September," Ray said.

"I was in the library and Betsy texted me." He looked up at Ray. "I had already given her the number of the new phone because we'd texted before."

"What time was this?"

"About nine-thirty. She was having a lot of trouble with the math for our introduction to animation class and she wanted me to help her. I told her I was busy."

He took a deep breath. "She started to flirt with me. Like she would make it worth my while if I'd help her. I said I would come to her room but she didn't want her roommate to know. So we agreed to meet outside."

"You're doing great, Kyle," Ray said. "Keep going."

"She didn't want anyone to see me with her. I was too nerdy for her. So we met over by the side of the cliff, and we sat down and I explained the problem she was having. It took her a while but she finally got it."

He looked down. "I asked her for a kiss."

"Not unreasonable," Ray said. "She was flirting with you in the texts, right?"

"I thought so. We stood up and I leaned over to kiss her, and she turned away. I was so angry."

He looked at us. "She was so two-faced. Like anybody who wasn't handsome or pretty wasn't worth her time. I just grabbed my backpack with both hands and swung it at her head. I never meant to kill her."

He started to sob again.

"It's okay," Ray said. "Get it all out. What happened next?"

"She fell down and hit her head on the gravel, really hard. There was all this blood and I freaked out."

He looked at Ray. "I know I should have called 911 or something but I wasn't thinking. Just that I had to get her out of sight. So I grabbed her feet and dragged her over to the cliff and then pushed her."

Neither of us said anything.

"And after she was gone, it was like the whole thing hadn't even happened," he said. "I ran back to my room. And I didn't see her again until the next morning, when I volunteered to identify her body."

He looked from Ray to me. "That has to count for something, right? That I was willing to do that?"

"We'll explain everything when we get to headquarters," Ray said. For the purposes of the recording he ended the conversation and we all got into the SUV, and I drove us back down the twisty road through Manoa.

Chapter 30
Blue Light Special

We didn't speak to Kyle Goodman again on the way to headquarters. He subsided into a funk, and we had all we needed from him for the time being. I drove into the sally port, the underground driveway where we drop off prisoners, and delivered him to the officers there for booking.

I parked in the garage and Ray and I went back upstairs to our office. We went immediately to Sampson's office and knocked on the door frame. "Can we come in?" I asked.

"I hope you have something useful to report." He was back to a bright green polo shirt, and I hoped that our information would be equally as cheerful.

"We do." Ray pulled out his phone and played the recording for Sampson.

"He just spoke to you? After you Mirandized him?"

"His father told him not to say anything, and that he'd have an attorney come here as soon as he could find one," I said. "But when I went to take his backpack from him, he broke down and he admitted hitting Betsy."

"That's when I asked him if it was okay if we recorded him," Ray said.

"It looks like you did this by the books," Sampson said. "Congratulations. But you've still got to establish your case. Is that the backpack?"

He pointed to the evidence bag on the floor.

"It is," I said. "I'll take it downstairs. But we wanted to fill you in first."

"Good. And I want you to follow up with that dean at HAC, the one who has the mayor's ear. We're arresting one of his students – he'll want to do some damage control."

I nodded. "I can do that after I drop the bag off."

"What about the other woman? Any chance he's responsible for that?"

"I doubt it," I said. "His phone wasn't within the geofence specifications, and we have nothing to connect him to Ravenna Cannon. He doesn't seem like the kind of guy who'd be texting mature women, or have the motivation to get down to Waikiki with a knife." I looked down. "We have a partial print from a potential suspect in that case."

"You do? Why haven't you brought him in?"

"Because that's all we have," Ray said. "A partial print on the victim's blouse. All he has to say is that she was passing him and she stumbled, and he helped her up."

"We got a warrant to put a tracker on his car," I said. "We know where he works and where he lives. We don't want to spook him by pulling him in too soon."

"You're learning," Sampson said. "God help you, it's been years, but you're learning some patience. I credit Detective Donne for that."

"It's been a struggle," Ray said, and he had to work hard to keep a grin from forming on his face.

"Go," Sampson said. "Work on your evidence. And don't let the other case slide."

"I credit Detective Donne for that," I mimicked as soon as we were out of Sampson's earshot. "Suck-up."

"Hey, he said it, not me."

I took the evidence bag containing the backpack downstairs and handed it over to Ryan Kainoa. "Am I looking for anything in particular?" he asked.

"We have a suspect in custody who admits to hitting Betsy Lawrence on the head with this backpack. So please check for blood and see if fibers from the pack match what Doc found on her head."

"I can do that." He turned to his computer and pulled up a form that documented chain of custody for the backpack. I sat down and started typing, pulling up the case number from my phone, adding my name and badge number, along with who I had confiscated the property from and when. I attested that the property had been in my exclusive possession since I picked it up.

Ryan pulled on his own gloves and the two of us examined the backpack. It was a Yeti brand, the Crossroads model. "Fancy pack for a school kid," Ryan said. "This retails for two-hundred-fifty bucks."

"And it weighs a ton," I said. "His dad probably bought it for him because he carries heavy textbooks."

The backpack was in good condition, probably only purchased at the start of the school year. There were a few scuff marks on the base where it might have been dragged. No visible signs of blood.

We inventoried the contents together. Four college textbooks, a spiral-bound notebook of math equations, and an oversized Strathmore pad which contained sketches of a warrior character wielding an axe.

In a separate compartment we found an iPad with a drawing pencil, and numerous pens and pencils used for artwork, along with a bottle of white-out. Miscellaneous other debris like candy wrappers and breath mints.

"Come into the lab with me," Ryan said. "Let me put this under a blue light. It won't be definitive yet, but at least you'll have an idea if this is possibly your murder weapon."

I followed him down the hall and he put the empty backpack on a table, then turned out the overhead light. He picked up a spray bottle.

"We've already got water and Luminol in here," he said. "Let's see if anything shows. Any idea which surface was used to hit the victim?"

"The suspect says that he swung it around accidentally. So the side?"

He sprayed one side lightly, and nothing happened. He turned the bag over to the other side and repeated the process. Once again, nothing.

"That doesn't mean anything," Ryan said. "It's possible that the blood we found is the result of her hitting her head on the pavement, not the initial impact from the backpack. So even if this pack is the murder weapon, there might not be blood on it."

He turned on the lights and looked along a shelf. "I have a small telescope here for things that are too big to fit under a microscope," he said. "Let me examine the surface."

He peered through the scope, moving it slowly and methodically along the fabric. "Aha!" he said. He grabbed a pair of tweezers and pulled off a long pink hair. He held it up to show me, and dropped it in a bag.

"That looks like it might match Betsy Lawrence's hair," I said.

"I thought so. I'll keep looking and work on documenting the match. But I'd say you're on your way."

As I get close to the end of a case, I always have mixed emotions. I was excited that Ryan had been able to find that hair on the backpack because that fit with Kyle's story and would be excellent evidence for his prosecution.

But at the same time I recognized that Kyle's life as he had known it was going to end. At the very least, he'd be charged with manslaughter, which Hawai'i statues defined as recklessly ending the life of another person. The maximum sentence for that crime was ten years in prison.

Even if he had a great attorney who could argue about Kyle's otherwise good character, he was still looking at prison time. That would have a dramatic effect on who he was and what his future would hold.

I returned to my desk and told Ray what I'd discovered. "The poor kid. All for an accident."

"He may have hit Betsy by accident, but what he did afterward was wrong," Ray said. "If he'd called 911, she might have survived, and if the assault was accidental he wouldn't have even been charged."

"I know. But we were talking about how teens' brains aren't fully wired yet."

"Vinnie is ten years old and he knows the difference between right and wrong."

I sighed. "I know. But I still feel bad about the loss of his future."

Ray had copied the recording on his phone onto the case database while I was downstairs. He checked the geofence data for Waikiki at the time of Ravenna Cannon's death for Kyle's unregistered phone, and it was no surprise to either of us that it didn't appear there.

I left to return to HAC after that. The sun was bright, glinting in and out of the trees and I couldn't help thinking that Kyle Goodman would only see the sun on supervised yard time in prison. And all because he acted impulsively—which sadly resulted in the death of a young woman who wouldn't ever see the sun again.

It had started to drizzle by the time I climbed all the way up to HAC, and I struggled into my rain jacket before getting out of the SUV. I hurried through the lot as the rain turned into a torrent.

I was in a foul mood by the time I reached the student life office. My face was dripping and the legs of my khakis were soaked. I didn't look like an exemplar of the Honolulu Police Department.

Medeiros was on the phone, and I was asked to wait, and the student worker gave me a couple of paper towels to wipe my face. When I was finally called into his office, I said, "I wanted to bring you up to date on our investigation into Elizabeth Lawrence's' death."

He motioned me to a seat across from him. "Sorry about the water," I said. "The rain caught me by surprise."

"It catches us all," he said. "It may not be far between these buildings but you can get soaked quickly."

I nodded. "I have good news and bad news. The good news is that we have identified the person responsible, and he has given us an oral confession, after being warned that he was being taped." I took a breath. "The bad news is that it's another student."

He steepled his fingers. "Miss Lawrence's death has initiated a number of reforms with regard to campus security," he said. "I've already notified her mother that we will be adding more lighting, more cameras, and several panic stations connected to the security office."

That was probably to forestall Kerry Lawrence from suing HAC for liability in her daughter's death, but I didn't say that.

"In addition, we will be placing a memorial plaque in her name in the meditation garden."

"I'm glad you're going to be able to protect your students better," I said. "That's at least a positive outcome."

"I can't say I'm happy that the assailant is another student. On the one hand, if it was an outsider, that could have been very damaging for the college's reputation. Can you tell me who the student is?"

"Under the circumstances I can," I said. "His name is Kyle Goodman, and he lived on the same floor as Betsy in the dorm, and was in her introduction to animation class."

"Did he give you a reason?"

"He said she flirted with him to get him to help her with homework, and when she denied his request for a kiss, he struck out at her in anger."

For the first time, I saw real pain in Medeiros's face. "It's a very difficult thing, being in loco parentis for a few hundred young people, many of them away from home for the first time," he said. "As you may have noticed, there's a real dichotomy between our male and female students. Many of the young women are here to study fashion and design, and they're focused on external beauty."

"I've seen that," I said.

"And as we know, young men often mature later. Our male students are overwhelmingly interested in computers and game design, and often lack the social skills the young women have cultivated. We've had to develop programs on hygiene, for example." He smiled. "You don't want to see what some of the boys' bathrooms look like."

"I raised a teenaged boy, so I have a good idea."

"We've made a counselor available to students who want help with grief or fear, but I think we're going to have to increase our social programming as well. And I'm going to be encouraging our faculty to make sure all their team projects are balanced. If we can get the boys and girls to see each other as real people, maybe we can avoid this kind of problem in the future."

I thanked him and apologized for getting his floor wet, and returned to my SUV. I thought about Medeiros's ideas as I drove back downtown. I was glad that Owen was growing up with a sister, so he'd be better equipped to deal with girls when his hormones kicked in.

If they did trend that way. Mike and I occasionally looked at both keikis and wondered if either might be gay. They had four gay parents, after all. But so far, they'd both been cisgender kids. Owen liked trucks and soldiers and Addie swooned after princesses. But those were no guarantees.

I didn't care what they were—I just wanted them to grow up knowing that they were loved. All four of us, in our turn, tried to model good behavior. Kindness, honesty, ohana.

I hoped that would be enough.

By the time I reached headquarters I had shifted my thinking to Ravenna. I wondered if I'd been wrong about the incel group. But I decided that even if no one from that subreddit had been involved in Betsy Lawrence's death, it was still worth following through the people there.

I always kept a change of clothes in the back of my SUV for days when I got soaked, or spattered with mud at a crime scene. I'd come home once too often with someone else's blood on me and scared the shit out of Mike.

After a quick change in the men's room, I returned to my desk and told Ray what Medeiros had said. "Julie and I have enough trouble with one kid," he said. "I can't imagine being responsible for a few hundred."

I turned to my computer, pulled up the subreddit, and read more posts. A few new ones came in while I was in Manoa. The one that interested me was from Waimea_Falls033, the poster who'd complained about being called a kissless virgin. "Who wants to go out and make some trouble?" was the lead.

"A group of Beckys is having a makeup event Friday evening at the Orange Lotus in Waikiki," Waimea continued. "Starting at 6:00. I say we get a bunch of guys together and show them how vain they are."

The post already had several thumbs up, though no one else had yet committed to attend. I couldn't say that I'd be there because that was moving dangerously close to entrapment, encouraging someone to a place where they might commit an illegal act. But I made a note of the message so I could find it again.

I went to the Orange Lotus website. It was a private venue with rooms available for rent, on the edge of Waikiki where the Ala Wai Canal curves out to the harbor. They also sponsored regular events, like salsa dancing on Thursday and a Friday night dance party with a local DJ.

Nothing about a makeup event at their site, so I started Googling. Quickly I came up with "Honolulu Women, Look Your Best." A half-dozen influencers and YouTube stars would be at Orange Lotus to demonstrate the best looks for fall. Manufacturers were donating gift bags, and you could win a makeover from one of several participating salons.

At the bottom they listed all the presenters who'd be there, starting with Tay Talaxian, who had risen to fame with her mother and her sisters on a reality show, *Taking on the Talaxians*. She and her sisters regularly tried to outdo each other with extravagant makeup and hair, but when someone attacked one of them, the others came out with claws.

I could see it was going to be a popular event, probably chronicled on the family TV show. I didn't recognize any of the other names, but the last one shot an arrow through my heart.

Apikela Kanapa'aka, aka MissApi on social sites.

Chapter 31
MissApi

I didn't know what to do with that information. Call Api and ask her to back out? But on what grounds? A couple of ugly guys might show up at her event and throw produce at pretty girls?

Then again, what if Ricky Kuapi was on the subreddit, and he showed up at the event ready to choose another victim?

I turned to Ray. "I've got a problem."

He shifted his chair to face me. "A new one? Or one of your old problems coming back?"

"Ha." I told him about the makeup event, Api's participation, and my fear that the guys from the subreddit would show up and cause trouble.

"So we set up a police presence to protect the speakers and the audience," Ray said.

"What if that's not enough? It would destroy my family if anything happened to Apikela."

"I think you're overreacting," Ray said. "Listen, I know she's your niece and you're looking out for her. But maybe we can turn this into a way to arrest Ricky Kuapi."

"What do you mean?"

"Let's say he shows up, and he has a crew with him. That gives us a chance to pull in a bunch of guys who have violent tendencies toward women. It's an opportunity to arrest him without bringing in Ravenna Cannon at first. When we get him here, he's already off kilter and we can hit him with the fingerprint."

"We've got the tracker on his car," I said. "So we'll know if he's on the move before the event."

"We could ask a couple of the female officers to go undercover in the audience in case anything happens."

I nodded. "And my family will probably show up to support Api so my brothers can look out for her personally."

"And in the meantime, we keep digging into Ricky Kuapi, so that when we pull him in we've got enough to hold him."

I still wasn't thrilled at the idea of my niece in the spotlight at an event that might attract angry incels, but I felt confident that we had enough in place to protect her and the other women.

The sergeant at the front desk called to say that Kyle Goodman's attorney had arrived, and we arranged to meet with him in an interview room on the ground level, near the holding cells.

Michael Arden was young, probably only a couple of years out of law school. Neither of us knew him, though he presented his card and said that he was from Fields and Yamato. "One of the most prestigious firms in the islands," he said, as he shook our hands.

"We've had many interactions with your firm," I said. "We're pursuing another case that involves the firm. Working with Sarah Byrne."

He wrinkled his nose, as if he didn't approve of Sarah's promotion from paralegal to attorney. Or perhaps that she'd gone to law school at night.

"We can make this brief," I said. "We have a taped confession from your client, after Miranda warnings, in which he admits to the crime."

"You know he's only eighteen," Arden said. "You should have waited for his father to arrive. He's on a flight this evening from Seattle."

"Kyle is legally an adult, and he chose to confess," Ray said. "Everything else is up to the Prosecuting Attorney."

"As soon as we can get before a judge and get bail set, I'll be bailing him out. But we'll make him available for any further questioning you have," Arden said.

"That you will." I stood up. "Anything else, counselor?"

He shook his head.

And with that, we were free to move on to Ravenna Cannon's murder, and let the Prosecuting Attorney and his investigators pick up anything else they needed.

Chapter 32
Taking on the Talaxians

We finished up soon after speaking with Michael Arden. Because of the boy's age and the accidental nature of the assault, I presumed Arden would be able to bail out Kyle and wondered if he would take the boy back up to his dorm, or put him in a hotel room to await his father. Either way, out of my hands.

Once again, I got home before Mike, and it was up to me to deal with Griffin. I wondered if maybe I'd been too hasty in agreeing to get another dog if this was going to be a regular pattern. Then Griffin rushed at me in a flurry of love, and I realized that I was just as much of a sucker as Mike.

We repeated our walk from the evening before, though this time we ran across a springer spaniel named Aslan, and after a preliminary sniff, Aslan went down on his front paws in the play position, and his mom and I let go of both leashes so the dogs could romp together. They raced around a neighbor's lawn, darting around trees and hedges, having a blast.

I finally retrieved Griffin's leash and led him home, where I fed him more of Roby's chow and went online to order a fresh bag. He collapsed in a furry white heap at my feet as I checked the incel subreddit. Six others had agreed to join Waimea_Falls at the beauty event the next night. One guy asked how they would recognize each other, and someone else posted a laughing emoji. "You think there will be a lot of ugly straight guys at this shindig?"

I would rather they'd made a plan to meet somewhere so I could keep them all under surveillance. But I'd have to wing it.

Over dinner, I discussed the event the next evening with Mike. "Do you think I'm overreacting?" I asked.

"You've been a cop for a long time. If you have a sense there's a problem, then you need to follow through, no matter what other people say."

"But am I putting Apikela and the other women in danger because I'm not arresting Ricky Kuapi before the event?"

"First of all, do you have any specific knowledge that this guy is going to show up at Api's party?"

"No."

"Do you have enough to charge him?"

I toyed with my pasta. "Not really. Just the fingerprint."

"Will picking him up at this party give you anything else?"

I shrugged. "I don't know. At least it will give us a pretense for bringing him in, and we can work our way around to the murder later."

"I don't see you have much choice other than to move forward the way you have been."

After dinner, I called Haoa, because Apikela was his daughter, and if he thought she was in danger, it was up to him to get her to pull out of the makeup event. But he was as unconcerned as Ray and Mike.

"Some weirdo wants to protest because these girls are wearing too much makeup?" he asked.

"It could be more than that." I told him about following the incel subreddit, but he'd never heard of Reddit and didn't think it was worth upsetting his daughter. "Tatiana and I will be there," he said. "Lui and Liliha, too. So we'll look out for her."

"You're having a family get-together and you didn't invite me?" I said, feigning surprise.

"It's not always about you, Kimo," he said. "I invited Mom, but you know she's been feeling frail since her last fall. She wishes she could come and I promised to film Api's speech and send it to her."

"I saw mom the other day," I said. "Are you and Lui as worried as I am?"

He sighed. "She's seventy-eight and she's had a good long life, Kimo. We're not going to have her forever."

"I know. It just makes me sad, you know. Thinking of losing her."

"You'll still have Haoa and me. I'll see you tomorrow night."

I turned to Lieutenant Sampson's stepdaughter, Kitty Cardozo. She was a sergeant in district four, which encompassed the Waimanalo area where Ricky Kuapi lived.

I had known Kitty ever since she was a student at UH, determined to follow her stepdad into the police force. Because she was a lesbian, I'd mentored her off and on over the years.

"We're interested in a guy who lives up near Maunawili," I said, after we'd traded introductions and caught up. "Ricky Kuapi."

"Ah, of the famous Kuapi family," she said.

"Really? Are they trouble?"

"The opposite. His father, his mother, his two brothers and his two sisters all perform at the Islands of History."

I knew it well—it was a twenty-acre park near Laie, a heavily Mormon area at the top of the Windward Coast, due north of Waikiki. We had run into some trouble there a few years ago. "They sing and dance?" I asked.

"The father is a headwaiter at the restaurant, and the brothers paddle a raft in the parade along the canal, and they also do some drumming in the show. The mother and sisters demonstrate crafts and they also dance."

"And what? Ricky's the only one who doesn't have rhythm?"

"Something like that. He's always been the black sheep of the family. We've caught him poaching Tahitian prawns and illegally harvesting rare orchids. What's he up to now?"

"Let me ask you a question first, since you know him. Do you think he's an incel?"

She laughed. "Involuntary celibate? I wouldn't be surprised. His family think he's a loser and his father has already told me he's done bailing Ricky out of jail."

"Is he dangerous?"

Kitty was quiet for a moment. Finally she asked, "Dangerous in what way?"

"We found a partial fingerprint that matches him on the blouse of a woman who was murdered in Waikiki," I said.

"Wow. He's a big guy, you know, and he's full of anger most of the time. I could see him punching someone and not realizing it was a death blow."

"If he was the killer, he didn't punch her. He used a knife."

"Pocket knife?"

"More like a kitchen knife.

"That would imply premeditation," Kitty said. "The last time we arrested him, he had a wicked-looking trowel with him, with a sharp blade. You think that might be your weapon?"

"Did you confiscate it?"

She laughed. "It's a garden trowel, Kimo. Yes, it could be a dangerous weapon, but we were looking at someone who digs up plants. Not a murder case."

"That's good intel," I said. "So listen, there's this makeup influencers event tomorrow evening in Waikiki."

"With Tay Talaxian," she said. "*Taking on the Talaxians* is one of my guilty pleasures."

"How would you feel about attending the event, then?" I asked. "My niece Api is one of the speakers, and I've seen some rumblings online about protests there."

"I would not mind at all. I might be a lesbian but I can still appreciate a good makeover. I'll drive down after my shift is over in Kaneohe."

"Thanks, Kitty. I'd appreciate it. Also good to have extra eyes in the audience."

"My pleasure. And I'm also a *Star Trek* geek, as you know, so I'm eager to meet a Talaxian in the flesh."

"What do the Talaxians have to do with *Star Trek*?"

She laughed. "Probably nothing, but Neelix, the morale officer on the Voyager, was a Talaxian. I keep wondering if someone who worked on that show knew Tay's family and named the race after them."

"See you tomorrow," I said, and ended the call.

I had one more call to make. "Hey, Doc," I said, when he answered his cell phone.

"This must be an emergency, if you're calling after hours."

"Sorry, but I didn't have your wife's number. Is she there?"

I heard him call, "Lidia, it's for you. Your favorite homicide detective."

Her voice was lighter than his, with a hint of an island accent. "Hello?"

"Aw, that's sweet. I didn't know I was your favorite," I said.

"Sometimes I could kill him," she said sweetly. "But someone in his office would be able to pin it on me. What can I do for you?"

"There's a makeup show tomorrow evening at the Orange Lotus," I said. "You think I could entice you to be in the audience?"

"Me? Makeup? Are you trying to tell me something?"

I explained about the threats from the incel group, and that my niece was going to be on stage. "I'd really like to have some extra eyes and ears in the audience."

She called, "Paul? Are we busy tomorrow night?"

I heard them have a conversation but couldn't make out the words.

"My husband thinks it would be a good idea for me to get some makeup tips," she said. "He and I will deal with that issue separately. But yes, we'll both come to the Orange Lotus."

"I hope we won't need his professional skills, but I appreciate both of you taking the time," I said. "My brothers and my niece don't think this is a big deal, but the online group gives me a bad vibe."

I didn't know if Ricky Kuapi had killed Ravenna Cannon, and I didn't know if Waimea_Falls and his group would cause any real trouble at the makeup event. But as Mike had pointed out, I'd learned to trust my instincts when it came to criminal cases. Like Griffin, I had my nose down and I was following a scent. It was smart to bring as much backup as I could to the event in case anything happened. And I was lucky to have an ohana around me, of family and cops, who could support me when I needed it.

First priority, though, had to be to protect Apikela, even if it was from some jerks throwing produce. Ravenna Cannon's murder investigation would have to come second.

Chapter 33
Wicked-Looking

Friday morning after Ray and I rolled into work, I called Doc Takayama, at his office this time. "Any progress on the weapon used to kill Ravenna Cannon?"

"It's a strange one," he said. "Sharp point, filed down for maximum impact. Probably about three inches in length. The sides were sharpened as well."

"Could it be something like a garden trowel?"

He thought for a moment. "I suppose. I'd have to see a similar one to make the comparison. You have a weapon in mind?"

I told him what Kitty had said, that Ricky Kuapi had been arrested for illegally collecting wild orchids.

"I can see that," he said. "There's a City Mill hardware store a few blocks from here. I can send someone over there to look for similar trowels, but we're backed up after that shooting in Wahiawa last night. I probably can't get someone onto this until Monday."

"I'd rather not wait that long. How about if I bring some over to you? Could you take a look?"

"For you, Kimo. Sure."

I hung up and pushed back my chair. "Field trip," I said to Ray. On the way to the garage I explained what we were looking for.

City Mill was a sprawling lumber yard and hardware store on the Nimitz Highway in an industrial neighborhood near Honolulu harbor. We parked and walked in, roaming the aisles until we found the right area. There were at least a dozen different trowels on the walls.

A guy in the kind of sleeveless orange vest my brother called a pinney came up to us as we looked. "Can I help you find something?" he asked.

I showed him my badge. "We're looking for the kind of trowel that might have been used in a homicide," I said. "Blade about three inches long, able to be sharpened on both sides."

He looked at the display. "If it helps, we think the person who wielded it might also be using it to harvest wild orchids."

"Then you'd want this one," he said, pulling down a wicked-looking trowel with a red handle from the display. "Premium stainless steel, pointed blade for digging." He pulled a tape measure off his belt. "Three-inch blade."

I held it in my hand and I liked the feel of it. I might even be able to use one like it for some gardening in our backyard, to replace an ancient one Mike had been using for years.

I turned to face Ray, and put my hand on his shoulder, pressing my thumb roughly where I'd seen the print on Ravenna's blouse. I pointed the trowel upwards toward his chest.

The guy helping us stared at me open-mouthed. "Just trying something out," I said. Of course I didn't slice into Ray, but I saw this was the right kind of weapon.

"How come I always have to play the victim?" Ray asked as I lowered the trowel.

"If I'm Ricky and you're Ravenna, we've got the right height difference," I said. "The next time we have a short perpetrator you can be the one with the weapon."

"I'm not short! I'm five-eight."

I patted him on the shoulder. "I know, Napoleon," I said, and the clerk laughed.

I bought the trowel and we drove around the corner to the ME's office. After a wait of a few minutes, we were sent back to Doc's office, where he was stuffing a bloody polyester gown into a medical waste bin.

"Let's see what you've got." He took the shrink-wrapped trowel from me and used a knife to expertly slice the plastic wrapper. He held it up, turning it back and forth.

"Looks good." He walked over to a workbench along the wall and found a whetstone. He rubbed it against the blade for a moment. "Takes a good sharpening." He measured the blade. "Right length."

He looked up at us. "When can you get me an actual weapon to compare?"

"Very soon," I said. "Thanks, Doc."

When we got back to headquarters there was a message from Michael Arden, the attorney for Kyle Goodman. "Kyle's father arrived late last night, and he'd like to meet with you. Please call me as soon as you get this."

I relayed the message to Ray. "What can he have to say to us?" I asked. "Our part is finished. We can't influence the Prosecuting Attorney on the decision of what charges to press."

"He's a father, and he's worried about his son," Ray said. "At least we can give him the courtesy of a conversation."

I looked at my watch. "It's almost noon, and we've got to be at the Orange Lotus at four to stake it out. Call Arden and see if we can meet early this afternoon. Otherwise it'll have to wait until Monday."

While he did that, I went back to the incel subreddit. Several people had posted in opposition to causing trouble at the makeup event, but there were at least six guys who were planning to be there. The original poster had done his homework—he provided information on parking at the Eaton Center garage, around the corner from the venue. It was free to attend, but you had to provide your name and email address, and he warned the other guys to have a fake address ready to present.

He even posted pictures of the four speakers, including my niece.

None of them were flattering, in my opinion. A paparazzi had shot Tay with her thong panties showing beneath her dress. Another girl had lost a false eyelash so it looked like a spider had landed on her other eye. The worst they'd been able to find of Api was a photo where her black hair was windblown and had fallen over her face in black strands.

Kind of matched the Halloween makeup she'd been testing when I saw her at her dorm, and I wondered if even this shot had been carefully staged.

"Two-thirty at Fields and Yamato," Ray said when he finished the call. We got sandwiches from the cafeteria downstairs and put together everything we could find on Ricky Kuapi. He had left Kaiser High School after ninth grade and transferred to the Olomana Youth Center, which served at-risk students from Windward Oahu's secondary schools. He'd only lasted there a year, and dropped out at the start of eleventh grade.

He had accumulated a significant juvenile record by the time he turned eighteen, mostly for car theft and drug possession. In the six years he'd been a legal adult, he had been arrested three more times for minor offenses such as drunken behavior and possession of marijuana. His most serious arrests were the ones Kitty had mentioned, poaching Tahitian prawns, and illegally harvesting rare orchids.

Tahitian prawns were an invasive species that competed with and preyed on native stream animals. They had been introduced to Hawai'i from the Marquesas Islands via aquaculture as a potential food source in 1950. His arrest wasn't so much about the poaching as the method he used—he dropped ant poison into a stream to kill a large number of prawns.

It was the pollution charge that got him. It's a bad idea to tamper with our waterways, which are a vital support to island life. And it was also stupid—who wants to eat prawns you've poisoned? He was turned in by a chef when he tried to sell his harvest and explained to the man how he'd gotten so many of the prawns.

His orchid theft was similarly clueless. Orchids are especially vulnerable to overharvesting because many species occur in one location and have low population densities. I read one expert on the subject who said, "You only have to collect a few here and there to potentially wipe out an entire species."

It's also not easy to sell stolen orchids. You can't take them to a pawn shop, for example. Even if you knew a collector, that person might turn you in rather than buy from you. I couldn't imagine Ricky setting up a booth at a farmer's market either. Any real orchid fancier would immediately be suspicious of an unknown variety.

I sat back in my chair to share what I had found about Ricky. "He has a history of committing stupid crimes, especially when you add in those public intoxication charges," I said, after I'd described the business with the prawns and the orchids.

"It's like what we were talking about with Kyle," Ray said. "Adults process information with the prefrontal cortex, the brain's rational part. That's the part that responds to situations with good judgment and an awareness of long-term consequences. Kyle wasn't thinking about the long-term consequences of his actions. He was using the emotional part of the brain, the amygdala."

"But Ricky's older," I said. "Nearly twenty-six."

Ray shrugged. "This kind of study isn't perfect yet. Some guys, like Ricky, might take longer to build up the prefrontal cortex. And remember, he dropped out of school after tenth grade, so he didn't have teachers pushing him into logical thought patterns."

"Great. That makes me see Ricky as a real loose cannon."

"Whatever he is, we've got to get over to Fields and Yamato."

We drove over to the high-rise building that housed the law firm and parked in the garage. We told the receptionist we were there to see Michael Arden, and he appeared a moment later to shepherd us to a conference room.

Derrick Goodman was a larger version of his son. Similar features, but much taller and bulkier. He wore a well-tailored dark business suit and had a strong handshake. Kyle cowered at the far end of the conference table, looking down instead of at us.

"Thank you for agreeing to see me," Goodman said. "I wanted to give you some insight into my son and his behavior."

Ray and I accepted cups of ice water from Arden and sat down across from him and Goodman, with Kyle still at the far end.

"This is merely a courtesy," I said. "Your son's case is in the hands of the Prosecuting Attorney. He'll decide what charges to pursue."

"I understand that. But I have a brother who has been in and out of the criminal justice system since he was Kyle's age, and I know how much influence the police have in presenting evidence."

"I'm sorry for your situation," Ray said. "But the evidence we have collected is clear. On a recorded phone line, your son accepted his Miranda warning. He then walked us through how he hit Betsy Lawrence in the head with his backpack. How he dragged her across the pavement to the cliffside. Where he pushed her over."

"She didn't die instantaneously," I continued. "The medical examiner will testify that if Kyle had called 911 instead of attempting to hide her body, Betsy might be alive today."

Goodman's face paled. "I understand that you can see things that way," he said, after a moment. "But my son is an avid video gamer. I believe that when he plays a game, he takes on the persona of the character. In his games, he often has to fight to save himself, and in the process kills other screen characters."

I took a sip of water.

"When the video game moves on, the dead character is no longer visible. I believe that my son thought he was playing a game online, and after the other player was dead, he moved on."

"Unfortunately, life is not a video game," Ray said. "And Betsy Lawrence wasn't merely an avatar who wouldn't accept a kiss from Kyle's character. She was a living, breathing human being – until she wasn't."

Goodman tried to frame his argument several different ways, but our response was always the same. Finally I said, "Mr. Goodman, I have two children of my own, and Ray has a son. As fathers, we can understand what you're going through, and both of us would do anything in our power to protect a child. I suggest that you and Mr. Arden provide all these insights to the Prosecuting Attorney."

I looked at Ray, and he nodded slightly.

Both of us pushed our chairs back and stood up. "I hate to see a young man with potential have his life destroyed," I said. "I hope you're able to work with the Prosecuting Attorney on Kyle's behalf. But any decisions are out of our hands."

We said goodbye to Arden, and to Kyle, who didn't respond, and we walked out. "That was tough," Ray said, as we stood by the elevator.

"I know. I hope and pray neither of us end up in his situation."

"You think Goodman made a mistake in letting his son play those games?"

I shrugged. "I'm no psychiatrist. But I saw the distance between Kyle and his father in that room, and that said something to me."

The elevator came and we rode down in silence. As we exited into the garage, I said, "Time to focus on Ricky Kuapi again. Let me see what I can find about his location through the tracker you installed."

I picked up my phone and found the right app. It took a while to connect to the server, and to overlay his location to a map of Oahu. "It looks like he's still at the place where my brother's company was working, the Koa Tree Diamond Head Hotel."

The screen blanked for a minute. "Hold on, he's on the move," I said. "He's on Diamond Head Road, heading toward Waikiki."

"Then we'd better get a move on," Ray said.

My stomach was tied in knots. I was worried about Api and her safety, and about feeling foolish if nothing happened at the Orange Lotus. I didn't want to be the boy who cried wolf.

Maybe Ricky wasn't on his way to the beauty event. He might be going to Waikiki to grab a beer, or maybe throw produce at couples like Brandon Paikai.

But what if he was instead on his way to the Orange Lotus to cause some trouble with guys from the subreddit? It was up to Ray and me to catch him before he could slip away.

Chapter 34
Gender Reveal

Ray and I arrived at the Orange Lotus at four. It was a square two-story building that had probably once been a theater because there was a triangular marquee over the entrance. A big banner outside announced that the event was free to the public, with a long list of sponsoring makeup companies.

I badged the pretty young woman at the ticket desk and asked to speak to the manager. An African-American guy I recognized came out a moment later.

"Jamal?" I asked. He nodded. "Kimo Kanapa'aka. We met when you were dating Gunter."

"A very brief experience, but delightful." He was about forty, slim, with a high puff of curly hair and an otherwise shaved head. Very much Gunter's kind of guy, and I wondered why it hadn't lasted.

Oh, I reminded myself. Because Gunter was all about the next sexual experience, rather than holding on to what he'd found.

We shook hands and I introduced Ray. "Is there some kind of problem?" Jamal asked.

"I'm probably being over-protective, because my niece is one of the speakers," I said. I explained what I'd read on the subreddit.

"That's disturbing," he said. "Do you think we should restrict the audience to women only?"

"The people on this subreddit are all what we call involuntary celibates," I said. "They feel that because of their appearance no one will want to have sex with them. Some of the posters are clearly female, while others aren't specific. So a couple of the protesters today could be women who are against the objectification of their looks."

"The organizers have told me they've had some protests by women at similar events in the past," he said.

I nodded. "I was at Kapiolani Park last weekend and passed by a beauty pageant, and people were protesting there. Though very peacefully."

He frowned. "There are so many positive things people could be putting their time toward," he said. "I see women with signs in front of abortion clinics and I think, 'why aren't you home taking care of your own children?' Not to mention gay rights protesters. I read a study that half of the people who show up at those events are either single or divorced. So why do they care if we get married?"

"You're preaching to the choir, brother," I said. "Can you give us a quick tour of the layout of the facility?"

"Absolutely." He led us inside, where workers were setting up a dais on the stage and testing video equipment. "Three doors at the front which can be used for entrance or exit." He pointed along one wall. "Two doors on that side go out to Hobron Lane, while two on the other side lead out to an alley alongside the parking garage."

"Do you have any other security precautions?" I asked Jamal.

"I have two big guys at the entrance examining over-large purses and any other big bags," he said. "Mostly to make sure they don't bring in food. But we make everyone go through metal detectors and there's a statement by the front that says no weapons are allowed inside."

His cell phone buzzed. "Sorry, have to take this," he said. "Any of the crew can get me if you need anything else."

He walked away and Ray and I looked around the room. A mezzanine level stretched around three sides. "If I wanted to cause trouble I'd head up there," Ray said. "You could drop stuff down on the audience."

"I hope Jamal's guys would stop anyone from coming in with a bag of ripe tomatoes or a couple cartons of eggs," I said.

We did a quick circuit of the building as a video of Tay Talaxian began playing on a big screen behind the stage. Then we walked back outside.

Ray had arranged for Julie to join us so that we'd appear less conspicuous than two guys in a sea of women. We kissed cheeks, and I complemented her on the elaborate French braid in her hair.

"I was worried we'd be in a room full of beauties and I didn't want to look drab," she said.

She was Italian, like Ray, and had classic Sophia Loren looks. Doe-shaped eyes under neatly trimmed brows, elegant cheekbones and a long neck. "You'd never look drab in any crowd," I said.

We stepped up to the registration table. In exchange for our names and email addresses, we each got a gift bag full of product samples. Tiny lipsticks in the newest shades. Butterfly clips with the name of a hair color company. Hotel-sized body wash, shampoo, and conditioner. Sample packages of eye shadow, concealer, night recovery, and something called liquid whip that made me think of mayonnaise.

"I'd like to keep this for Addie when she gets a little older," I said.

"As long as Cathy supervises, Addie will love all the tiny samples," Julie said. "Give me the bag and I'll hold it for you."

"Really? She's only ten."

I remembered her reaction to the beauty pageant we'd passed at the park the previous weekend after Mike's 10K run. She'd been entranced. "Ten going on twenty," I added.

Julie squashed all three of the bags we'd been given into her backpack and she and Ray went inside, while I stayed out on Hobron Lane and watched the attendees stream in from the Eaton Square parking lot. They were mostly pretty, young women like Apikela, though there were lots of soccer moms and teenagers, too. A few guys who gave off a gay vibe.

I wondered if I did. Since my conversations with Api I'd been wondering what other men thought of me. If I was with Mike and we were standing close together, we were sending off signals that we were a couple. I had a couple of outfits in my closet, like a tight-fitting tank top and tiny shorts, or an aloha shirt with rainbows, which might have marked me. But overall I was a cisgender guy who dressed like a guy. I had so far resisted any beauty products, though I was willing to consider the under-eye concealer Api had mentioned.

The very fact that I knew about under-eye concealer probably marked me as gay.

Lidia and Doc arrived, and it was surprising to see them in civilian clothes. He wore a Tommy Bahama aloha shirt in a subtle wave pattern over khakis. Lidia had on a red silk blouse with a plunging neckline like the one Ravenna Cannon had been wearing, and carefully applied eyeshadow and lipstick.

The crowd started increasing, mostly women, and I had to move to the side of the building to stay out of the way. Kitty Cardozo arrived, looking more like a downtown businesswoman than a police sergeant, in a pencil skirt and chocolate-brown blouse. Between her and all the other women passing by, I felt underdressed as she came up and kissed my cheek. "Anything happening yet?" she asked in a low voice.

"Not that I've seen. I may have made a big fuss over nothing."

"Not sure about that. Did you see those two guys over by the side of the garage? I haven't seen him for a while, but I'm pretty sure one of them is Ricky Kuapi."

I moved around so that I could look at her, and over her shoulder at the men she noticed. Yeah, one of them looked like Ricky. And the guy with him was Brandon Paikai, who had been pelting eggs and tomatoes at couples leaving the Sailors' Rest. As I watched, two other guys, one tall and skinny and the other short and round, approached them cautiously.

I couldn't hear the conversation but it looked like they were members of the incel group, too. "Damn, I wish I could go over there," I said to Kitty. "But Ray and I had a conversation with the guy in the aloha shirt last week, and I know he'd recognize me."

"Ditto for me and Ricky."

She went inside, and I spotted my brother and sister-in-law, arriving with Keoni. It was great that they were there to support Apikela, though from the crowds streaming along she was going to get plenty of support from her audience. I kissed Liliha's cheek, shook Lui's hand, and pulled Keoni aside. "You guys go ahead inside," I said. "I need a favor from my favorite nephew."

"I'm your favorite?" Keoni asked. "But I'm the worst surfer."

"My favorite niece or nephew is the one I currently need a favor from," I said, as his parents walked away. "Could you go over and talk to Ricky and his buddies, see what they're planning?"

He looked toward where I'd nodded. "No way," he said. "He already makes fun of me at work."

"If things go as I plan, he won't be coming to work anymore," I said. "I really need you to pretend to be part of this subreddit for *Noho male'ole.*"

"Unmarried men?"

I nodded. "It's an incel group, and I think they're planning something to disrupt your cousin's event. It would really help me to know if they're just going to make noise, or if they've got something more dangerous planned."

He looked over at where his employee stood. "For the record, I hate this," he said. "I am not an incel. Just a guy who has trouble getting dates."

"I believe that," I said.

I watched as he turned away from me and headed toward Ricky and Brandon and their crew. As he approached, Ricky spotted him and his body began to shake with one of those big-bellied laughs. He reached out and wrapped his arm around Keoni's neck, and pulled him close.

I couldn't hear what they said, but it looked like Ricky was introducing Keoni to the rest of the guys. Keoni put his arm around Ricky's back, then pulled away.

I felt bad that I was forcing my nephew to do something that he didn't want to, but I'd find a way to make it up to him.

There were seven guys now, with Keoni. Six of them began moving toward where I was standing, and as I stepped back behind one of the building's columns I saw Keoni pull out his cell phone.

The guys had almost approached where I stood when my phone pinged with an incoming message. I glanced at the screen, saw it was from Keoni, and turned my back to the six men so I could read it.

"They have smoke canisters like you use at a baby party," he had typed. "Pink and blue."

Why bring those? To cause chaos, then stand back and watch all the Beckys and Stacys stumble over each other? Or something more? I turned around but Ricky and the other men had been swallowed by the crowd.

Chapter 35
Nowhere to Run

I typed a quick thumbs-up to Keoni. Then I sent a text to Ray about Ricky's smoke canisters. A few weeks before, I'd accompanied Mike to a gender reveal party for his pregnant secretary. The firefighters there had made a lot of jokes about the canisters and the smoke they set off. But the secretary's husband had been careful to point out the safety features, and the fact that the canisters were biodegradable.

So they wouldn't set off any metal detectors, and they were small enough that they could fit into a pocket of the kind of baggy cargo pants that the guys were all wearing.

I began hurrying through the crowd toward the entrance. The crowd was thick and I didn't want to upset anyone by holding out my badge and announcing that I was a police officer. So I shuffled forward, surrounding by happy, chattering young women. As I turned the corner I saw the front entrance.

Ricky and his cohort were at the registration desk, receiving their gift bags. I couldn't see any faces but I imagined they were chagrined to be given such dainty pink bags. I watched as I moved forward and they tossed the bags into a trash can. A tween girl behind them immediately retrieved the bags and I shook my head.

By the time I got to the front, the guys had gone inside, and the crowd behind me had thinned. The event was about to start. I showed my badge and my holstered gun to the security guard, and he let me walk through.

When I got inside, I spotted Ray and Julie toward the back. "Waiting for you," he said. "I saw the guys. They're over toward the right wall."

I looked in that direction. "Keoni said they've got a bunch of those gender reveal smoke bombs, but I have no idea what they're going to use them for."

"They could cause a lot of trouble if they frighten people. Look at this crowd—some of the younger girls or the older women could get run over in a stampede."

"I'm going to see how close I can get to them," I said.

"I'll stay back here near the exit. If something happens and people want to get out fast, they'll need crowd control. I told Lidia and Kitty to stay by the other doors."

"Good man. See you later."

I began to move through the crowd. It wasn't easy because there were a lot of women all around me, but I kept saying, "Sorry, need to get to my wife."

It was a small lie, but women stepped aside to let me pass.

A petite Asian woman stepped up to the microphone and introduced each of the influencers. I wanted to cheer for Api but I had my head down, apologizing, and I heard my family yelling her name. I was glad so many of them had turned out to encourage her, though the crowd seemed to love her, too.

Tay Talaxian took over at the podium and told a couple of stories about behind-the-scenes drama from her family's TV show. Then she stepped aside slightly so that the big screen could show one of her makeup demos. I was almost up to where the guys from the subreddit were standing in a rough circle around Ricky. As I watched, Keoni stepped away from them, heading toward where his family was.

Because of my height, I could see over the heads of the women ahead of me, and I saw Brandon lean over to say something to Ricky. Then Ricky reached behind himself and under his shirt. The movement reminded me of the way I would reach back to pull a gun out of a holster at the small of my back. But he'd gone through the metal detectors at the entrance, so he couldn't have a gun.

Or could he?

Years before, a company had released blueprints online for a 3D printable single-shot handgun called the Liberator. Legal efforts to restrict it had come and gone, but the blueprints were still available on the dark web. Someone like Ricky, who had a lot of gripes and spent time online, could probably find them if he wanted.

You did need ammunition for it, which should have set off the detector. However I'd seen examples online of how a bullet could be hidden inside a keyring or other device that would be easily explained away.

My heart rate quickened. I couldn't see if there was anything in Ricky's hand because he was surrounded. I was focused on him so it took me an extra minute to register that the other five guys were acting, too.

The items that the guys pulled out of their pockets resembled the smoke canisters I'd seen, decorated in such bright colors and patterns that they looked harmless. Brandon pulled a lighter from his pocket and began lighting the wicks on the canisters.

In succession, they went off, and pink and blue smoke filled the front area of the room. Apikela and the other women began coughing and waving their hands in front of their faces.

I looked back at the guys, and saw Ricky raise his hand and point it toward the dais. I wasn't close enough to see what was in it, but I doubted it was another harmless smoke canister.

All around me women were coughing and trying to clear the smoke away. The air handlers for the building had picked up the smoke and were moving it all around the room.

I pushed closer, apologizing to women as I did. I kept glancing up to see if I could tell what was in Ricky's hand. Could it be that wicked-looking garden trowel Kitty had caught him using to harvest orchids? Was he planning on throwing it at one of the women? Turning to a woman near him and stabbing her, the way we believed he had stabbed Ravenna Cannon?

The air ahead of me cleared a bit and I saw clearly that Ricky had his hand wrapped around the grip of a pistol. How the hell had he gotten it past the metal detectors? I couldn't see clearly enough to determine if it was made of plastic or not.

I was only a few feet away by then, but the clearing air allowed Ricky to take his shot.

He must have hit Tay Talaxian, because she crumpled to the floor. I couldn't see what he did with the gun because the five men formed a cordon around him and began pushing toward one of the side exits, which had been propped wide open to allow the crowd to escape the smoke.

I grabbed my badge from my pocket. "Police!" I called, as I raised it above my head. "Let me through!"

The crowd was so thick, and pressed together so closely, that I couldn't get any further. I heard girls crying, women screaming.

Fortunately the guys were stuck a few feet back from the doorway by the press of the crowd. I called Ray's cell, and over the noise of the women around me I yelled, "They're heading for the exit along the right wall."

I couldn't hear what he said, but he ended the call. I hoped that he, Kitty or Lidia was close enough to the back door to get outside and around the building. The crowd finally eased enough that I could begin pushing women aside, waving my badge in one hand and my gun in the other. But Ricky and his crew got out ahead of me.

By the time I got through the door, they were halfway back to the parking garage. I took off in pursuit, and realized that Ray was a few feet to my right. "Stop, police!" I yelled, and women around us froze, but the crew kept going.

Ray and I met up, and I saw Lidia and Kitty a few dozen feet behind us as we all ran. "Ricky Kuapi! Honolulu PD! You're under arrest!"

He didn't even look back, but two of the men with him peeled off to the right. It didn't matter; we'd find out who they were eventually.

Brandon Paikai ran out of breath, and bent over, gasping. Lidia cuffed him as Ray, Kitty and I passed.

I called out to Ricky again. "We know who you are, Ricky! We're coming for you!"

I was glad that I'd been running with Mike because I didn't even feel winded. Ray had always been in good shape, and Kitty was younger and fitter than both of us. She gained on us.

"Ricky! It's Sergeant Cardozo. I'm taking you in!"

There were only two guys left with Ricky, and as they approached the entrance to the garage they stopped and turned to face Kitty, blocking her way.

Ray jumped over to help her subdue them, and Ricky disappeared into the parking garage. I decided it was time to start using my head, so I stood by the exit ramp and called for police car backup. I grabbed my phone and opened the app that tracked Ricky's crummy Nissan.

Sure enough, it registered in the garage.

He didn't know we were tracking him, so I bet that he would lie low in his car until he could get into a long line of cars trying to exit the garage, and stay below our radar.

Wrong move on his part.

The first dozen cars got out of the garage before patrol cars arrived to block the exit. After that, officers checked each car, asking to have the trunk opened, before they let anyone out.

Horns were honking and women were yelling, but it didn't matter to us. Ray, Kitty, Lidia, and Doc joined me at the garage. "Brandon Paikai and two of the other guys are in custody," Ray said. "Kitty was an ace. She hardly needed my help."

"I'll go to headquarters to help with the booking," Kitty said, and she walked off.

I turned to Doc and Lidia and shook both their hands. "Thanks so much for your help."

"I don't get much opportunity to see my wife work," Doc said. "Reminded me all over again how magnificent she is, and how lucky I am to have her."

Lidia blushed, and I said, "Aw, that's sweet. But you're right, Doc. She's amazing."

He took her hand they walked into the garage.

By then it looked like every uniformed officer in Honolulu was with us, though I'm sure that wasn't the case. We allowed the garage to open a back exit and officers staffed it. Ray and I stood on the sidelines, waiting.

It took nearly an hour for the dot on my phone to begin moving. I walked over to the sergeant supervising the operation and showed him my screen. "You can let anyone through who's not in a beige Nissan," I said.

Things moved more quickly, as officers waved cars through. Once I spotted Ricky's car on the ramp, I notified the sergeant. Ray and I stood off to the side until Ricky got to the end of the ramp, when we stepped out, our guns poised. "Ricky Kuapi! Exit the vehicle now!" I yelled.

He looked from me to Ray and realized he had nowhere else to run, so he got out of the car with his hands up. We got him on his knees, cuffed him, then searched him. He didn't have a gun with him but that didn't matter.

A pair of officers took him in for booking, and Ray and I took another four back to the venue to hunt for the gun. The rest left and the garage was able to empty easily.

I hadn't seen my family anywhere, so I texted Haoa to make sure they were all okay. He called me a minute later. "Api's fine," he said. "Jeffrey, Keoni and Chesa jumped up on the podium and surrounded her."

"That's great. Where are you now?"

"We wanted to avoid the crowd so we walked over to the Queen of Canton," he said. That was a smart move; the Chinese buffet was a few blocks away, and they wouldn't be stuck in the garage. "Come on over when you're finished. We'll be here for a while."

"Will do."

One of the uniforms found the gun near the podium after a search of only a few minutes, and Ray bagged it. I spoke to Jamal, the manager who had dated Gunter, and let him know he could close up the place. "What happened to the woman who was shot?" I asked. "It was Tay Talaxian, wasn't it?"

"It was. An ambulance took her to the hospital," he said. "She was still breathing when they left though she was in pain."

Ray said, "You go join your family. I'll swing past downtown and put the gun in the evidence locker and make sure that Ricky is booked."

He held it up and looked at it through the clear plastic evidence bag. "I've never seen one of these in person before. It's so light."

The simple grip had a textured surface for better handling. The gun had an angled barrel, and no sights or safety mechanism. It looked like something out of a science fiction movie. He looked inside the barrel. "Must not be an extractor mechanism, because the spent casing is still in here."

"Scary to think Ricky could get the plans for that online and make it with a 3-D printer," I said. "At least they only fire one shot."

"Enough to knock that poor woman down," he said.

I nodded. "Thanks, brah. I appreciate all your help today."

"Back at you. We make a good team."

Chapter 36
Baby Girl

I walked over to the Queen of Canton. It was a touristy place, with a big red-and-gold Chinese gate over the front door. A half-dozen parties were waiting to be seated, but the hostess directed me to a room at the rear, where my family had taken over a couple of tables.

Lui and Haoa were laughing at one corner, drinking glasses of what looked like plum wine. I was beginning to get accustomed to this new, slim Haoa, glad that he was looking after his health. Their wives were toward the other side, while Apikela, Jeffrey, Keoni and Chesa were all at a central table, still eating. I was surprised to see Su-Kim, the dorm manager at HAC, with them.

Api jumped up to hug me. "You were right, Uncle K," she said. "Thank you for looking out for me."

She held onto my waist and pivoted to face the other young people.

"Keoni deserves a lot of credit," I said. "He's the one who told me about the smoke canisters."

"He and Jeff and Chesa were amazing! I am so fortunate to have such a protective family." She made a face. "Though sometimes I don't think so."

Everyone laughed.

Api dragged me over to where Su-Kim and Keoni were sitting. "Do you know my friend Su-Kim?" she asked me. "She's the dorm manager at HAC."

"We've met." I was pleased to see her with Keoni, and I hoped that he'd broken that single-guy dark cloud he thought was over him.

"Api is so kind to invite me to the event tonight," Su-Kim said. "And to join your family here for dinner." I noticed she had managed to hold onto her pink bag of goodies in the rush out of the theater.

"How is everything up at HAC?" I asked. "Are the students upset about Betsy's death?"

"We had counselors come in to talk," Su-Kim said. "It's interesting, the boys are taking it harder than the girls. But we're planning some ways to bring both groups together in a non-judgmental way, to teach them how to get along with each other better."

"That's good," I said, thinking of what Owen's teacher had planned for him and the boy who had taunted him. "It's a cliché, but sometimes good things happen because of bad things."

Su-Kim nodded. "And the most interesting change is in Kimora. She was really upset over Betsy's death, and she told me that she has vowed to be nicer to other girls. She was at the event but had to leave early because Api arranged to give her gift bags to distribute up at the college."

My brothers came over for big hugs. "How come that guy got a gun inside the theater?" Haoa asked.

"My guess is that it was a 3-D printable gun," I said. "Probably got the plans online. Doesn't have any metal parts so it went through the metal detector."

"So many offices have those 3-D printers now," Lui said. "We did a feature on them last month. They use them at all kinds of crazy places. The Queen's Medical Center, labs at UH, even the Islands of History theme park, where they recreate artifacts from the different islands."

"The suspect's family works there," I said. "That's probably how he got access to a printer."

"Is it true, what Keoni said?" Haoa asked. "The shooter works for me?"

I nodded. "I'm afraid to tell you he won't be able to report for work on Monday."

"I wouldn't want him, even if he gets out on bail. Anybody who threatens my baby girl…"

"Daddy," Api said, and everyone laughed.

As I got a plate at the buffet, Mike walked in. "Tatiana texted me that you were all here," he said.

I leaned up and kissed his cheek. "I'm glad you're here, too. Not a family event without you."

"Well, we have a whole other family up in Aeia Heights who will be glad that you came through that mob scene without problems."

We loaded up our plates and looked for a place to sit. Keoni was deep in conversation with Su-Kim, so we chose to sit with Jeffrey and Chesa. "It was nice of you guys to come out to support Apikela," I said, as we put our plates down. "I'm really pleased to see that all you cousins are staying close."

"They have group chats," Chesa said. "Complaining about their parents, making plans to go out. It's very sweet."

Jeffrey elbowed her. "Chesa's family is very conservative. She has one cousin who thinks her tattoos are the work of the devil."

She smiled sweetly. "Every time I get a new one I send him a picture." Then she got serious. "Though I'm worried he might end up like one of those guys at the event tonight. He needs a girlfriend, but his parents – my white aunt and uncle—are fundamentalist Christians and they don't believe in sex before marriage. They have to approve anyone my cousins date, and because he's overweight and has some low-level Asperger's, no girl wants to get near him."

"Sadly, that's what happens to a lot of these guys," I said. "Of course, they're not all overweight or have disabilities. But our society puts so much pressure on sex and attractiveness. We really need to do something about that."

"Bankoh puts a lot of emphasis on ethnic, racial and sexual diversity," Jeffrey said. Bankoh was short for Bank of Hawai'i, his employer. "I wish there was a way we could reach out to other people who feel isolated."

"There's a subreddit for people who feel that they'll never get married," I said. "I did some research there when I was learning about guys like Ricky Kuapi. That's where he recruited the other guys who helped him out tonight. Is there a way to reach out through that group for some kind of social event sponsored by the bank?"

"You really think guys who can't get a date will show up for a party?" Mike asked.

"There's a way to approach it," Jeffrey said. "Something like financial planning for single people. Rent, mortgages, furniture, utilities – all kinds of things are more expensive if you have to pay by yourself. And women as well as men could show up and have a chance to talk to each other about something other than dating."

I nodded. Finances had gotten easier to manage once I was sharing costs with Mike.

Jeffrey was excited. "We could educate people about that, encourage different ways of living. Look at Tutu Lokelani—she's been all alone in that big condo, and now she has Reiko living with her. I know that's because she's sick, but I'll bet there are other elderly people who are alone and wouldn't mind sharing a house with someone younger, who could help with errands and meal preparation in exchange for a lower rent."

"Jeff has an amazing social conscience for a banker," Chesa said, smiling.

"When you have something concrete, let me know," I said. "Maybe I can get HPD or the court system to partner with you. If we identify some single adults who could be swayed to violence, we could divert them into activities that would help them with money and socialization."

Other family members joined the conversation, each of them with ideas, and I felt like something positive might arise from the two deaths Ray and I had investigated.

Chapter 37
Additional Charges

Tay Talaxian had suffered a bullet wound to the chest and a punctured lung, and she was recovering at The Queen's Medical Center, where a camera crew from her family's television show were already filming.

In the case of a warrantless arrest in Hawai'i, a district judge must determine whether there was probable cause for the arrest. Monday morning, we met in front of Judge Yamanaka, along with Daniel Francois from the Prosecuting Attorney's office. We had already briefed him on what we were going to say.

The public defender was a twenty-something haole we'd dealt with before named Tyler Hix. Back then he'd been fresh out of law school and new to the islands. In the intervening two years he'd gained a few pounds and a level of certainty.

Ricky's family declined to put up bail for him, so he had been in our holding cells until that morning. When a bailiff brought him in, he had cuffs around his hands and wore orange prison scrubs in what had to be a size XXL at least.

Daniel stood and recited the charge against Ricky. He mentioned the plastic ghost gun, and how the police had uncovered the directions on how to manufacture one, using a 3-D printer, in Ricky's room at his family house. His office had a subpoena pending for the history of the printer at the Islands of History theme park.

Then it was my turn to stand and provide my eyewitness account of the shooting of Tay Talaxian. I sat down, and Hix stood.

"Your honor, my client does not dispute the events of last Friday evening," he said. "His single condition, compounded by the pressures of his large family, led him to commit the act at the Orange Lotus on Friday, which he sincerely regrets. He wishes to plead not guilty by reason of mental disease."

Francois stood again. "Your honor, if I may? We have additional information to add to the charges against Mr. Kuapi." He handed a sheet of paper to the bailiff, who took it to the judge. "Detective Raymond Donne can recap for you."

Ray stood. We had both dressed up for the appearance, in button-down shirts instead of our regular aloha wear. "Mr. Kuapi had two cell phones with him at the time of his arrest," Ray said. "One of them was registered under his name and at his address. The other is what is referred to on the street as a burner phone, an inexpensive mobile phone designed for temporary, sometimes anonymous, use. Burners are purchased with prepaid minutes and without a formal contract with a communications provider so it is difficult for law enforcement to trace them."

He looked up at the judge. "Fortunately, Google has a new technology called the Sensorvault, which uses location sensing to identify when a phone is in a particular area at a certain time. I was able to match the second phone in Mr. Kuapi's possession to one used to communicate with a woman named Ravenna Cannon."

I stole a glance at Tyler Hix. It didn't look like he recognized the name, so he had no idea what was coming.

"Mr. Kuapi used the burner phone to arrange to meet Ms. Cannon behind the Waikiki Bandshell last Thursday night, where Ms. Cannon was stabbed to death. The Medical Examiner found one of Mr. Kuapi's fingerprints on Ms. Cannon's blouse, and described the kind of weapon he thought was used to kill her."

Ricky was looking down at the table in front of him.

"Saturday morning, I put together a search warrant for the sharpened object the Medical Examiner described, and accompanied by a pair of HPD officers, I searched Ricky's apartment and his parents' home."

Francois handed another sheet of paper to the bailiff.

"What you have in front of you is a photograph of an exceptionally sharp trowel we found in the Kuapi family garage," Ray said. "His parents disavowed knowledge of it. The trowel is now at the Medical Examiner's office waiting to be confirmed as the weapon used to kill Ravenna Cannon."

Ray sat down and Francois stood. He looked directly at the judge. "Based on this additional evidence, which puts Mr. Kuapi in contact with the victim before the murder, his fingerprint on her blouse and the nature of the weapon, we wish to add the charge of homicide in the first degree in the death of Ravenna Cannon. This was a premeditated act which does not fit with a pattern of mental disorder."

I stole a glance at Ricky Kuapi. His eyes were wide and his mouth in the shape of an O. His shoulders were shaking.

Hix immediately requested time to confer with his client, which was granted. I watched as he leaned over to Ricky and asked him questions. Ricky nodded at each one. After only a couple of minutes Hix announced that he would need more time to address this new charge.

"I rule that there was indeed probable cause for the arrest on the initial charge . However due to the new information provided to the court I am not willing to set bail and potentially have Mr. Kuapi released. Detectives, you have forty-eight hours to provide me with information on this new charge." He banged his gavel.

Ricky was sent to the Oahu Community Correctional Center to await his next court date. Ray and I went back to headquarters where we filled in Lieutenant Sampson on what had happened. "Kitty did an outstanding job of subduing two individuals," Ray said. "By the time I made it to her side to help she was almost finished."

"She's a hell of an officer," Sampson said. "As soon as a detective position opens up I'll be lobbying for her. Just not under my command."

We promised to let him know as soon as we had the details wrapped up, and he sent us back to our desks to continue assembling the evidence the Prosecuting Attorney would need for the murder charge against Ricky. Later that day Doc verified the weapon and found Ricky's fingerprints on it.

That night, I met Mike at home. He had already been to his parents' house to retrieve Griffin, and he sat on the sofa ruffling the dog's ears. "How was your day?" I asked.

When he looked up I saw that he had tears in his eyes, and I immediately went over to sit beside him. "What's wrong?"

"I didn't bother to knock when I went in to pick up Griffin," he said. "I just unlocked the door and walked in."

"And?"

"My father was on the floor, and my mother was trying to lift him up. They had this gadget, almost like a car's steering wheel, with grips on both sides. He had one side and she had the other, and she was leaning back and trying to leverage him up."

"Wow."

"I rushed over and grabbed him under the arms and lifted him up. It turns out this isn't the first time he's fallen."

"Not if they already had a gadget on hand."

He nodded. "He said he didn't want to worry me. He's been having some trouble with his blood pressure going up and down, and he got up too quickly and got dizzy."

"They say doctors are the worst patients," I said.

"You better believe it. I had a very strongly worded discussion with both of them. That he needs to get some testing, stat, and find out what's going on."

"He's always kept himself in good condition," I said. "I'm sure once he gets some tests, his doctors will figure out what's wrong. Or he will."

"He's seventy-six. Ever since he retired it seems like he's getting progressively worse, and now I think that's why he retired. That he knew he was getting into trouble."

"You were by my side when my dad died, and you've been with me as my mom is getting sicker. I'll be here with you whatever happens to your parents."

He took my hand and squeezed it. "I appreciate it. And I know this is inevitable but I don't want to lose him. I want him to see Addie and Owen grow up and graduate from college and…"

"I know, sweetheart. And we'll do what we can to make that happen, and if we can't we'll work through things together."

He stood up. "I could use a run. Want to come with me?"

"Sure."

We took Griffin with us, and went up Aiea Heights Drive to a mountain path where we could let him off the leash. He rushed ahead of us, leaping from stone to stone with the agility of a mountain goat. Of course, by the time we got to the top of the hill, he was exhausted, and collapsed at our feet.

"I don't know if he's going to be a good running partner for you," I said.

"Then you'll have to pick up the slack," Mike said with a smile.

With Tay Talaxian out of commission, Api had been tapped to handle Tay's other public appearances in Honolulu and Maui, and she even made a cameo appearance on *Taking on the Talaxians* as she visited Tay in her hospital bed. They shared tips on putting on makeup using an around-the-neck mirror while hospitalized.

When I went out to a job site in Salt Lake to interview Keoni about Ricky, he was looking very happy. "I really like Su-Kim and she seems to like me," he said. "We're going to a concert this weekend."

I thanked him again for his courage on the night of the attack. "What are the other guys you work with saying about Ricky?" I asked.

"A couple of them have already apologized to me for laughing along with him." Keoni smiled. "I made sure to show them a picture of me and Su-Kim at that restaurant on Friday night."

The cousins were all taking turns visiting their tutu. Though Reiko was taking good care of her, every time I spoke to my mother she seemed more frail and closer to joining my father. She was looking forward to seeing him, and in her less lucid moments she had begun talking directly to him.

Dominic went to a doctor he knew at the VA and got a full workup. There was something wrong with his autonomic nervous system which was wreaking havoc with his blood pressure and his heart rate, but he was put on a regimen of medication to handle it.

Ray had spoken with Sarah Byrne, who was the one who'd recommended the singing teacher. Since she was the closest to a friend that Ravenna had, he had called her to let her know that we had apprehended Ricky for her murder.

Sarah mentioned during that conversation that her singing group needed a tenor to replace one who had dropped out, and he had auditioned for the group the day before. "It's not a big commitment," he said. "Weekly practices and performances every couple of months. It makes me happy just thinking about it."

"Me, too. And it's what you were looking for, isn't it? Something of your own, that you can share with Julie and Vinnie when you want?"

"It is. My first gig with them is going to be next month at the Kennedy Theater at UH. Julie's promised to invite all her colleagues and students." He looked at me. "You and Mike will be there, won't you?"

I put my arm around his shoulder. "You may be my work husband, but I can see you out of work, too," I said.

Acknowledgments

A big mahalo to Joanna Campbell Slan and my Facebook ohana for help with how Addie and Owen behave as ten-year-olds. Thanks also to Jim Born for sage advice on police procedures. I am grateful to my Hawaiian friends, including Cindy Chow and Annette Mahon, for all I've learned from them.

I'm a big fan of Scott Galloway's Prof G podcast, and I've learned a lot about the problems of young men by listening to him. I've tried to incorporate some of those ideas here, and in my college teaching.

I also appreciate the many fans who have told me how much they enjoy these books, and how many of them want to marry either Kimo or Mike. Sadly they are both fictional—and taken!

As always, Randall Klein has provided excellent editorial advice, and Kelly Nichols designed a gorgeous cover representing the fictional Honolulu Arts College.

Readers I meet are often surprised that there is a real subgenre for Hawaiian music. I encourage you to check out some of Kimo's and my favorites: Keola Beamer, Paula Fuga, Hapa, Kui Lee, and Kalani Pe'a.

My loyal crew of beta readers always help me make these books better, and any errors that remain are my fault. Thanks to Andy Jackson, Timothy Brehme, and Sally Huxley for their eagle eyes. Judith Levitsky has been particularly vigilant about sentences ending with prepositions. If you find any that remain in this version, they're on me.

As it did for many people around the world, the pandemic

changed my life. My college classes became fully online, and the time I saved from commuting and sitting in my office waiting for students went into writing. The return to face-to-face teaching coincided with my 65th birthday and I decided to pivot to a full-time writing career. I am grateful for the support of my husband to be able to do this, and delighted that it gives me more time to spend with him and Brody and Griffin. (Yes, my own dogs have snuck their way into my work—Griffin here, and Brody as a trouble-making English cream golden in my golden retriever mystery series.)

Thanks for reading!

I'd love to stay in touch with you. Subscribe to one or more of my newsletters: Gay Mystery and Romance or Golden Retriever Mysteries and I promise I won't spam you!

Follow me at Goodreads to see what I'm reading, and my author page at Facebook where I post news and giveaways.

Learn more about Mahu Investigations Series:

You'll fall instantly in love with Kimo, from his scrupulous approach to his job to his easy way with his nieces, nephews, brothers, and friends, even when some turn against him on his new path. What's happening to him is the late-breaking realization that he's gay. If he's going to accept that and live as he's meant to, he has to upend everything and learn a whole new culture. It's a rocky path, and that's what makes a good story. Author Plakcy, creator of The Golden Retriever Mysteries, weaves a very different kind of tale here —realistic and hard-boiled, yet also empathetic and warm. **MAHU is a taut, ingenious, many-threaded mystery, each unexpected plot twist leading believably to the next, yet**

Thanks for reading!

nothing telegraphed—in other words, an extremely satisfying read.

The entire series is here: https://amzn.to/3Gokhsa

∽

Looking for something new to read? Neil has a series just for you!

The Golden Retriever Mysteries? You'll find the entire series here: https://amzn.to/3Kki7w6

∽

Author of over 50 romance and mystery novels and short story collections. **Neil's entire catalog of books are here:** https://amzn.to/3I7qOIf

About the Author

NEIL S. PLAKCY is the author of over fifty mystery and romance novels, including the best-selling golden retriever mysteries and the highly acclaimed *Mahu* series, a three-time finalist for the Lambda Literary Awards. His stories have been featured in numerous venues, including the Bouchercon anthology Florida Happens and Malice Domestic's Murder Most Conventional and several Happy Homicides collections.

He is a professor of English at Broward College in South Florida, where he lives with his husband and their rambunctious golden retrievers.

His website is www.mahubooks.com.

www.ingramcontent.com/pod-product-compliance
Lightning Source LLC
LaVergne TN
LVHW011948060526
838201LV00061B/4251